CHOICES

A NOVEL

BJ KING

*Phoebe,
my dear old friend
since childhood.
Enjoy Jessie's journey.
BJ King
07-14-16*

Valentine Press ∾ Greenville

A VALENTINE PRESS BOOK

Book and Cover Design by
Julie Felton

Author photo by
Stephanie King Yearwood

ISBN 978-0-9846748-1-7

For my husband, Del King.
My champion, my hero, my love,
and my best friend.
Del, you saved my life. I love you.

Gisehun'yi, "where the female lives."
Cherokee

Chapter 1

PRESENT

Until the Autumn I turned thirteen, I was devastated I had been born a girl. Before that October, I existed in my own world of make believe, and was, at times, Roy Rogers, galloping on a horse named Trigger, his golden mane flying in the wind. At other times, a straw broom could be a guitar when I was Elvis; or an old rope hanging from a huge oak was my vine and jungle when I was Tarzan. In 1959, I was Mickey Mantle.

Charlie, my younger brother, would turn beet red in the face with anger when I refused to play unless he was Jane or Dale. I, Jessica Grace Jordan, refused to be the weaker sex. Slapping, kicking and punching were common in our daily life. I learned to fight early. We fought like cats and dogs, and I loved him deeply.

I remember one doll as a child, a Tiny Tear that peed and cried real tears. Santa Claus left her under the tree one Christmas and I was thrilled for a while until I grew tired of her and went back to strapping on toy guns and romping through the woods with Charlie.

Then, in October of 1962, I was instantly smitten over a boy and no longer wanted to be one. Pale pink lipstick became indispensable and Sandra Dee was my new idol.

The boy, with shaggy blonde hair was oblivious to my existence. I would sit on the porch and wait for him and his friends to ride by on their bikes. Once they had threaded sunflowers in the wheel spokes. When one fell into the street, I ran out to retrieve it and saved it pressed between waxed paper in a huge book. I kept that stupid flower for years, although the boy never spoke more than a few words to me.

* * * * *

I'm well into middle age, now, as I lazily I flipped through the blank pages of a new journal, mulling over how to begin writing my life story. Not, that my life had been extraordinary, by any means. Recording a family history for our only grandchild was my goal.

Soon our only child and grandson would be arriving back in the states from Germany. The thought of them safe under our roof was a long awaited event. The anticipation of our reunion and meeting our grandson for the first time left me with a desire to put pen to paper. Memories flooded my mind, some painful, others not so much.

Where should I start? Barton Quinlan, my

second husband? He had been a Green Beret, a hero in Vietnam, a cop, an honest man, a debatable father, and a dreadful husband. I started leaving Barton the day we met. He worried incessantly that I would leave, and I would weep, reassure and vow I never would, until the day I did.

But, long before Barton, there was Momma. Momma prepared me well for weeping, promising, and constantly *fixing* relationships. She instilled a relentless guilt and angst of impending doom and my interminable aspiration to right every wrong. It would take years and a therapist before I realized she had been the architect of the majority of the real and imagined transgressions in my young life.

Momma was incongruous with all that was our life. A blue collar Prima Donna southern belle, she was perpetually burdened by life itself. She grew up dirt poor during the depression and her view of the world was permanently dark and gloomy, unless it involved her own desires. Her two children were certainly an inconvenience in her life.

Charlie and I learned early to stay as far away from Momma as we could, for Momma was not a happy woman. The momma of our childhood wore a constant scowl with an unremitting annoyed edge to her voice. She was a fast walking, angry little woman who stood five feet one and could stare down a mad dog.

Momma had the fairest of skin, sky blue eyes and dark auburn hair. She had been a tow head blonde when she was a toddler. My grandfather called her Cotton. I often overheard others describe Momma as a beautiful woman, but I could not see that beauty. She appeared shrouded in deceit to me, and my own fear of what I might see prevented me from looking too closely.

At an early age, I knew Momma had a secret life. She thought no one knew about her forbidden trysts. However, Charlie and I knew and I suppose Daddy did as well. She was not as clever as she thought. The most benevolent label for Momma was Narcissist; although, as I grew older I learned there were other words that were not so kind.

Involuntarily my thoughts go to another child. A child I became a mother to, but, who would never be mine. A child I had loved with my very soul. The possibility of another reunion added to my desire to write.

I brushed the sudden tears away and concluded it would be no picnic putting my story on paper. *No picnic.* A phrase I used often and I smiled at the memory of a man whose voice I had not heard in many years. Captain Cleve Crowell.

"Do you see any fried chicken, potato salad or pimento cheese sandwiches out there in that street? No! And you won't, cause it ain't no picnic out there."

That is where I would begin—with the epiphany of my soul.

The day I became a cop.

Chapter 2

1975

As I walked out of Reedy View Community College, the oppressive June humidity hit me like a hot wet blanket, and it was barely noon. July would be unbearable as most summers were in the piedmont of South Carolina. I had worked eight hours on third shift, before another four discussing Evidence and Procedure in the classroom.

I crawled into my most treasured possession, a 1969 Chevrolet Malibu SS I called Blue Moon. When I ended my first marriage, I drove away in Blue Moon with nothing else. I rolled down the windows, started the car, flipped on the radio and Helen Redding blasted out with *"I am woman hear me roar…"*

Momma had been offended and disapproving when I left a comfortable job as a customer service rep for a large national company to take a civilian position with the local police department. I could still hear her nagging voice, *"You were making good money, good benefits, why would you do that to me?"*

I had refused to discuss it and tuned out her tiresome rants. I had never been more exhausted or had so little time for a personal life and had never been happier.

The brutal Vietnam War was over. The United States had surrendered Saigon to the communist in April. I still could not believe the war, the war we lost, had taken so many. They were mostly just boys my age and as they graduated, they were shipped to 'Nam and too many returned home in a box.

I was twenty-two years old and a divorcee the first time I entered a college classroom. When I enrolled, I did not have a clue what I wanted to do with the rest of my life. I changed my major twice, before taking a course in Basic Law Enforcement on a whim. The third time I changed it to Criminal Justice and knew I had found my passion.

Many were shocked or surprised, but I don't know why. Following typical female traditions had never interested me. The only time I emulated those television fifties female role models, was when I had married my high school sweetheart. Later I determined I had married more as an escape than for love. What does a teenager know about love?

Picturing the clichéd white picket fence and yellow roses, I tried to perform all the expected wifely endeavors portrayed on television and I failed miserably.

I married Jonathan Morrison Greenfield when I was a senior in high school, much to Momma's dismay. We had eloped when Momma made it explicitly clear, she was dead set against me having my daddy, involved in any way with a marriage ceremony.

A Family Living class in my high school senior year had the girls writing their wedding announcements, a rather fun project since the ultimate goal for most girls was finding a husband and have a family. Hopefully in that order. A few had dropped out of school, when they got the cart before the horse, as my grandmother used to say.

When Momma began to read my assignment, she was smiling at the A+ I had received, then I saw her face contort with anger when she got to the part about the bride, me, being walked down the aisle and given in marriage by my father. She had one of her conniption fits that were customary, especially since she divorced my daddy.

We ended up in a screaming match and I ripped the paper to shreds. Five months later Johnny and I eloped. I was seventeen years old.

Johnny grew up on his family's farm near Spartanburg South Carolina, the son of a loving Christian family. In retrospect, I think I fell in love with his family as much as I did with him. We had dated two years and I saw the Greenfields as, unquestionably, what my family was not.

Until Johnny, my view of love, contentment and happy endings played out on the big screen. I lived vicariously through old movies and like many imaginative teenagers, the difference between fantasy and reality tended to blur. I wanted a life like Doris Day and Rock Hudson or Sandra Dee and Bobby Darin and a magical, happily ever after ending. Secretly, I think I will always be a little bit in love with Rock Hudson.

However, even as Johnny and I began to talk about a family and I tried unsuccessfully to conceive, I began to grow restless, I felt stymied and more than a little disillusioned. After a conversation with my gynecologist, he recognized that my desire to have a baby was more about trying to make myself happy. He told me it would not.

So, it was torture when I first made the decision to leave Johnny, because he had done nothing wrong.

Who was I? The only thing I knew for sure, I was not Mrs. Jonathan Greenfield.

The realization left me immersed in an almost crippling guilt. Momma declared I was trying to kill her and raged that I could not love her. First, I ran off and got married, and now that she had finally started to like Jonathan, I wanted to hurt her and leave him.

With a consuming guilt and a raging anger at my mother, I broke Johnny's heart and therefore

CHOICES

my own when I walked out on a perfect husband
on a journey to find me.

CHAPTER 3

1975

It was my third semester of college when one of the adjunct professors announced the local police department was hiring civilian dispatchers for their communication center. I jumped at the chance and landed the job. Again, I was restless, knowing that I wanted to be on the other end of the radio microphone. Opportunities for women were slim to non-existent in the slow talking, slow moving south.

Then in the fall of 1974, word was out that the Reedy View Police Department would begin accepting applications from females. The Equal Rights Amendment and a little thing called federal funding gave me hope. I did not classify myself as a feminist nor did I make noise about demanding my rights, I only wanted to be a cop. When the city manager was interviewed by a news reporter and asked if they would begin accepting applications for police officer from females, he responded, *"they better do more than that, they better start hiring some."* The article said *"The chief of police had no comment."*

I was thrilled and jumped at the opportunity, but such an incredible prospect that Reedy View would hire women seemed hopeless. The all-male uniform patrol division, was still reeling from hiring the first black officer just a few years before. Adding females was unlikely in 1974.

The Reedy View Police Department had the most modern state of the art radio equipment and updated dispatch center in the state. Reedy View was nestled in the upstate of South Carolina, spooning with the mountains that spanned into North Carolina and the Great Smokies.

Usually two of us worked a shift, rotating operating the police radio, and taking phone complaints. I was working the phones this particular day and when an in house line rang, I grabbed it.

"Give me Echo-2's case number on that burglary little girl." Most of the veteran officers treated me merely as a helpful child.

He was probably using one of the police call boxes, and there was one outside a coffee shop that I was sure he was using. Not a bad place to be out of service, (unavailable for a call) writing a report and having coffee with the proverbial donut. I was in awe of all of them; I loved their toughness and bluster, their compassion and self-deprecating humor. I loved that they chased down bad guys and made our town a little safer. More than that, I loved that I was a small part of it.

"The case number is 74 dash 13241."

"One, three, two, four, one, got it. How many times you seen Walking Tall so far." He asked. Then belly laughed.

"Hush! It's a wonderful movie. Don't you want to see it? I've only seen it 4 times." He laughed harder.

"Why are you laughing? By the way, did I tell you I've applied to come on as an officer?" I changed the subject

"God Almighty!" He bellowed. "I heard they were taking applications from women. Do not for one minute think they will actually hire one. They will take the applications but hell will freeze over before this department starts hiring women."

"Why not?" I challenged.

"Women got no business being cops, Jess. No offense to you, but policing is a man's job. A woman could get killed or worse, get one of us killed. Those are mean streets Jessica and no place for a woman. Why in the world would a pretty little gal like you want to be a cop?"

"Why did you become a cop?" He was silent; the question seemed to give him pause. I glared at the phone and was equally quiet.

Finally, with his voice cooler he said, "Well don't go getting measured for a uniform yet. Like I said, I been around a long time, and it will be a cold day in hell, yes sir."

* * * * *

But the department was forever changed one hot July night in 1975 when I walked into roll call for a third shift tour of duty as the first female uniformed patrol officer in Reedy View, South Carolina. Me, little Jessica Grace Jordan, stepped proudly into that inner sanctum and I could not hear a thing but the pounding of my own heart. No one spoke a word. Even the usual shuffling and scraping of chairs came to an abrupt halt. It even seemed that the whirr of the air conditioner ceased. *Maybe hell was freezing over.*

CHAPTER 4

1975

An hour before roll call my hands had literally trembled as I placed my badge and name plate on the standard navy blue uniform of the Reedy View Police Department. My streaked strawberry blonde hair was to my shoulders. In uniform, an officer's hair had to be off the shirt collar, so to comply with regulations, I had French-braided it and tucked the remainder underneath. Tiny sliver studs in my ears struck the right balance between professionalism and femininity. Taking stock of myself in the full-length mirror, I pulled on the Sam Brown gun belt that weighed about fifteen pounds. I felt every ounce of the leather and metal and loved it. Frowning, I wished that I was taller than five feet four inches and stood as erect as possible with shoulders back. *Here we go kiddo.*

The guys had already made a production of me being hired, teasing me unmercifully, and calling me a "cop-ette." All of it I accepted, still smiling and a shrug, but inwardly there was a tiny prickle that made me determined to do a good job, to prove myself to them and to me.

Before roll call and inspection, officers would sit around ancient wooden card tables, chewing tobacco, spitting in paper cups, guffawing at crude jokes, puffing on cigarettes, cigars and the occasional pipe. Deep male voices echoed in the heavy smoke filled room.

I spotted the one other new rookie, Mark Carlton and took the long walk toward him. Silence and eyes followed me as I fell in beside Mark, and helped him hold up the back wall. One older grey haired officer, shuffling cards at a table, shook his head with a disgusted expression and mumbled.

"This is going to be a disaster."

Still, I had no qualms and remained unflappable as I lined up that night with thirty male officers on a roughhewn pine floor, in a building constructed in 1902. I could not help but ponder the history and yes, the irony, as I imagined all the *men* who had tread these floors before me. The law insured I had a chance and the training had been rigorous. I was ready. Being born female, I could not change; I only wanted to be a good cop.

CHAPTER 5

1975

Lieutenant Russell Burdette was young and zealous, and the troops loved him. He entered roll call with his two sergeants, one white and one black.

"Fall in!" the black Sergeant bellowed. Sergeant Brady was over six feet, and built like a Mac truck.

I tried to calm my thudding heart and stood erect placing my 8-point hat in the correct position on my head. Two fingers between the bill and my nose. *Oh, God please do not let me throw up.*

I kept my eyes straight ahead and prayed I did not betray the knot of cold hard fear that tried to consume me. It did not seem possible four months had passed since I was called to Uniform Patrol Command and Captain Crowell's office. I would be in awe of this great lawman throughout my career. He exuded professionalism but could be brutal in his reprimands with an inept officer.

I had stood in front of his desk and as I heard the words, my ears started to ring and my mind started racing.

"Jessica, you've been chosen to attend the department's rookie school and from there the South Carolina Criminal Justice Academy. You will be sworn in as our first female uniform patrol officer. Congratulations." He leaned over the desk and shook my hand.

His words had hit me like a blast and I had difficulty breathing and processing them.

"Sit down." He smiled.

Finally, I found my voice, "Uniform patrol, and my assignment..." Front desk duty sounded good, they had a female in juvenile, a former meter maid who had recently received a degree in psychology. *Uniform Patrol? Did not sound like desk duty.*

"You will be assigned to a regular platoon and work with a training officer on a beat for a few months after the academy."

"You mean riding in a patrol car?" *What a stupid comment to fly out of my mouth.*

"Unless you're walking Main Street," he deadpanned.

Captain Crowell was all business and his Navy background meshed perfectly when he moved into a police persona. He would prove to be my principal critic when I screwed up and my mentor and biggest supporter when I did not.

Now after all the long months of posturing for television spots and newspaper articles about the first female uniformed patrol officer in Reedy View, my first tour of duty had arrived.

"Attention!" the Sergeant bellowed once more.

Lt. Burdette and the white sergeant, Sgt. McIntyre, walked slowly down the front of the line and then down the back as they inspected the troops, a daily ritual. Sergeant McIntyre was of a slighter build than Sergeant Brady. He would be retiring in the coming year. The lieutenant stopped in front of a five-year veteran, silently looked purposely at the officer's boots, then at his face and continued down the line. *What was that?*

The two fell back and took seats behind an old battered wooden podium, where the second sergeant was standing arranging report copies and teletypes. It was his duty tonight to brief the troops before our tour began. I was ready and inwardly praying my rubbery legs would not fold.

"At ease men...uh...as you were." There was a smattering of snickers as all eyes turned toward me. *Holy God, I am dying.*

"I'm just one of the guys Sarge..." I quipped, but the words stuck in my throat. All my life I had tried to cover my insecurity with humor.

"Two new officers are assigned to our shift, Carlton and Jordan." Sergeant Brady continued.

"Sarge, if she's just one of the guys, my oh my can this *guy* ride with me?" There was rowdier laughing and low level hoots and whistles.

"Enough, as you were." The sergeant barked, obviously flustered. I could feel my neck and face flushing red and I gave the smart-ass joker who was leering my way a go to hell look. My defiance delighted the room even more and more laughter erupted.

"Guess that look will shut you up Clark."

The sergeant began reading off a couple of stolen vehicle descriptions and thankfully, the moment of amusement passed as we all began writing hurriedly in our notebooks.

"Barron's Liquor at the corner of Main and Elm, alarm's 10-7. Extra patrol throughout the night. Two 45s (Armed Robberies) this afternoon..." He continued. "And I do not want to see more than two cars at the Koffee Klatch tonight."

Police code added to southern colloquialism sounded like a foreign language. I was thankful my stint in dispatch had afforded me the opportunity to learn the *language.*

"Fall Out!"

A line of dark blue made its way to the alley adjacent to Police Headquarters, where patrol cars were parked, one behind the other. Two early units were already in service to cover emergencies while the platoon going off duty transferred equipment to the platoon going on duty. In those days, patrol cars ran 24/7 and really took a beating. A few of the officers grumbled that their assigned beat car was ready for the junk yard. As for me, I was thrilled to have one. I had not forgotten Captain Crowell's comment about walking.

My first night the lieutenant assigned me to ride with a young five-year veteran, Ted Evans, whose boots Lt. Burdette had inspected so intently during roll call. Since working at the department as a civilian, I already knew many of the officers. But that night all the dynamics had changed. I had become a fellow officer.

CHAPTER 6

1975

"Jess, looks like you're stuck with me tonight." Ted shook my hand and gestured toward our assigned car. He was friendly and well liked. I was thankful he was my first partner and not Parnell. Parnell was the older grey hair who was disgusted I was breathing.

"Ted, I think you mean you're stuck with me and I know that's not good for you." I said.

"Nah, you ask me it's time women got out here doing their share of crime fighting. You will be fine. My wife is your biggest fan," he said.

"Really?" I smiled.

"Yep, remember your training, well most of it. Some you need to forget. I will let you know which is which. And, by the way, remind me to get my boots shined when Ayers opens up in the morning." Ayers leather shop had been in Reedy View for years and had a shoe stand set up in the rear. The shine boy got there early for downtown businessmen.

"That's what the L.T. meant?"

"Yep, and if you need a haircut, he'll take off his hat and ask you if you think *he* needs one." He trailed off and I noticed him looking at my strands hanging loose from the braid and the hat. Self-consciously, I shoved the strands under the hat with my finger.

"But the L.T. is a good guy, fair and square and we respect him. You are lucky you got The Blue Machine. He's a huge Cincinnati Reds man, so we've nicknamed ourselves the Blue Machine." He grinned until he noticed my bewilderment.

"What?" He asked. "You're not a Reds fan?"

"Baseball I know, but I don't keep up with it much anymore. I loved it when I was a kid, especially the Yankees." *I did not tell him I used to be Mickey Mantle.*

"Okay, I give, what's the Blue Machine meaning?"

"What? The Reds...Red Machine...Blue Machine? Get it?"

"Oh."

"Oh, she says." He was smiling and I was thinking this might not be such a bad night after all.

"Fox 100," the radio crackled to life in the silence of the night. Dispatch sent us a call before we had driven two blocks. A disturbance at a local nightspot, well known for drunken brawls that routinely erupted as the night progressed. I was familiar with the location from dispatching. The popular bar was in the 100 sector of the city. The city was divided into eight sectors for the police, with one or more cars assigned to each sector. Each car had a phonetic identifier attached to the specific platoon on duty. My platoon was Fox and our sector was 100.

"Fox 100, go ahead Headquarters."

"Fox 100, fight in progress, Zodiac Club, 724 Rushmore Street."

"Fox 100 10-5 (en route) 724 Rushmore Zodiac." I repeated, fearing my stomach would jump clear out of my throat when I opened my mouth. Adrenaline surged and the excitement was overwhelming. Being afraid did not even register. Without thinking, I was pushing my foot into the floorboard, wishing I could make the car go faster. Why didn't Ted turn on the blue lights? It was an in progress call. Of course, there was hardly any traffic downtown. He seemed to have the driving under control, although if I were driving I would put the pedal to the metal as they say. Then I realized that is why they probably did not let rookies drive. Abruptly I stifled a giggle. *God! Do not giggle!* However, I could not wipe the grin off my face as the patrol car flew through the night.

CHAPTER 7

1975

"Fox 100, 10-6" (on scene), I spoke into the mike.

"Fox 100 23:40 Hours," replied the dispatcher.

We pulled into the lot of the Zodiac and a second patrol car sped in from the opposite direction. Before Ted or I could exit our vehicle, an unmarked unit slid in as well. I recognized one of the undercover officers. I began having thoughts of making my first drug bust, confiscating pounds of marijuana, speed, LSD. Before I could even speak, another patrol car arrived; it was Sergeant Brady.

Ted and I began making our way toward a large crowd. I was vaguely aware of two additional patrol cars pulling to the curb. *Why did we need so many officers?*

All of my attention focused on the crowd we were approaching. Like tunnel vision, I put eyes on two men in their early twenties who were arguing loudly. A few were pointing toward them. Two other young men were holding the drunken staggering fighters apart from the other. The taller of the two was bleeding from the nose, the other had a busted lip, but were not seriously hurt. They continued pulling against their human constraints, cursing and making threats to each other.

We pieced the story together, and the argument was over the ex-girlfriend of one, now the current girlfriend of the other. I spotted a skinny peroxide blonde with three inches of black roots showing, sniffing, and waiting with two other girls, who were angry, their nostrils flaring, flinging curses of their own. This was the subject of the squabble and seemed to be enjoying the drama. If possible, she was drunker than her two paramours. Her friends assured us they would get her home safely, so it was a simple matter of cuffing the current boyfriend and the scorned lover. As I placed cuffs on the latter, he went perfectly still, as if seeing me for the first time. He continued to strain his neck to look at me as if I was a figment of his imagination. He was rendered mute. So this is how someone reacts to the first female cop they have ever seen.

I pushed him into the back seat and before crawling into the passenger side; I scanned the lot and grew suddenly still. All patrol units on duty, east, west, north, and south sector cars were either parked in the lot or leaving. Even the lieutenant.

What the hell? They had all responded to observe my first call.

I was taken aback and not sure how I felt. Amused? Angry? Grateful? Angry I decided as I slammed my door. My jaw tightened and determination filled me. I set a protocol for myself that night that would remain for my entire career. I would, by God, do this job and I would, by God, do it well.

"Fox 100 10-5 to detention with prisoner in custody." I advised the dispatcher. *By God!*

CHAPTER 8

1975

With our prisoners booked into the jail, we called back in service and started a slow crawl down Main Street.

"Asshole!" Ted jerked the car left wheel to curb and stopped in front of a women's apparel shop. The entry alcove was dark. I jumped out to catch up with him, I saw a drunken man, probably one of the homeless winos, zipping up his pants, and the stench of urine hit me in the face.

"God!" I gasped.

The drunken man swayed slightly and looked at us as if we were rather dense.

"What? Can't a gentleman take a piss any more without getting harassed by the cops?"

I rolled my eyes at the drunk and took one arm as Ted and I pushed him against the glass, patted him down, and cuffed him. I was not sure what shocked me more, a man peeing in public or the coarse language that most of the cops spouted, seemingly to cope. Looking back, I had led a rather sheltered life until I joined the police department. Even though I had been married, in some areas I was chaste and naïve. I had read a risqué novel by Harold Robbins when I first saw the "F" word written and learned what it meant. I was already 16 years old. I had never heard anyone actually say the word aloud until I started to work at the police department. I joked that I initially thought that was everybody's first name.

The remainder of the night was uneventful except for our meal break. After we cleared from locking up the last drunk, we headed for IHOP, the only place open 24 hours on our beat. After eggs and pancakes, Ted reached for my ticket along with his. He insisted on paying. Then to my horror, as we approached the patrol car, he walked to passenger door and opened it.

"I've got it Ted." I said pointedly

When we pulled out of the IHOP lot, I decided it was time to clear the air.

"Look Ted, you are a true southern gentleman, but we are not on a date. I buy my own meals and I open my own car door."

He looked at me sheepishly and smiled.

"It's a little hard to know what and when…" He said.

"No." I interrupted. "It's easy. You treat me like any other rookie and I will treat you like the senior officer you are. Simple. Chew me out if I

28

screw up and let me do all the crappy stuff that rookies have to do. If you get out of the car, I get out. If you get in a fight, then I will be fighting with you. If you get your ass kicked, then mine will get kicked also…Okay?"

"Okay partner, works for me." He smiled and I think he was a little relieved.

We drove silently for a while and then thankfully it began to rain, cooling off the muggy night. After a while, Ted announced we were at the half tank mark on the fuel gauge.

"You never go below the half full mark rookie." He said.

He pulled up to the department's fuel station and looked at me with a grin and a hint of devilment.

"Hop to it Rookie. I'm going to catch a couple of winks while you fill'er up." Then he proceeded to do exactly that. *Be careful what you wish for Jessica Grace.* As I stood in the pouring rain pumping gas, I thought grudgingly about the one uniform item still on back order, a raincoat.

CHAPTER 9

1975

I had been a cop less than a week when my partner and I rolled on my first domestic call.

"Fox 100, 10-80 532-B Pennsylvania Avenue, weapons unknown."

"Fox 100 en route 532-B Pennsylvania Avenue."

It was after midnight when our blacked out patrol car pulled slowly to the curb one house down from number 532. According to the type call, an officer would cut off the headlights and a switch turned off the taillights. So at times, we could glide in like a ghost.

"Fox 100 on scene."

"Fox on scene 00:51 hours." The radio crackled and fell silent.

Ted and I exited the patrol car without a sound and walked toward the house. The only sound was Ted snapping his keys on his Sam

Brown with a belt keeper. The shabby Victorian had probably once been impressive. Reedy View's elite inhabited these houses at the turn of the 20th century, but most now stood in near ruin. This one had long since been divided into small apartments, that were occupied by those down on their luck, ravaged by too much whiskey, too many cigarettes, lost jobs, and hopelessness.

An ancient magnolia secreted one end of the long covered front porch. Its boughs were heavy with blooms draping the nearly bare ground and its fragrance filled the air. As a slight breeze swept the upper branches, they rubbed against the porch roof producing the only thing we could hear, an eerie ghostly scraping.

We cautiously approached the side of the large house, where a screened door hung loosely from its hinge. Someone had painted the letter "B" crudely beside the door in bright blue paint, also used on two of six shutters; a third one was half-blue. The night remained silent except for the crickets in full chorus and intermittent sounds of distant interstate traffic. I briefly wondered if we were at the correct house.

Inside apartment B, a faint light from a black and white TV flickered through thin curtains covering beveled glass in the front door. Silently we took positions on either side of the door. Our stance automatic, safety drilled into us through persistent training. Statistics proved domestics were one of the most dangerous calls to which a police officer would respond. Ted rapped loudly on the door with his flashlight.

"Police!" he announced.

The door slowly opened and a small framed woman stood in the doorway. Her hair was shoe polish black with roots that were stark white. She stared at us blankly.

My first impression was a grandmotherly figure clad in haphazard clothing, but the garish hair color somehow cheapened what once had been a pretty face. Half expecting the smell of lavender-scented talc, my senses were assaulted with the repulsive stench of cheap whiskey and sour body odor and urine. Her eyes were vacant as she stared at us. Upon scrutiny, I noticed blood caked around one nostril and her lip and right eye were swelling and already turning purple.

"Ma'am, we received a call about a disturbance in this apartment. Are you alright?" Ted spoke.

At first, she did not answer, then in surprising defiance she said, "We ain't called any po-leece."

"We got two calls." Ted continued, "Why don't you step outside and talk to us?"

She looked back nervously before stepping onto the porch.

"Me and my old man got in a little fuss." She admitted. "When he gets drunk he gets loud and a little mean."

She made a dismissive gesture with one frail arm. "Aw, go on now; he's already in bed. It's over."

"Ma'am is there anywhere we can take you where you'll be safe, you really should be checked by a doctor." I pressed.

"No." She said emphatically.

I was incensed by her obvious injuries and perplexed that she would ignore what had happened and stay. It was maddening that we could take no action unless an assault occurred in our presence. It would take years before South Carolina law changed allowing police officers to make an arrest on the probable cause of an injury or evidence of violence in the home. However, in 1975, we could do nothing.

One last time I tried to convince her to leave, but she would not.

"He'll get madder'n hell and it'll be worse next time."

"Well, you better keep the noise down; we better not have to come back out here." Ted said

"We can't leave her..." I looked at Ted incredulously.

"We can and we are." He deadpanned. "We will get his name for the report and make sure she hasn't killed him, but that's all we can do Jessica."

"Does he have any weapons in there?" Ted asked.

"Nothing 'cept a mean mouth. He won't hurt nobody. He's a good man till he drinks."

"Do you have any family here?" I was persistent if nothing else.

"Hun, I got a son in Texas, but I ain't got money

for a cab to the liquor store, much less Texas."

We made note of her name, Loretta Wilkins, date of birth April 12, 1920. Hard to believe she was only 55 years old. She looked 70. Her common law husband's name was Dewy Gosnell, she told us.

"Loretta, you wait out here while we go have a word with Dewy." Ted said.

We entered the apartment that turned out to be one large room with a bathroom. This was probably the foyer and parlor when the grand house was younger. The walls were in need of paint and a good cleaning. The original crown moldings were still in place around the high ceiling. They had once been beautiful, but now caked with layers of paint and grime.

I took in the rest of the room; a deep laundry sink was in one corner adjacent to a makeshift cabinet fashioned out of plywood. A hotplate was on the crude unpainted counter along with a cheap and battered toaster and a partial loaf of white bread. A small table stood beneath a window with two ladder-back chairs with the cane bottoms sagging. A small refrigerator with a rusty handle and rust along the bottom completed the kitchen.

On the opposite wall was a bed with a thin mattress, stained sheets and the air filled with the stench of body odor and whiskey. Ted opened the door to the bathroom to clear it of anyone lurking there.

I thought I might gag each time I had to take a

breath. Our focus was on Dewy, the suspect, who was supine in bed with a sheet pulled to his chin and he was holding the edges firmly in his fists. At first, he pretended to be asleep, but we could see his eyes twitching. An empty bottle of Wild Irish Rose was on the bare wood floor. He looked to have a couple of days' growth of beard. He was not wearing a shirt and was either in his skivvies or in the raw. I hoped we did not have to find out. Ted addressed the man authoritatively.

"What's going on here? We got calls saying y'all were raising hell in here. It looks to me like you beat the shit out of your wife but for some reason she wants to keep your sorry ass out of jail."

Dewey appeared to be not much taller than my own five feet four. His beady eyes were angry and his lips tight with outrage. Suddenly he blurted out.

"That old whore ain't my wife and she called me a son of a bitch. Ain't nobody got the right to call me a son of a bitch."

My anger blazed compounded by the fact we could not take him in unless Loretta agreed to press charges. Keeping my eyes on his hands as they gripped the sheet, I walked over to the side of the bed where he lay. The mere indignation of the situation and the audacity of his words enraged me.

I shoved the departmental issued flashlight under his chin, stretching his neck back into an awkward angle. He did not move but his eyes widened.

I leaned closer and whispered, "understand this you son of a bitch. If you lay another hand on this woman, I will personally drag your drunk, sorry, piece of shit ass out of that bed, out the front door, onto the sidewalk, and then kick your sorry ass within an inch of your worthless, pathetic life.

"Then I'll lock your despicable, useless ass up for assaulting a police officer, disturbing the peace, public drunkenness, and imitating a human being. Do you understand, you Son. Of. A. Bitch?"

As we crawled back in the patrol car, Ted let out a low whistle.

"You're alright partner."

Suddenly filled with remorse and dread I turned to Ted.

"Sorry, I lost my cool. You think he will make a brutality complaint?" I was beginning to feel sick at my stomach.

Ted guffawed, "That old rooster will never admit a female roughed him up, which you didn't or even manhandled him." Ted suddenly stopped speaking looking thoughtful.

"Is it still considered manhandling if it's a woman doing the handling?"

"Oh shut up Ted." However, I was laughing and feeling a whole lot better. I started filling out the Uniform Incident Report that had four copies. I stopped, now it was I being thoughtful.

"Are there any agencies that would assist

Loretta financially, to get her to Texas? Damn, I should have gotten her son's name and phone number…"

"What? You working for Social Services? We don't get involved in that shit."

He turned and looked at my determined expression and began to shake his head. "Oh hell! We will check before we get off duty when social services open. Do not tell me you're a bleeding heart. Remember she's got to want help first of all."

I began to smile, and he continued. "And I'm not spending a lot of time when I get off; I go home get a cold beer and hit the bed."

"A cold beer at 8 in the morning?" I wrinkled my nose at him.

"Yep, damn rookies think they can save the fucking world." I was not sure if he was talking to himself, or me but I had a big grin on my face.

CHAPTER 10

1950s and 1960s

Arguing, cussing, spitting and yelling were normal in our house. I grew up listening to Momma and Daddy, behind closed doors, them believing Charlie and I were asleep. Me wishing I were. My stomach was in an endless knot, heart thumping so loudly, that my ears felt like they were vibrating. I would lay motionless in bed, wishing they would shut up and stop being so mad with one another. I knew they did not like each other, but I was too afraid to ponder for long what that meant.

Small Southern communities held few secrets. If somebody's 'old man' ran off, got drunk, or beat the hell out of the wife, most people knew it within a day or so. At least I often heard Momma, Daddy, or our grandmother talk about such things.

Sharing this information once ended with my

humiliation in second grade. It all started one Sunday afternoon with Nell Bryson. Nell was a sweet woman who would come and stay with us when Momma was having her sick *'spells'*. Momma was sick a lot and always tired. The way I saw it, she was mostly sick and tired of Charlie, Daddy and me. One could never be sure when we would commit despicable acts in Momma's mind.

"Jessie! Charlie! Don't slam that screen door! I'll make your teeth rattle you run through this house one more time."

" Jessie! Charlie! You better not be tracking dirt in on my floor! Stay outside!"

However, Nell was always a step ahead of Momma and us. Nell was a country woman, behind her back Momma called her a hillbilly. She reminded me of a witch, because she often went without her teeth, and her hair was long and grey and she would wear it loose at times. She kept her fingernails painted red and would sometimes paint mine. Charlie and I loved her and when Nell was there, it was an adventure. When she finished her chores, then all she had to do was *'keep us kids'*. We did not have baby sitters, we had Nell, or grandparents, who *kept us* for whatever reason necessitated it. This is when the adventures began, walking in the woods, Nell pointing out plants that were poisonous like poison oak and ivy. *Leaves of three leave them be.* As we shuffled through dense forest, she pointed out certain plants that you could chew to freshen your breath;

we would hike through the woods, chewing on a stick and being ever vigilant for snakes. The black snake was a good one, but others were deadly. We seemed to learn something new each time we went into the woods.

On one particular Sunday, we traveled to the foothills to pick up Nell, since she would be staying a few days. Nell did not have a car. I overheard Momma say Nell never learned to drive.

As we drove along, I was listening to Momma and Daddy talk. Momma was in a good mood, probably the prospect of reinforcement from Nell.

"I had a crazy dream last night." She said. "I dreamed Nell ran her old man off." I knew Nell lived with a man named Otto, but I had never seen him.

"Why?" I inquired.

"It was a dream Jessica, be quiet." She turned around and glared at me. I was always a curious kid, and talked constantly. Half of my second grade, the teacher banished me to stand in the hall, outside the classroom, for talking. However, there were usually others sent to stand in the hall for minor infractions from other classrooms. Therefore, we waved and talked in loud whispers.

Nevertheless, I knew exactly what it meant if someone ran his or her old man off. It was usually because he was out drinking or running around with a whore. I did not dare say that aloud, I knew it was not kind, although I was not sure why or what a whore really was. It was through my observation, that when the church sang the 'invitation' song, "Just As I Am", if they went down in the front of the church, it meant God had forgiven them and they probably wouldn't go to hell. Some returned to the marital home if they had found salvation.

The road, or more like a red dirt path, that wound its way to Nell's little cottage, was rough and sometimes it felt like our 1957 Ford had fallen in a ditch. Momma would frown the entire time, sitting on the edge of the seat watching for bumps in our path.

Finally, we reached her house and as Daddy was turning around, Nell came out waving. She climbed in the back between Charlie and me and we began to retrace the route home.

"You doing alright Nell?" Momma asked

"Yep, purdy good, 'cepten for having to run my old man off yesterdee." Nell responded.

My eyes grew wide and my mouth was hanging open. Charlie and I always suspected momma had eyes in the back of her head, but this took scary to a completely new level.

Nevertheless, I was thunderstruck momma had dreamed about Nell and it had really happened. Therefore, I thought I had something to share, for the first time, the next day at school.

I proudly raised my hand, and Mrs. Barton called on me to stand for show and tell. I did not have anything to show, but boy did I have a story to tell.

"Yesterday, my momma had a dream about Nell, the woman who keeps us. She dreamed Nell had run her old man off, and when we picked Nell up, she really had run him off."

I looked at the teacher and her face was horrified.

"Jessica Grace, we do not refer to a husband as an old man. That is impolite and disrespectful. You will not say that again. We do not discuss others' misfortune."

My face grew red and hot from embarrassment. Some of the brats giggled and I sat down trying not to cry. However, I placated myself, smugly, because I was pretty sure Nell was not married.

CHAPTER 11

1950s and 1960s

My source of wisdom in all things, especially marital discord, came from my paternal grandmother, Momma Alex. She was my guiding light all of her life, my most important female role model. Charlie and I bestowed the love for a mother upon Momma Alex. She could shoot a gun straighter than any man, prayed faithfully, and if it were a crisis, she prayed aloud. *Oh, Lord help us we pray...* even as she took care of business. One did not go to Momma Alex's house after dark without calling first. She made that clear.

"I hear anyone messing around my house I'll put a bullet in their ass." When she was older, she would shoot through the floor or wall if she heard strange sounds. Moreover, God have mercy on your soul if you ever hurt any of her family.

Momma Alex stories abound, and were repeated often. My favorite concerned Momma

Alex and one of her sisters. According to all accounts, it was after the war. That was the big war, WWII. All of her brothers were Navy veterans who served during the war.

My Great Grandfather, Alexander Dugan, was sitting in his cane rocker on the front porch of the home place that still stands north of Travelers Rest, South Carolina. He was surprised when he spotted Momma Alex's Chevrolet approaching rather rapidly, the dust billowing behind her 1937 Chevrolet Coupe.

Papa Dugan walked to meet her as she pulled into the drive. He was puzzled as to why his daughter was visiting in the middle of her workday.

Papa Dugan had four sons and three other daughters, but Alexandra was his favorite. They were like two peas in a pod, was the general consensus. Being his namesake, they both felt they were more akin than the others were.

"Is anything wrong Alexandra?"

"Yes Papa, I had to beat hell out of your son-in-law. I told Lamar, if he ever touched Ella Jo again, I would be back with my pistol."

"Let me shake your hand Alexandra, I should have killed that bastard myself a long time ago. Did you hurt him bad?

"I wish I'd hurt 'm worse, but he'll live. You might want to go check on sister though. That piss-ant blacked both her eyes before I got ahold of 'em."

According to her brothers, Momma Alex had "beat the hell" out of him. They were a little ashamed they did not get to him first. No one ever knew why Momma Alex went to her older sister's house that day, but when she arrived, she had found Aunt Ella's face swollen and bruised and Uncle Lamar sitting in the kitchen drinking coffee.

Quite a ruckus followed. I am not sure anyone ever knew exactly what happened next, except that Uncle Lamar ran limping out the front door, holding his private parts with one hand, and covering his mouth and nose with the other; bleeding and squealing like a stuck pig. I do not know if Uncle Lamar ever hit Aunt Ella again, but they lived out the rest of their lives together, unlike Momma Alex and her husband, grandfather Jordan, whom I would lay eyes upon only once.

CHAPTER 12

1950s

Momma Alex was an independent woman, long before the world considered an independent woman a good thing. She had dared to divorce my grandfather during an era when divorce was not only disgraceful, but also illegal in South Carolina.

Although I had heard stories of my infamous, ne'r-do-well grandfather, I had never met him. I was told he was dark and handsome, a heavy drinker and the meanest man in South Carolina when he got drunk. The few pictures I saw showed a good-looking, square chinned man with olive skin, deep dimples, and a sly smile showing perfect white teeth, the spitting image of my own handsome father.

My grandfather, when drunk, was prone to strike my grandmother. After this happened one time too many, she went to her papa and he and her brothers paid him a visit and warned him to never touch my grandmother again. The next time, and I have learned there will always be a 'next time', she packed up her two children, one who was my father, and drove to Papa Dugan's house north of Travelers Rest, South Carolina.

"I've left the son-of- a-bitch Papa. Can we stay until I find a place?"

"This is your home as long as you want, girl. I never liked that bastard anyway." Therefore, that was the end of it. When Aunt Eunice began to lecture Momma Alex about what the church might think, Papa Dugan told her to shut up. The story was, Aunt Eunice left in a huff, but never dared mention Momma Alex's situation again in front of her father.

Momma Alex moved her little family to Ohio for a year or so. I heard bits and pieces about the time they lived there, but never understood why. I mean, Yankees lived in Ohio. Years later, while researching South Carolina divorce law, I discovered that divorce was illegal in South Carolina until 1949. I was stunned. Ohio was one of the states where divorce was legal if you were a resident of the state. I had always been proud of my grandmother and was in awe of how she had survived alone for so many years. I longed to have a conversation with her about so many things, but by then she was no longer with us. When she returned from Ohio, she had started a new chapter in her life.

My grandmother was a paradigm, and the

Momma Alexism I would carry with me always, was, *"Remember Jessica Grace, a strong woman can be weak, but at their weakest, can become their strongest."*

Papa Dugan had a large farm with about a hundred acres. He gave her about twenty acres and she built a little cottage, where she lived with her children and when they left home, she remained there until her death.

Momma Alex went to work for Valentine Meat Packing Company in Reedy View. She worked out in the plant grinding meat, making sausage and from there she learned to butcher meat. The owner recognized her work ethic early on and promoted her to supervisor on the packaging line.

When he discovered customers were asking for Mrs. Jordan, instead of him, if there was a problem or if they wanted special cuts, the boss promoted her to travelling "salesman." Again, her siblings were aghast. Why, traveling jobs were for men! The unconventional idea of a divorced woman driving the back roads of South Carolina, calling on customers in little country stores, and staying in hotels and motor courts alone in the 1940s and 1950s South was unheard of.

Her sisters touted the dangers befalling a woman traveling alone. However, Momma Alex was never alone. She carried a 38 pistol in her purse. She always kept her money tucked in the cut out toe of a silk stocking, pinned to the inside of her brassiere, hidden safely in her considerable bosom.

After the depression in the thirties, our great-grandfather became a warden at a prison camp. Times were hard. The year before I was born, Momma Alex finally met her soul mate. Graham O'Dooley. He was a Captain at the prison camp where Papa Dugan worked. It was actually called a chain gang camp. Like most aspects of life in the Jim Crow South, even prisons were segregated. The camp Papa Dugan oversaw was for the *colored* prisoners. We would come to call Graham O'Dooley Papa, and he would be the only grandfather we knew on our daddy's side of the family. Although our grandmother's beau was a constant visitor, Momma Alex refused marriage until well into the 50s. Actually, it was only after my paternal grandfather died.

Prisoners were a common sight; plowing and planting vegetables for the prison. From the time we were young children, there was a constant flow of trustees working around the property. After Graham O'Dooley had officially become our Papa, he came home one afternoon to see one of the trustees with a rifle thrown over one shoulder and carrying a duck from the pond. He came bursting into the kitchen a short time later, carrying the rifle and the duck.

"Alexandra, what in the hell are you thinking? These are prisoners. You can't give them a gun!"

"Oh hush Graham, Titus is a good man and he wouldn't hurt a fly. And I wanted duck for supper."

"Dammit, Alexandra, don't do that again. It doesn't look right."

CHAPTER 13

1950s

It was a cold winter day in the late 50s, Charlie and I were off on our bikes when Daddy hunted us down to tell us we had to go to Momma Alex's house. Our grandfather Jordan had died. He had to help plan the funeral. This was big news since we never talked about our Grandfather Jordan. Never discussed why he did not live with Momma Alex. No one had ever explained why we had never met him but the talk overheard within the family was that Momma Alex had run him off years before. Therefore, after this momentous event, Papa O'Dooley married our beautiful grandmother. I never knew why she waited so long.

But, I'm getting ahead of myself. The first time I laid eyes on my Grandfather Jordan was also the last. I had seen one or two dead people at funerals before, so approaching a corpse in a casket was no shock. Nevertheless, this time was different. This was my grandfather. I was a little apprehensive, but more curious. I took a good long look at this familiar stranger, my father's father, lying still as a statue in a flower covered casket, wearing a dark blue suit, his jet-black hair combed neatly to one side. Even dead, he was surprisingly handsome. Momma Alex walked up to me and put her arms around me as I stared at my grandfather.

"Jessica Grace, remember if you live in the gutter you die in the gutter."

Momma Alex was puzzling during this time. She smiled, a lot. Greeted old friends at the funeral home, many she had not seen in years. She bought a new black dress and a hat to match and black lace gloves. I knew there was nothing like a good Baptist funeral for dressing up, visiting and eating mounds of food people would haul in. It was a little disconcerting that Momma Alex appeared to revel in the festivities.

Momma Alex found her ex-husband being dead suited her much better than him being alive. She declared herself a widow and many people who came to know my grandmother in later years, never knew she was divorced before marrying Papa O'Dooley. Her widowhood pleased her high and mighty Baptist siblings as well. So, I learned as a child that dying was the only respectable thing my paternal grandfather ever did.

Years later, I looked up the police report chronicling his death, long transferred to microfilm.

When the clerk handed me a copy, I noted the cause of death was labeled unknown. He was found dead, a short distance from the front steps of what was known in the South, as a liquor house. A liquor house is an illegal operation, usually in a private residence, where derelicts would gather to purchase and drink moonshine or distilled spirits. The practice originated during prohibition and continued when it was illegal to purchase liquor on Sundays in South Carolina. Much like crack houses, it was the same dissolute dwelling, a different drug.

It was a bitter January morning when the Reedy View Police responded to what was possibly deceased person. The complainant was anonymous. The brief yet austere report documented the temperatures had dipped in the low twenties during the previous night and into the morning. The officer documented the victim had the usual puffiness and swelling around the face from acute alcoholism, and scarring, possibly from past barroom brawls, however the coroner determined he died of hypothermia. Acquaintances identified him as Luther Jordan, address unknown. My grandfather.

I never had never forgotten what Momma Alex had whispered to me on that long ago night at the funeral home. My grandfather had literally died in the gutter, or at least two feet from the curb and ten feet from the front steps of 7 Hollis Avenue in the City of Reedy View, South Carolina.

One need not be a cop to know a person could be killed in ways other than with a weapon. It could be slow and insidious, from substance abuse or a broken heart. The soul dies first. When the body follows, it is merely a postscript.

CHAPTER 14

1975

The hoopla surrounding Reedy View's first female on uniform patrol seemed to go on long after I grew tired of the notoriety. Every month or so another reporter, with a slow news day, wanted to do a feature. When a few other women were hired, the news media would ask to take pictures of us together, walking up the steps into Police Headquarters. They asked about make-up and hair; whether we had boyfriends or husbands and how they felt about our jobs. I had neither.

While the brass encouraged these positive public relations, there were unwritten rules an officer didn't discuss with the press. Open cases, any unrest within the department or names of victims, were never released to the press without approval from the chief. Being on constant exhibition got old fast. I began to feel like a resident alien.

Days and nights turned into weeks and months. My platoon had grown accustomed to a female on the shift. For the most part, I was accepted and my worth as a cop proven, yet most of the male officers were still overprotective. I was still referred to as a female cop, but as one officer told the media, I was an *'exception'*. That was a thorn in my flesh...sure, some women could not cut it. However, neither could all men. I just wanted to be a good cop.

"If 'man shall not live by bread alone'," I said, "woman shall not exist for her career alone." I was getting tired of frozen pizza for one, and I began to think if I ever had to look at another pancake, I would puke. Rushing to a bar fight no longer caused the rush of excitement it once had. In fact, bar fights became routine. I never looked forward to days off. I would have preferred working straight through the week. Ted and his wife, Linda, sometimes invited me over, but without a date, I felt like a sore thumb.

Mark Carlton, remained a good friend since we had survived rookie school, the police academy, and were assigned to the same platoon. He constantly pushed me to date Ben Davis and I finally did. Ben was in the latest rookie class and it seemed strange that I was already a senior officer to a group of newbies. He was a quiet, down-to-earth person from a great family. Mark would always point him out and then move his eyebrows up and down comically. He constantly reminded me of what a great catch he would be. However, the fire was not there. Ben and I had fun, I felt relaxed with him, but I knew we would never end up in the bedroom. Ben wanted more out of the relationship and was patient to wait until I decided. I knew his patience was futile. It would never happen.

I was never much of a party animal and I preferred staying home to going out on mind-numbing dates, or to loud discos with friends from work. I was not a big drinker and I disliked dancing. I obviously had two left feet.

Occasionally I made the mistake of going out with someone other than a cop. Most were nice, charming, intelligent or good looking, sometimes all of these, but they all lacked one important essential, they were not cops. I found myself comparing all non-police dates to the cops I knew — and the non-cops never measured up.

The truth was, my occupation got in the way. They were either intimidated or we failed to connect on any level. They always asked the same dumb questions. *Why did you want to be a cop? Do you like it?* The last usually asked with an incredulous voice inflection. *Have you ever been in fight, shot your gun...*some wanted gruesome details, but those were shared only within an exclusive police ethos. The date was usually over for me within the first half hour when even if he did not ask the same questions, he would joke, *I had better not speed with you in the car, I will get a* *ticket* then snicker thinking that was so funny. One of my least favorite, *you have a gun on you now?* I was never sure if they were dating me or dating a 'cop'. I was a non-person. I accepted that my world had fundamentally changed and that was perfectly fine with me.

I began to spend more and more time with a veteran group of officers who met for coffee after work. On a whim, we all signed up for Karate classes. Once we went flying with an acquaintance who had his pilot's license. They all howled when I was sick for the rest of the day.

One in the group was Barton Quinlan. While I considered them all friends, I especially liked Barton. He was a three-year veteran who was quiet and unassuming. He had joined the Reedy View Police Department right after a tour in Vietnam. He was three months older, and we had graduated from our respective high schools the same year. Me from Reedy View High and him from Junction City High in Kansas. He had been an Army brat and had lived all over the world. I referred to him as my big brother and mentor. On days when I partnered with Bart, we kept a competition going, trying to outguess each other on car make, model, and year. He was delighted that I knew as much about cars as he did. He claimed he had never known a female who could tell a Chevy from an Oldsmobile, and he for sure never knew one who knew a Bel Air from a Cutlass.

Barton was polite, yes ma'am, no sir—polite, almost to a fault. Good manners were never a negative. It would be a long time before it dawned on me that his politeness and introversion masked serious self-esteem issues. In uniform, he could hide his true self. Being painfully shy, he would often give a crooked grin and shake his head in lieu of answering a question; I realized later, I was mistaking his silence as manly confidence.

Bart would open up to me and we talked endlessly about football, his gridiron success, making All State defensive end his senior year. His father, being career military, Bart grew up on bases in Germany and France; this was all very intriguing to someone who had lived her entire life in the same small house in the same middling town.

As suddenly as he would open up, he would withdraw. For no reason I could fathom, he would curl inward as if he were in a shell and become unusually quiet. I felt it added to the mystery of this kindhearted, strong, silent hero who had risked his life for our country. Looking back, I should have delved deeper into those dark places, where he locked out those closest to him.

It did not start out as a romantic relationship, far from it. He was married, but separated and living with his mom. He seldom mentioned his marriage but did constantly brag about his son who was beginning to take his first steps.

We talked about my dates, with me either

complaining or crowing, and Bart giving his opinions on who he thought was good enough for me. When a brief relationship with another officer ended after he cheated on me, Barton quickly voiced his dislike for the detective and vehemently declared that was no way to treat any woman. I clearly remember thinking, *yep all the good ones taken*. Years later, I would remember that conversation and the disconcerting paradox.

CHAPTER 15

1975

Bart was not handsome in the traditional sense. He was not one to automatically turn a woman's head. However, once you knew him, his quiet demeanor and crooked smile was enchanting. One day it dawned on me, *Barton Quinlan was quite a hunk.* But he was so reserved and timid, he got lost in the shadows.

One night, working the third shift, the radio was unusually quiet. The rain fell steadily. The weather seemingly had driven would-be criminals inside and there was a hiatus for both sides of the law that night. As we checked buildings on the beat, he began to tell me about his stint in Vietnam. He had been seriously wounded but never talked about it. With a fresh thermos of coffee in the seat between us, our mugs filled, Bart began to smile to himself as memories obviously flooded his mind. The rain, he said, always made him sad. I thought I could still glimpse the pain—a pain I would never understand regardless of how hard I tried. A pain buried so deep, it would at times consume him. He looked into my eyes and in a deep Southern drawl softly recanted the time he spent in a hell called Vietnam.

"You can't believe the rain in 'Nam, Jess." He shook his head as the sound of rain steadily pelted our car roof. Water gushed and flowed down the dark gutters as we crept through the midnight hours in the city.

Bart was second in command of a platoon of Army Green Berets, sent into the jungle to establish the location of a cell of North Vietnam's regular army. If they found it, their orders were to take them out. Kill them all or die trying.

"We were in skirmishes throughout that first day. Dog-tired could not start describing how we felt, and it was the monsoon season. I carried a M-60 and the load seemed to get heavier as the day went on. Of course, I was in better shape then, still had my muscles from football," he chuckled.

"You almost welcomed a skirmish, so you could put down the load and kill Vietcong. It was hot as hell, sticky, and so wet. There was no place dry. I prayed to God, I would never see rain like that again, if I ever got out of that jungle. I really hated the rain. But, when it wasn't raining, it was a beautiful country, you know?

"You never really slept while out on patrol. We were pretty far north of Saigon, the North's

border. We were in bad need of reinforcements. I
left before first light with a fire team to scout a
trail. I was an E-7 and on the second day out, the
rain had lightened a little. It felt like we had been
walking for days when all of a sudden we were
ambushed by Viet Cong coming up from behind
us. It all happened so fast. They hit us first. We set
up a line and began returning fire. I was praying
air support was close. We radioed our position
and requested help. After what seemed like
forever, but I guess it was only a few minutes,
their shots grew sporadic. We figured there had
been fewer of 'um than we first thought. We made
the decision to continue up the trail. I was
bringing up the rear. My buddy, we called him
Duck, cause he sorta of waddled when he walked,
was ahead of me. Then it was like hell rained
down, gunfire was coming from behind us. I felt
something like a hot flame hit my back. The
impact threw me to the ground but I managed to
turn my M-60 around and took out the last two.

"Next thing I remembered was the helicopter
and I was on a gurney being lifted into that big
bird. I can still hear Duck yelling for me to hang in
there; he would see me in Hawaii. "hang in there
Sarge'..." He grew quiet for a long while. And
when I thought he had finished, he added, "Never
saw any of them again. They medevac'd me out
and within weeks sent me stateside to a hospital in
Texas. Don't remember much of the time when I
first arrived. They said I was critical for days.

Guess I was one of the lucky ones." But his laugh indicated he was not so sure he was lucky.

"My girlfriend, or so I thought she was my girlfriend, came from Kansas to visit me. We had dated all through high school. She was beautiful. I played football and she was a cheerleader. She came in, we talked, and when she walked out, I never saw her again. History. I sure would like to know how many of those guys made it home."

As suddenly as he had begun his story, he fell silent. For a long time, all that could be heard was the rain. I realized there were tears on my cheeks and Bart noticed them as well. I was embarrassed but he just smiled and nodded his head, in what I came to know as his trademark characteristic when he was deep in thought. He looked at me so intently for a moment, that I knew we had just shared something deep, something I did not fully understand. I just felt such great admiration for this man.

When I finally found my voice, I asked. "Bart, why don't you try to contact your old friends? I am sure there is a way...write Washington or the Army? Have you tried?"

"Nah, I wouldn't know where to start and the war is over. No sense poking a dead dog. We wouldn't have anything to say now."

I could not help but think that was not true. I could not imagine not wanting to contact comrades who had been through such hell with me. I came to realize that Bart was his own man and private about his past and his family. It would be a long time before I heard him speak of those times again.

CHAPTER 16

1975 - 1977

Camaraderie between cops and our sometimes sick humor is a bond most civilians never understand. As I demonstrated my abilities, I was slowly accepted, and being a female became less and less a point of contention or distinction. We worked together, fought together, and played together. We formed a softball team that challenged other platoons to games, and then we gathered for choir practice after second shift tours, and would sit until the late hours drinking beer or wine, telling war stories, some told the same story more than once.

When a cop, turned author, Joseph Wambaugh, coined the term 'choir practice' in his novel, THE CHOIR BOYS, it became a best seller and then a movie; the name for those after shift gatherings stuck. We covered each other's back and knew things about each other that even families did not know.

When one of our own drank too much, they were loaded into a vehicle and driven home. Those good Samaritans were often met with cold stares and silence as the wife opened the door so her husband could be poured into bed.

Barton attended the gatherings sporadically and he and I would talk as we watched many of our cohorts drink themselves into oblivion. I hated the taste of beer and preferred wine or Sangria. Barton usually chose a soda increasing my respect for him. Yes, I liked Barton immensely, but not in a romantic sense, even later, it was never romantic. Was I blind to the darkness in those days? Did it even exist? If it existed, I did not see it.

Our friendship progressed gradually. We began as teacher-student. The training protocol called for new officers to have exposure in all areas of the city. Barton worked the train depot area. It was a rough section of town with constant fight calls around the bars and plenty of domestic disturbances. Many of the calls involved drunk and disorderly—put that with volatile domestic situations and the danger quotient increases tenfold.

An inner city housing project, two streets over from the depot, increased the foot traffic of young hoodlums who sought haven in the area. There were constant shootings and robberies at nearby liquor and convenience stores. The bus station was only a few blocks from the train depot, making muggings and strong-armed robberies of unsuspecting travelers, routine.

Lieutenant Burdette regularly assigned me to the west side and the train depot area. On those rare occasions I worked the East side of town, I was miserable. The majority of calls were shopliftings at the mall or a hit and run in the mall parking lot. I diplomatically got the word out, I preferred a specific area and the majority of my training would be on the violent west side.

Most of the rookies on other shifts and even Mark had the opportunity to ride solo. I had not. The L T was backed into a corner when I kept asking when I would patrol solo. I was still technically in training, but all rookies would go into a solo phase, but I knew the Lieutenant was apprehensive about putting a female on patrol solo. What could he do? It was past time.

When the third shift tour of duty rolled around again, I got into a patrol car alone, picked up the mike and called in service. My heart was in my throat, as I pulled out of the alley adjacent to Police Headquarters. The alleyway was plenty wide, but I carefully checked all my mirrors to insure I did not scrape the sides of the buildings. This time, I giggled aloud.

As the night progressed, I began to have déjà vu feelings of my first night on patrol. Bart and Ted, who worked as partners when they were not training, began to show up on all of my dispatched calls. The first couple of calls, I was appreciative. Then, when I volunteered for a couple of calls, since I was the nearby unit, predictably, Bart and Ted would come sliding into the location.

After a couple of those incidents, I decided I would not advise dispatch I was responding, until I arrived on scene. I had always been a rebel. Although against General Orders, at least the other units (including Ted and Bart) would not know until I advised dispatch over the shared police frequency of my location. The next call was a reported prowler, dispatched to an adjoining beat. I was first on scene. In less than four minutes, I could hear tires squealing and shortly two additional patrol cars slid onto the street. So much for a silent response. When the area was secure and it was confirmed that the prowler was gone upon the officer's arrival, I walked over to where Bart and Ted were standing by their patrol car.

"What in the hell are you two doing...?" I began as soon as I drew near.

"Dammit, Jess, you know you are supposed to advise headquarters before you backup on a call!" Ted cut my tirade short and began his own.

"Do you mean headquarters or you, Ted?" I felt my face growing hot from anger. This was beginning to get ridiculous and I told them so. Both had the civility to look a little chagrined and finally Ted explained.

"This is just between us three." Ted began.

"What?" I asked once again, exasperated.

"Just between us?" Ted asked once more.

"For the love of... yes! Get it out already!" I shrieked.

"Well, the Lieutenant was worried about his little girl, I guess. Anyway, after roll call, he called us over and explicitly ordered us and his exact words were, 'where she goes, you go'. So how the hell can we keep up if you don't tell us where you're going?"

I didn't know whether to laugh, cry, claw my face, or pull my hair. When I finally felt I could speak, I calmly told them.

"I do not need a baby sitter. Understood? I am not the Lieutenant's 'little girl' and if you ever want to hear my voice on the radio again tonight, stop hounding my calls!"

"Jess, if we stop, you promise to call out from now on and call for backup before jumping into anything?" Bart asked evenly, speaking for the first time.

"Yes! What is this, elementary school? I'm a cop for God's sake. Furthermore, I'm not stupid. I don't intend to get myself hurt just to prove I can do this job."

I finished my impromptu speech suddenly weary of being stalked and protected by cops who were supposed to be my friends. Seemingly satisfied, they left me alone and it never happened again. True to my word, I never went into a situation without advising dispatch, at least for the remainder of the night.

CHAPTER 17

1977

In the spring of 1977, the mayor and council decided there were too many whores, queers, winos, drug addicts and drag queens wandering the downtown streets of Reedy View. The chief's words, not the council. The decision came after a group of business owners stormed the council meeting on two consecutive sessions. The Reedy View Herald devoted an entire page in its metro section to the derelict problems. The headlines read, "Council Says Downtown Streets Depraved." Then just below that, "Police Promise Prompt Action Ridding City Of Troublemakers."

Down on their luck, many homeless, the winos and drug addicts often took up residence in kudzu thickets that sprouted on various empty lots. The fire department had fought fifteen wild fires set in the last year by these kudzu dwellers trying to keep warm by a campfire. In the same article, the newspaper reported an increase in strong-armed robberies, solicitation, and begging. The chief, according to scuttlebutt, cussed out the statistics officer, threatening to shove his red and blue stickpins up his ass for releasing negative information to the media. Apparently, the chief took his own ass chewing from the mayor for not informing him about the increase in crime at the last staff meeting. The bottom line was that something had to be done.

With an aggressive downtown economic development project in the works, city hall demanded that the so-called "dregs of society" to be dispatched from the business district, ideally out of the city limits entirely. The mayor directed the chief of police to provide constant police presence. Of course, the department must achieve this with no increase in personnel or overtime pay, according to the mayor and council.

The solution was a temporary squad of three two-manned units, assigned during high crime times, such times gleefully supplied by the statistics officer. The chief reassigned Bart and me to work from 1800 hours (6 PM) until 0300 hours (3AM). The department assigned a duo from each of the three platoons. I was excited to be working a coveted time slot and partnered with Bart on the special shift assignment dubbed the XRAY shift. We were officially 2-XRAY.

Bart and I started the XRAY assignment comfortably together, and began to make cases steadily for loitering, littering, panhandling, public intoxication and traffic citations for a sundry of violations. The objective was to discourage undesirables from flocking downtown. The one difference in Bart's style of policing and mine was that he was not as pro-active as I thought an officer should be.

Although he was no longer one of my training officers, we were friends and felt at ease continuing our discussions and debates on anything from sports to famous personalities. These were usually sprinkled with good-natured joking, However, I was somewhat taken aback when a week into our assignment I became frustrated when Bart took a laissez-faire attitude toward volunteering for calls. He was content to amble along quiet streets until dispatch assigned us a call.

"Bart, do you never go on a call unless you are specifically dispatched?" I laughed, only partly joking, but we joked often about me being such a hotdog cop. For the first time I saw a black mood settle over Bart and I realized he was angry, although he never said a word. Apparently, he was not fond of criticism, whether implied or direct, and no matter how minor or well meaning. At first, I tried kidding him out of his churlishness but he was having none of it. His reaction was so disproportionate that at first I thought he was putting me on.

We spent much of the rest of the night in

loaded silence. Each time I tried to start a conversation he lit a cigarette and said nothing. He purposely alternated his attention between the view from his driver's side window and the roadway ahead. His sullen behavior left me bewildered. This behavior was so uncharacteristic of the person I thought I knew the last couple of years.

Finally, about an hour before the end of shift, he discussed a traffic accident we were investigating. This was the first conversation in almost three hours. After we cleared, he asked if I could do with some coffee.

"I definitely need a cup, maybe two." His suggestion and the conversation were music to my ears. We headed to the Koffee Klatch and I fully expected him to apologize—or at least explain. We sat in a booth and sipped our coffee while he made pointless small talk. Neither of us mentioned the earlier incident. Momma Alex would probably call him a strange bird, but I was surprised at the relief I felt that he was acting somewhat normal again. Yet, it was unsettling. Then I became annoyed with myself for even giving a rat's ass. All these emotions were swirling about but went unspoken.

After the coffee break, we both seemed to have forgotten the incident. It was over, but a kernel of misapprehension lodged deep in my psyche. Later I would look back on that night as a defining moment in our relationship, a red flag I failed to recognize. I did not yet know his darkness would haunt my days for years.

Chapter 18

PRESENT

My fingers grew stiff from writing, a subtle reminder of middle age. As I glanced at the clock on my porch, I was surprised it was already noon. I had filled nine pages in my journal and it was time for a break. I smiled at the pleasant memories and grimaced at the painful ones.

My husband was cutting grass. And I think about how much I love this man. Even before I knew he existed, he slipped into my life as quietly as the sun slips into the day with those first golden tinges of warmth and light. The warmth, after a numbing cold. When, at long last, you finally turn your face and revel in a glowing passion that left you with an ache at the thought of losing it. Yes, flowery and poetic as it is — that is my heart.

Suddenly I heard the roar of a motorcycle rounding the corner. The sound was loud and seemed to shake the foundation. As the engine grew louder, I could tell it had to have pulled into our driveway. My husband waves and turns off the riding mower and climbs off. I started out the back but before I could get down the steps, my best friend Casey rounded the side yard with a motorcycle helmet tucked under her arm.

"Dear God in heaven, Casey, what are you up to now?" I asked, giving her a hug. I was hoping her latest boyfriend was with her--but, no, she was alone, on a motorcycle. "Are you crazy?" I asked as I descended the steps from the porch.

She was laughing like a kid. "You've gotta see my new toy," she boasted . "I told you I was gonna do it and I did!"

"Had to be a Harley." My husband eyes the motorcycle appraisingly. Sure enough, there sat a huge cream-colored Harley Hog, shiny chrome, and brand-new.

"You've lost your damn mind, Casey. You're almost what...over 50, for Christ sake!"

"I am not; you're closer to... 50 than I am." Then she threw her head back and howled her infectious laugh. My adventurous husband was already walking the motorcycle backwards out of the driveway to try it out.

"You don't mind, do you?" he asked. She nodded, knowing he was an experienced biker.

"Wish you would reconsider lunch, Casey."

"Nope, it should be just you. The only reason you want me is because you're such a chicken," she teased me. "But I brought a gift. I spent half the night going through boxes, knowing it was there somewhere." She handed me a five by seven framed picture I had not seen in years. As soon as I saw it, I could feel tears brimming.

"Oh, stop your bawling,'" she said. "I hope it's all right." Her own eyes were damp, I noticed.

"It's absolutely perfect. Thanks Casey." I gave her another hug, this time not so quick. This would make the perfect gift for that old acquaintance I was meeting after twenty years.

I could not have loved Casey more if she were my own sister. We shared so much history. She still wore her hair long and straight although those dark tresses, were now sprinkled with gray. She was still as beautiful as she was the first time I met her, over thirty years ago.

CHAPTER 19

1976

As often is the case, my circle of friends was a small group of other cops, and most of them male. The department had hired a few other women, spread out to make sure each shift had a 'token' female. A few made it through probation, many did not.

One of these rookie female officers threw herself into my life quite unexpectedly. When Acacia Demarches was not patrolling the streets of Reedy View, like me, I discovered she was going through her own domestic crisis. One crisis that brought her to my attention launched a lifelong friendship.

Acacia long ago, shortened her name to Casey. She was tall, athletic with classic Greek features. Her black hair was long and she had piercing dark eyes. Over the years, we would consume dozens of Greek cookies, Baklava, and her killer rice pudding. I put on the pounds, while she remained slim.

Casey's grandfather, born on one of the Greek islands, moved his family to America in the 1930s. Her grandfather had owned and managed a restaurant in Reedy View for more than forty years. His well-known establishment, The Greek Isle, fed and clothed four children and sent them all to college. Casey's father was now a prominent attorney in Tampa, Florida.

After college, Casey had worked briefly with the Florida State Bureau of Investigations, carrying out mundane duties and making a few undercover narcotic buys. Her father continued to press her to attend law school, but her desire to be a cop was too strong. When Casey realized that the connections her father had called on to get her the job was also preventing her from real assignments, she moved to Reedy View, where her grandfather still owned his restaurant and she began waiting tables until the Reedy View Police Department hired her as a police officer. Her resume spoke for itself, but far away from her father's over protectiveness.

The first time I met Casey, we worked a special detail at one of the malls, as decoys for a purse-snatcher. Recent attacks had escalated to violence when he had knocked an elderly woman down and she had broken her hip from a fall. Our job was to wander around the various stores and parking areas, with an expensive purse slung casually over our shoulder…trying to appear unsuspecting and vulnerable.

The only thing we accomplished were very sore feet from the spike heels we wore. Store security arrested the suspect the next day, but without our help. During the detail, it became obvious that Casey and I were alike, not to mention the whole police thing. I liked her down-to-earth personality and the serious attitude she had about law enforcement.

The first time I laid eyes on her, I thought she looked like a beautiful exotic bird, wild and free. We felt a connection from the beginning, but schedules usually meant only the occasional cup of coffee at shift change.

At times, my male counterparts could act rather juvenile, and thought I would be jealous of another female on the department-which I never understood. Sometimes I never could figure out the thought process of men.

"You got some competition now, huh Jess?" They would laugh, trying to get a rise out of me. "She looks like Cleopatra, don't cha think?"

"Cleopatra was Egyptian, not Greek." I deadpanned. While they stared at me without a clue, I continued. "You know, the ruler of Egypt."

"You read too much Jordan."

"It was a movie."

"What?"

"Cleopatra was a movie with Elizabeth Taylor."

"Who?"

I would just shake my head, roll my eyes, and walk off. Although their antics could be exasperating, they were joking good naturedly, so I took it in stride.

About a month after our joint assignment, my phone rang. It was my day off and I was trying to catch up on housecleaning, an activity I loathed.

"This is Casey; I need your help."

Her voice sounded raspy and I sensed something was not right.

"Are you hurt?"

My intuition kicked in and I knew something was very wrong.

"No, I..." Her voice broke and I knew she was crying.

"I'm on the way."

Although I was not positive, I had a suspicion what may have transpired and that it was domestic related. Before I headed for the door, I crammed my I.D. pack into the back pocket of my jeans. I pushed my off duty .357 Smith and Wesson into a shoulder holster and pulled on an oversized denim shirt as I flew down the steps from my apartment over the garage and to my car. I backed my seven-year-old Blue Moon down the rock-paved driveway, into the street and then floored it.

CHAPTER 20

1976

A short time later, I pulled into a parking space in front of Casey's apartment. Parking next to her Monte Carlo, I also looked for the car belonging to Jack Morris, another police officer she had been dating, but I did not see it. Rumors had circulated that Casey was involved with her former partner. After he received a transfer, Jack had moved in with Casey.

Jack was newly divorced, and this could be a predicable situation for cops. Typically, there was more divorce, adultery, suicide, and personal drama within police departments than on any television soap opera. Just some of many maladies plaguing cops, who in their personal lives, grappled with relationships, money problems and the atrocities they witnessed daily.

Jack Morris had once been a good cop. But, after he was promoted to detective, he started drinking heavily. Some suggested he was doing more than drinking. Whatever his drug of choice, when he was high, he got mean.

Because, my instincts were screaming domestic disturbance, I approached the apartment cautiously. I immediately snapped into cop mode, focusing on the apartment door ajar. Sunlight was streaming through the opening, from the patio doors across from the entry. I instinctively felt for the butt of my gun as I approached the door and stood to one side as I pushed it open wider with my foot, simultaneously calling Casey's name.

"I'm in the kitchen." Casey responded, sounding more like herself. As I peered around the door, I saw her walking to meet me and I relaxed as I entered. With the sun at her back, her face was in shadow. When I was closer, I suddenly stopped and gasped at the utter devastation, not only of the apartment, but also to her face.

Her once immaculate apartment was in shambles. Furniture was broken and littered the floor. Houseplants had been thrown askew and their contents emptied onto the cream-colored carpet. An end table thrown against a large wall and a large painting was hanging sideways and shards of glass hung precariously from the splintered frame.

A footprint was on the door leading into the master bedroom and the door was partly off the hinges, the casing was splintered and the knob on the floor.

I took all of this in as I rushed to Casey to determine how seriously she was injured. Despite the apartment destruction, she looked worse. Both eyes were bloodshot and blackened. Her left eye was almost swollen shut. She had a cut on her lower lip and blood was oozing from her nose and mouth. Her clothes were torn and patches of her dark hair had been ripped from her scalp. I was so enraged I was almost dizzy. I reached for the phone on the floor to call an ambulance.

"No ambulance." She pleaded. "Please don't."

"Will you at least go to an urgent care? You may need stitches."

"No, I'll be okay." She moved slowly and stared at the ruins of her home. She was almost in shock and far from fine, physically or mentally.

"Damn Casey, who did this?"

"You probably can figure that out." She replied, resigned to what had transpired. "Some cop I am, huh?"

"You're a good cop, Casey. But Jack Morris is a bastard, not a cop."

"Thanks for coming. I didn't know if he would come back. I guess I shouldn't have put you in the situation. But I'm scared..." Her voice trailed off, and she stared at nothing.

I was consumed by a rage that scared me. How could a police officer do this? How could a police officer allow this to happen to her? Then I was immediately ashamed for thinking that.

"I'm glad you called and I wish the son of a

bitch would come back." My anger continued to build. "He needs to be in jail Casey. You have to press charges.

"No. No report, no one else. I don't want anyone to know, please." The no was emphatic, but the *please* came out as a whisper.

"Of course it's your decision and I would never do anything you didn't want me to do."

"I'm going to that new Resident Inn tonight; I can't stay here. Will you just follow me to make sure he's not around or following me? I've packed as few things to get me through the next few days. I cannot go home. Mom and Dad are ten hours away and Daddy would kill him." She grew silent and several tears ran slowly down her bruised cheek.

I knew of nothing to do, but pull her into my arms and she began to weep. As her crying lessened, I firmly turned her around and told her to wash her face; we were packing a lot more than for a few days.

"You're coming home with me, no discussion." I looked around the room and felt sick at my stomach, knowing how much worse things could have been.

"It's going to be quite a while before anyone can live here again. I need a roommate anyway, so you don't even need to return." I could tell she was processing her options.

Someone else taking charge was exactly what she needed in her traumatized state. Without another word we began packing and making trips back and forth to both vehicles. The apartment complex manager had sent maintenance over to change the locks and they had already started some repairs inside.

The anxiety did not let up as I carefully scanned the parking lot each time I went out with another box, or heard a vehicle pulling into the lot. I found new packing boxes, still folded, in a spare closet, speaking volumes about her intentions before today. I wondered if her plans to leave had set off his anger and assault.

Regardless of what had transpired, I was seething at just who the hell Jack Morris thought he was to hit Casey or any woman. It was unthinkable and appalling. A cop? Inconceivable. But, even as I thought this, I also knew there would be those old school cops, the good ole boy system, that would help cover it up. Cops carried guns. I instinctively touched the butt of my weapon. My stomach roiled at the thought.

CHAPTER 21

1976

"Midnight, here kitty kitty, Midnight." Casey was calling her cat. Cat? Shit. I hated cats. Well, hate was too strong a word, I was afraid of cats. I stood watching Casey looking under her bed when I felt something rub against my leg. I almost had a stroke. I looked down a the most beautiful creature, with white down his face, one foot white and the rest solid black.

"Somebody cuss that damn cat." I could still hear my grandfather say as he made a cross on the windshield when a black cat would cross the road in front of us. But if it wasn't solid black, you were safe. I still looked down at Midnight skeptical. Casey didn't need me being a *scaredy cat*...so I didn't say a word. The last thing she placed in her car, was a litter box, litter and cat food. *Crap.* Briefly I thought Jack deserved the cat, then felt ashamed.

At last we finished and headed for my place five or six miles away. To be on the safe side, I circled blocks and did other maneuvers to make sure we weren't being followed.

When I was confident no one was following, I led Casey to my driveway, and directed her to pull her red, 1973 Monte Carlo into the double garage underneath the living quarters, then I pulled my Blue Moon in next to hers and pulled down the garage doors and locked them. Steps led up into the kitchen. The only other entrance had steps leading up the side that entered into the living room.

The place I called home was a bit of luck when I found it, and I could not believe my good fortune. It was in the middle of the city, yet it felt far removed. There was a private driveway off the back alleyway and was part of a four-acre estate. It was built in the early twentieth century and the garage apartment was constructed in 1930, away from the main house as servants' quarters. A couple who worked as the housekeeper and her husband the gardener, lived there until the health of the original owners required skilled nursing care in a facility.

It was bricked, with the same brick as the main house. A wide lawn and hedge of tall camellias separated the quarters from the main house. It was quiet and private and I loved it. There were two small bedrooms, each with a bath, separated by a large living room. The kitchen and dining area ran the length of the rear of the apartment, with a large pantry on one end and a dining nook on the opposite. It was cozy and unique, yet oddly spacious. The current owners remodeled it for their son while he was in college and added a large screened porch the length of the apartment with a tin shed roof that made music when it rained. The screened porch was twenty feet off the ground and I reverted to the old custom of using it as a sleeping porch on nights when it wasn't too muggy. I had simply dubbed it The Quarters.

I welcomed the secluded, relaxing atmosphere of my home. The only sounds I heard were the sounds of nature. It was silent enough to make sleeping on the graveyard shift easy.

The owners, a retired businessman and his wife, traveled extensively when they became empty nesters, so having a cop living on the premises appealed to them. Just the month before, they offered to sell me The Quarters and half an acre. I jumped at the chance and we were scheduled to close the next week.

With the garage doors down, no one would know Casey was there, if anyone even thought to check. Not that many officers were aware we knew each other, certainly not well enough to be roommates. I just prayed Jack had not circled the parking lot earlier and seen us loading the vehicles. I deduced he would have made a scene right then, because according to Casey he was very drunk. I hoped that he was sleeping it off somewhere.

"Welcome to The Quarters, first thing we need is an icepack, I have one somewhere." I led her into my guest bedroom and showed her the bath. I found an icepack and headed for the kitchen to fill it. I looked up and Casey was following me silently to the kitchen and back through the den, like a dog shadowing its master.

"Sit." I pointed to a rocker in the corner as I began to put fresh linens on the bed. Casey docilely did as she was told, no longer speaking or protesting. She moved almost robotically as she sat and began to take in her surroundings. I think I was a little in shock myself. My anxiety level was still high, but beginning to subside. I willed myself to calm down and get over my anger at Jack Morris. As I thought about how it might have ended my blood ran cold. I could hardly believe that another cop, sworn to protect, would do this to someone he supposedly loved. Yet I knew not to be surprised, some cops were bad.

Cops are human. Some humans are just bad. I had been a cop for less than a week when I first witnessed police brutality. Two veteran officers were processing an older man for public drunkenness. It is hard to determine age when hard living and excessive alcohol took their toll. Often these hardcore alcoholics lived in filthy squatter camps around the city, spending their days wandering, begging, and sometimes stealing.

The old drunk, with his hands handcuffed behind his back, was shamefully thin. He was having a hard time keeping his tattered pants from falling down. His face was sunken and red, with broken veins and he was almost toothless. As he lost the battle with his pants, they fell below his knees, as he struggled to catch them, made more awkward with his cuffed hands. There was no dignity left, as he wore no underwear.

The arresting officers turned around and began to curse him.

"Pull your pants up asshole!" and he punched him in the back. His partner turned and became as outraged as the partner toward the helpless, inebriated man. They threw him to the floor, and pounded his face until blood smeared on the floor. The scene made me physically ill, as I stepped back into the alley, not wanting to see anymore. Yet I felt disgust with myself, because I could do nothing. Would do nothing. I was just a rookie. A female rookie. I prayed I would never be assigned to ride with these poor excuses for men, much less for cops. One of those cops was Jack Morris. It was doubtful Casey knew that story. And I didn't bother to impart it now. I just knew brutality had no place in the police department, and cops who abused their families should not carry guns and be cops.

In 1996, Title 18 of the United States Code was strengthened by removing the exemption for Law Enforcement officers and military personnel convicted of Domestic Violence. In plain English, they can't carry a gun. You can't be a police officer if you can't carry a gun.

CHAPTER 22

1975-1976

I became an avid reader the first time I read a book about four orphans who set up housekeeping in a train boxcar. Gertrude Chandler Warner awakened my imagination and I never forgot living in that boxcar with those children. I graduated to Nancy Drew and rode around on my blue bike pretending it was a blue Roadster, imagining mysteries to solve. Then I discovered Victoria Holt and Gothic novels. From a little house in Reedy View, South Carolina, I would escape effortlessly into the past centuries in England's Cornwall and explore the windswept Cornish moors. My discovery of reading was 'a glorious gift.

It was a given I would consume Serpico the same way in 1973. Peter Maas wrote about good cop versus bad cops when he penned the true story of Frank Serpico, a New York City undercover police officer. Then it was brought to the big screen and reached an even larger audience. While police corruption was rampant in larger cities it was far away from sleepy, boring Reedy View. Or so I thought.

I was stunned as our own department struggled to overcome the disgrace of its own resident bunch of dirty cops in 1974. Seven were arrested and prosecuted six months before I went to the Academy.

As an adult, my heroes had become soldiers and police officers; I was consumed by my own idealistic desires to be part of the thin blue line. Therefore, when the facts emerged and the officers charged, I was shaken to my core. For a brief time, I was so disillusioned, I considered dropping my criminal justice major and pursuing another career.

Seeing each of these criminals tried, in court became my determined objective. I attended all of the trials. It was then I realized true cops were still my heroes. My admiration and pride swelled as I absorbed the facts of the case and listened to the testimony, how officers in our own department brought these charlatans and felons down and saw justice dispensed.

Yes, these fine police officers, symbols of truth and integrity walked to the witness box, and immediately restored my belief and faith about law enforcement, and my confidence in the men and women who wore the uniform. The undercover operation brought down the corrupt and made the Reedy View Police Department, one of the best departments in the southeast.

Corrupt cops are the dregs of society, criminals masked in cops' clothing, betraying the trust of citizens they had sworn to protect. Departmental Public Relations touted we had *cleaned our own door steps*. But, public opinion and support of the police took a nose dive.

The facts presented included the investigating Lieutenant had wire tapped the patrol cars of these thugs, and one of the dirty cops, turned informant, was wired and the full extent of criminality and ruthlessness was revealed. These criminals committed burglaries while on duty. If an alarm was activated at a business, they would simply call out on scene, and take the incident report after loading up the patrol car with stolen goods. The chilling tapes revealed the extent of the callousness when the informant had asked one of the 15-year veterans, what would happen if the Lieutenant or Sergeant ever rolled up during a burglary?

With quiet calm he replied, "Dead men don't talk."

Four of the infamous Reedy View cops even worked as training officers. A few of their well-trained rookies were eventually charged with receiving and possessing stolen property. They got a break when they agreed to testify against the senior officers who trained them.

Portrayed as impressionable young men, I did not care—their greedy weakness made me sick. I continued to pursue a career in law enforcement and did not allow common thieves to tarnish the badges of brave, courageous men and women who put their lives on the line daily. When I finally fastened my own badge to a blue uniform, I felt only pride.

In 1975, the first female police officer in uniform patrolling in a marked cruiser, right there in front of God and Reedy View, proved to be the greatest public relations tool the department could have imagined. Who knows—maybe it was why they finally hired me. I think it probably was twofold. This meant I was asked to speak at various functions such as local women's clubs and business organizations.

Before my first night on patrol, I had been interviewed by the newspaper and two local television stations. Suddenly there was Jessica Jordan, blond and twenty-something, photo on the front page and talking on the six o'clock news. I'm sure there were more than a few feathers ruffled among the old-timers.

After a continuous deluge of newspaper articles, morning and evening papers, Momma bought a scrapbook. I equally loved and hated all the attention. Eventually the notoriety grew tiresome. Although I was soon joined by a second female officer, we were still a minority of two among two hundred. Usually on each tour of duty, I encountered yet another person who would stare, be supportive, or recoil in total shock when they saw a policewoman get out of a patrol car. Such things just were not done in Reedy View.

The most memorable reaction was a disturbance call Ted and I answered at the local hospital emergency room. Ted wheeled to the door and I jumped out while he pulled the patrol car away from the emergency entrance.

"I'll be one minute, Jordan," he yelled as I went through the automatic doors. The receptionist was waiting and hit another automatic button opening an inner set of doors leading into the examination area. I headed down the hallway and could hear loud voices.

"In here!" a nurse shouted as she exited the exam room. She suddenly stopped and stared as I ran down the hall. "Oh my God, you won't do!" she wailed and ran back into the room. By this time Ted was through the second set of doors and fast catching up with me. We entered the small exam room and encountered a heroin addicted, skinny, short, white male, no more than eighteen or nineteen years old. He was doing karate chops in the air and shouting profanities as he made a sweep with the sides of his hands. He had a doctor and nurse backed against the wall, and the out-of-control addict continued to yell and do karate chops in the air. He was the textbook example of the extraordinary strength displayed by a person on drugs or a mental patient. Adrenaline makes them twice as strong as normal, no inhibitions. I could not believe no one was injured.

Neither Ted nor I spoke a word. We just looked at each other and in perfect tandem took him to the floor. In no time flat, we had the young man handcuffed and under control. The doctor pronounced him physically fit for a jail cell. He and the nurse stared slack jawed and relieved as we led him out of the room.

Our prisoner continued to scream at the top of his lungs, scaring the medical personnel and other patients. Then like Houdini, he somehow managed to get his cuffed wrists from behind his back to the front. It was a trick I never figured out, usually accomplished only by those high enough to feel no pain and lithe enough to twist like a pretzel. Off to the jail we headed, our prisoner doing his best to karate chop the bulletproof glass partition with his handcuffed hands.

To the delight of my fellow officers, my partner shared the story—with some embellishment, of course—at the end of shift. Although there was belly laughing, Ted ended by adding that I had carried my own weight, in other words, he established my credentials as a good partner. That made up for all the laughter. I was slowly earning the respect of the other officers, and their respect reinforced that I was doing a good job. Although it still rankled that they were surprised that a woman could be a decent cop.

For sure, I would never be lost in a sea of blue.

I stood out like a sore thumb whether in a patrol car or working a crime scene. Yet, it was a small price to pay for the marvelous journey.

CHAPTER 23

1950

My first memory was when I was barely two years old. I was sitting in my grandmother's big black '49 Mercury, Momma Alex and me, while Momma and Daddy went inside the hospital for my baby brother.

I've been told memories for one so young are impossible, but I know what I know. It's fate that I would remember the momentous event, my brother, my partner in surviving our family. Momma Alex told me all about my baby brother, Charles Edward. I would have a playmate. I remember Momma getting into the car holding a tiny blue-wrapped bundle with a white-knitted cap peeking out of the blanket. It was not clear if he was a pet or a toy, but I was pretty sure he wouldn't be playing for a while.

Charlie made a surprise appearance in September when he was supposed to have waited until November. He had to remain in the hospital for two months, in an incubator. It would be a few years before I learned what premature babies meant. Being born off schedule was his first transgression, and almost killing Momma was his second. Momma would remain angry at him for the next 48 years. That is when she finally forgot her anger along with most of her memory.

I remember nothing else about that day, but the mere anticipation of such an event burned deep into my sub-consciousness.

It seemed perfectly natural we should have fetched him from the hospital nursery as we would a sack of groceries from Winn Dixie. The story proved so captivating, I begged Momma Alex to tell it repeatedly. I loved anything dramatic, especially when it involved life and death.

There must have been nothing spectacular about my own birth because I never heard them speak of it. It annoyed me a little, that my brother got center stage getting-born.

CHAPTER 24

1950

The story of my brother's birth, is imprinted in my mind like a movie, although of course I have no recollection of those perilous hours when I almost lost my momma and my brother.

"The day began like any other," Momma Alex always began. "You could cut the heat and humidity with knife." In South Carolina, everyone is craving cooler days and the anticipation of autumn when September arrives, but it could sometimes sizzle right on into October. Momma's pains had started late that morning and at first she thought it was false labor. Then water gushed out first, then blood.

"Momma, did it hurt?" I asked her once, when she was present during a recounting. She glared at me and snapped, "Yes it hurt." So I never asked her about it again. Momma did not like pain and talking with Charlie or me could really piss her off.

Momma Alex said Daddy rushed the half mile to Valley Grocery to call an ambulance. We did not have a phone yet, but we sure got one after my brother pulled that little caper. I spent my early childhood crediting Charlie for bringing us rightfully into the modern age. We got a telephone before we got our first television set.

Momma Alex said Daddy slowed in front of her house, just a quarter mile from ours, and yelled to her that Momma was in bad shape, and he was following the ambulance into town. Momma Alex jumped in the car with Daddy and they both headed for the hospital. Doctor Woodberry, they said, frantically rushed to the hospital emergency room and his mouth was set in a thin line and his brows furrowed, as he rushed into one of only two examining rooms. I think Momma Alex embellished a little here and there over the years each time she told the story. I know more details about that day than I know about today.

The ambulance attendants carried Momma in on a stretcher, holding tightly to the wooden handles. The blood flowed heavily through the thick sheet of white cotton canvas. Momma Alex said she stayed right there with Momma and Daddy. I never knew where I was during all this; no one ever told me.

"Faye, hang on you're losing a lot of blood. We are starting a transfusion. If we stop the bleeding, you have a chance, but we've got to stop the bleeding." Dr. Woodberry had told her.

Momma Alex said the doctor's voice trailed off as he and the emergency room staff began giving Momma blood transfusions. Doctor Woodberry was short and fat with big ears and a jolly voice. He always reminded me of a large elf. He remained our family doctor until we reached adulthood and he finally retired. He was a heavy smoker who breathed loudly and heavily from the slightest exertion of rushing around. That is the vision I have of him, as he rushed around that day saving Momma and Charlie.

Momma Alex said Momma was pale and weak as a kitten. "No one thought she was going to make it," Momma Alex said.

As the second bag of blood flowed into Momma's veins, she looked up and pleaded — and this was a part of the story I particularly loved, "If I don't make it, Alex, please take care of Jessica."

"I will, sugar, I'll take the best care of her in the world. But don't you worry, you'll be all right," Momma Alex assured her daughter-in-law. "You were just twenty-three months old, Jessica Grace. I prayed to Jesus, yes I did. And Jesus was listening, yes ma'am he was."

CHAPTER 25

1950

Although it was a rough beginning for Baby Charlie, he arrived with a hardy appetite and began growing like a weed. To this day, he is a big eater and seldom sleeps past five A.M. The circumstances of his birth must be deep-rooted.

My favorite part of the story was how much formula Charlie would consume while he remained in the hospital. He ate so much that the nurses would joke about how much Baby Jordan could put away. Once, when an orderly dropped a metal bedpan on the tiled floor, one of the nurses was startled, then quipped, "Oh Lord, I think Jordan just blew up in the nursery."

My brother was my first best friend, even when we were trying to knock each other's block off as kids. We filled our days with adventure and exploration. Romping through the woods and clearing bike paths, then scrounging through the barn for scrap wood to make bridges across the ditches winding among the country lanes in our neighborhood. We worked for hours arranging rocks into rooms of imaginary playhouses. We loved each other, protected each other, became infuriated with each other, cried when we physically fought, and laughed often.

As a young child, I realized Momma was continuously mad at Charlie, and I wondered if it was because he created such a stir at birth. She was unyielding in her harshness toward him. The difference in the way she treated us was obvious to me and made me sick with guilt. I was always trying to make it better for him because I knew it wasn't his fault he almost killed Momma. The guilt was really bad, because sometimes I wished he had.

The feeling of culpability lingered long into adulthood as both Charlie and I struggled to correct the many transgressions only Momma seemed to recognize. As a result, from a very early age I learned to be a fixer, or at least try.

Life always seemed harder for my brother. He received more spankings, but we were equally lacking in maternal affection. Charlie would often times antagonize Momma, knowing the result would be a switching. I never remember warm hugs and I never remember the words 'I love you', until she was in the *home* many years later. She never played with us as most parents do with their small children. There was little fun and laughter in our house. Charlie and I made our own fun. That fun came from getting out of the house as soon as we could every day. We were either off to school, or in summer, off on our bikes until dusk. We were with Momma Alex every week-end. We were glad to escape and I'm sure Momma was relieved to see us go.

It was instinctive that I became Charlie's protector. I was older, and bigger. I remember one incident, when two hellions came upon us at the Mill Hill Park. They were maybe Charlie's age or a year older, but younger than me. For some reason, Charlie being Charlie said something derogatory while sitting at the top of the sliding board. One walked up the slide, and the other climbed the steps. One punched him in the stomach and Charlie started crying. I had already started running for the slide, screaming like a banshee. One ran and I dragged the other one, on the ladder, down by his legs and punched him before he broke away and ran. I screamed that I would kill them if they ever went near Charlie again. But the biggest bully, was Momma and I couldn't protect Charlie from her.

Momma's anger didn't need a reason, it just was. Charlie could make Momma mad over the slightest insignificant thing. She would scream at him, switch him and sometimes slap his face. I heard Daddy tell her not to ever slap his face again so she quit slapping him in front of Daddy. One of the repercussions from his premature birth were eye problems; surgery was required at Duke University when Charlie was three. Knowing this, I would clench my fists loathing her and wanting desperately to grab her hand away from hitting Charlie. I felt rage, wanting to hit her so she would know what it felt like, the sting of the slap. I dreamed about seeing those red imprints of my hand on her face. Whenever Charlie wasn't blinded after one of her rants, I was deeply relieved. But, I got my share of punishment. I regularly received a switching. Although she used various implements, a switch, she simply called a 'hickory', was her weapon of choice. They did not come from a hickory tree, usually, just Ligustrum stems or she could grab a fly swatter, if we were inside. When Charlie and I got into one of our spitting and slapping fights, Momma would spank us both, declaring that way, she got the right one. That is the only time I remember her being fair, and I did respect her for that, although I was mad as a hornet when it was not my fault.

Charlie could always make even the direst of circumstances funny. We would have to stifle our mirth many times until Momma was out of earshot. She would make us fetch our own hickory. We would walk slowly around trying to put it off for as long as possible. Charlie would always come back with a tiny twig gripped in his little fingers. Momma did not have a sense of humor. It would send Momma into one of her conniption fits, and we were usually spanked harder, but it was worth it to give her grief. As soon as she turned her back and out of earshot, we made faces, sticking our tongues out at her retreating figure. Then we would laugh uncontrollably with tears streaking our dirty faces. We learned early, laughter is a great and redeeming medicine.

CHAPTER 26

1950s -1960s

Both Momma and Daddy's families were hardcore Baptists. Any church other than Baptist was suspect. Catholics were particularly uncommon and worrisome. *"Don't want to have anything to do with those Catholics."*

The preacher constantly bellowed from the pulpit Sunday after Sunday about how we were going to hell. Momma and Daddy seldom attended church in those days. Momma would pack us off to church with our maternal Grandma. It was a conservative congregation in rural Taylors, South Carolina. I viewed it as just another form of punishment on us kids.

Although Momma Alex did not attend church regularly either, she prayed every day and she said the Lord knew she was a good woman. I always thought Momma Alex had a much more accurate outlook on religion and spirituality.

Grandma's country church had the pulpit enclosed with a wooden gate. The preacher would yell, red faced, with spittle flying every Sunday. He would perspire so heavily, he constantly wiped his face with a handkerchief. It was rather a relief that he seemed to be contained, because he scared me to death. He, much like Momma, was mad at everybody. My stomach would knot, knowing I was probably on my way to hell for one transgression or another, although I didn't know exactly what all the sins were, I was pretty sure I was a sinner.

Even our prayer we recited every night was terrifying.

"Now I lay me down to sleep, I pray the Lord my soul to keep. But if I should die before I wake, I pray the Lord my soul to take." I would lie there for a long time; afraid Jesus would snatch me right out of my bed.

One incident in particular would weigh on my mind and heart for many years. It began in Sunday school. I was seven years old, sitting primly, wearing my Sunday dress, my Sunday patent leather Mary Jane's, even my Sunday panties with ruffles on the back.

"Next Sunday is Mother's Day," the teacher announced. She was always as mad as that preacher, as she shook her finger at us, and said Jesus demanded we honor and love our mothers.

"Honor thy father and mother," she recited straight from the Bible. I was pretty sure you

112

could go straight to hell if you didn't. I did not think I could honor Momma, although I wasn't sure what that meant. I often pondered how well Jesus really knew my Momma. Seeing as how she did not go to church often, I hoped he would be understanding.

My Sunday School teacher was a tall, stern, dark-haired woman who never smiled. She wore no makeup and she wore her hair pulled into a severe bun at the back of her head. I would sit entranced by dark hair that quivered under her prominent nose, marveling at a woman with a mustache. Her dresses were always dark colored, the hem reaching well below her knees. I seldom listened to what she said, but just stared in fascination. She had a keen intelligence. She knew we were all horrible little sinners. I tried not to think about my bike waiting for me at home. I was pretty sure Jesus knew what I was thinking, I couldn't stop myself from wanting to be anywhere but that little room. So again, my stomach was in guilty knots.

"Next Sunday, boys and girls, I want you to get up from your beds and go into our mother's bedroom and tell her that you love her. Even if you don't have a gift, your words of love will be the only gift she will want."

Sitting there, I felt my stomach twist even worse than was customary. The assignment the teacher gave was incredibly difficult. Carrying out that difficult task was on my mind off and on all week.

The anxiety was almost unbearable as I went to bed the following Saturday night. Finally, the dreaded Mother's Day arrived. I could not even get out of bed. I laid there unable to move, paralyzed. Dismay spread through my entire being. I tried to make my feet hit the floor and move across the bedroom and out the door, but I could not. Lying there looking at my door, I knew I could not tell my mother that I loved her. I was awash with remorse. I was a terrible daughter. A horrible person. Yes, I was going straight to hell.

Later that morning in Sunday school, the teacher asked if we had all told our mothers that we loved them. Everyone's hands shot up. Suddenly mine rose as high as the rest. My stomach was hurting so bad I thought I might have to run to the bathroom. Somehow, I survived the Sunday School class, but later during big church, I kept a watchful eye out for either Jesus or the Devil. I was afraid one of 'em might just snatch my butt right off the pew after I had told such a bald face lie and in church.

CHAPTER 27

1950s -1960s

As I look back at my childhood, part of me remembers happy times. The happy times I remember are probably credited to Daddy, Charlie and Momma Alex.

There were never decorated birthday cakes. If Momma baked a cake, it was either coconut or the dreaded Christmas fruitcake. Charlie and I hated coconut and fruitcake.

I remember one birthday party as a child. It was the year I turned thirteen. A surprise party with friends from school and even the popular girls were there.

The first person I saw was my grandmother, and knew instantly that she, not momma, had orchestrated it. I don't remember Charlie ever having a birthday party as a child and I've always felt guilty about that.

Momma Alex would bake pies, apple and

peach. Chocolate and rainbow cakes, and we loved them and her. She stepped in to give us the only dose of normality and love we knew. So, we frolicked in our not so innocent life and grew up fast with a mother like ours.

Momma, unknowingly, was a great teacher. We learned to always be cautious, and always ask questions, and trust no one. Especially don't trust your momma. A good example was when Charlie started having fever blisters, Momma's older sister, had trained as a practical nurse when she was in her forties. That made her as good as a doctor to momma. My aunt decided he was constipated. An enema was the answer she said. We had no idea what that was, and Momma saw no reason to explain it.

She called Charlie into the bathroom and had this red rubber bag hanging, and filled with liquid. A long hose protruded with some ominous gadget on the end. Charlie hesitated about going in, and I just stared wide-eyed.

"Come here Charlie!" Momma commanded.

"No Momma, what is that?"

"I said get in here!"

"What you gonna do Momma?"

"When I get a hold of you, I'm sticking this up your little ass!" We both ran. She finally corralled him and gave him the enema; it did not cure his fever blisters.

Thoughts of *what if,* always pushed me into a dreadful sense of guilt, because in the dark of night, I thought about what if momma had not survived when Charlie was born. What if Momma Alex had raised Charlie and me? Would Daddy have lived longer? Darkness would overtake me. Then, the guilt.

As I think about the unhappy times, our unorthodox family life, I know we were never a normal family. No family game nights, no hugs, no "I love you" heard. But did we know we were lacking in these things? If they never were, did you miss them?

My brother and I, when we were away from Momma, were happy because we had each other. After his premature birth and eye operations, he was perfectly healthy. Charlie and I both were plagued with curly hair, his darker like Daddy's and mine strawberry blonde that was usually bleached mostly blonde every summer by the sun. He luckily also inherited Daddy's complexion, which turned a golden brown during the summer. I ended up with Momma's fairer complexion and with it, a tendency to burn and had an abundance of freckles. When I reached my teens, I was envious of how easily he tanned, while I constantly smelled of Noxzema, vinegar and Sea and Ski suntan lotion.

As a child, during the summer, Charlie was usually clad in shorts with no shirt and no shoes. I wore the same except Momma made me wear a tee shirt or halter top. The two of us were perpetually covered with dirt and grime. As the sun would rise higher, we grew sweaty from biking, playing, or the odd chores Daddy made sure we completed. By the end of each summer day, we looked like little soldiers after a fierce battle.

We fought those battles together with a vengeance, both real and imagined. Our imaginations were our escape. Sometimes we were commandos on a beach in Normandy, especially after seeing an Audie Murphy movie. Alternatively, we were the Cavalry, riding gallantly on our broomstick steeds, flags flying, trumpets blaring, on our way to save the wagon train from wild and savage Indians.

But, guilt would always be a component of my personality that I continued to struggle with and can never completely purge. My Baptist upbringing? The sins of my mother? I'm not sure. It can still rear its ugly head in the most ordinary of circumstances. For years, the simple custom of buying a birthday card or Mother's Day card for Momma was incredibly difficult. I would literally stand for an hour looking at one card and then another. No matter how difficult it was or how long it might take, I was determined to find a card with words that were true but not hurtful. Hallmark did not make those. I could not love a mother who was selfish and critical of everything and everybody. She was infinitely irritated at all things breathing.

The imaginary battles were easily won; the real ones were we lost.

CHAPTER 28

1975

Why does she stay with him if he hits her?

I cannot count the number of times I asked that question. Domestic disturbance calls were routine events. We became familiar with some of the regular domestic disturbance locations. Knew their names, their children's names, where, if anywhere, they worked.

"They always go back even if we arrest him," Ted would tell me about this victim or the next. "She's the one that bails him out of jail. Trust me, Jordan; you will see this over and over on domestic calls."

"I say, they make their bed, let them sleep in it." Ted made this speech when we had responded to Dewey and Loretta's second domestic call.

This was repeated often by one veteran officer after another. An attitude prevailed among many of my male counterparts that made these women a victim twice.

Why do they have kids if they live with or marry someone who beats them? Or, if they'd quit talking back, maybe he'd settle down.

The most infuriating reason was a holier than thou *Christian*, who liked to spout off quotes from the bible about *"the man being head of his house..."* The wife must be subservient to the husband or face the consequences. Incredibly, most often the reason was *because I love him.* So, the woman would go back and try to be a better wife, because so many came to think it was their fault.

Often, when a victim did decide to leave, the abuser wouldn't allow her. Stalking would follow and the violence would increase. Eventually, he would either wear down her resolve or threaten the children or her family. Some women went back because the fear of what might happen was too great. Often times these cases would escalate to murder, regardless.

It would be years into my career before I saw positive changes in domestic violence laws and their enforcement. How police departments across the nation handled domestic disturbance calls would be changed forever when a Connecticut woman, Tracy Thurgood, won a huge monetary award against her local police department after they failed to protect her from her estranged husband.

Although Tracy Thurgood survived the attack, she was left with permanent debilitating injuries.

CHOICES

It simply came down to a crapshoot-the plight of victims of domestic abuse. The only hope was that the vicious cycle of abuse could be broken by intervention, and the parties would seek counseling. As a rookie, I was a starry-eyed crusader with ideas and expectations that were seldom realized.

CHAPTER 29

1975

Three weeks after responding to several domestic calls to Loretta and Dewey's apartment, the sergeant handed me a note at roll call.

"Jordan, I've got a number for you, Loretta, no last name, East Pennsylvania. She wants you to call her ASAP." I glanced the slip of paper, and with dismay I recognized it as a pay phone number. The call was received at 1600 hours the previous afternoon. Somehow, I doubted Loretta was sitting on the curb by a pay phone for seven hours.

"Fallout," the Sergeant bellowed, dismissing roll call. Our platoon filed out, only to line up in the arsenal as we waited for the quartermaster to issue equipment. Each officer received round brass tags with badge numbers engraved. The quartermaster hung a tag in place of each piece of equipment issued. A hand held walkie-talkie, a patrol car, a shotgun. At end of shift, we lined up and reversed the process.

Before leaving police headquarters, even though it was after midnight, I tried the phone number Loretta left. As expected, it went unanswered. Ted and I made our way up the alley to our assigned patrol car. We performed the routine check of seats, gas and tires and noted the beginning mileage.

"Damn Taylor, if he eats chicken one more time and leaves the bones in the floorboard, I'll kick his ass," Ted grumbled. The car smelled like Church's Fried Chicken and reminded me I was hungry. I didn't respond because Ted said the same thing every other day about the officer who was assigned to the same patrol car on the previous shift. He never said a word to him or kicked his ass.

"The twenty-one Loretta left was a pay phone so I bet her old man beat the shit out of her again" After a while, cops begin to talk in code to each other like we do on the radio. Twenty-one for phone calls, thirteen for meal break. I continued around the patrol car and kicked the back tires.

"These damn tires need to be replaced again. Aside from the chicken bones, Taylor drives the hell out of this car." Now I was aggravated.

"I'll be glad when the city starts assigning each shift our own fleet of cars. The word was out, this was in the upcoming budget. Ted and I both liked a well-maintained vehicle; Ted liked them

123

neat and clean, that, I could care less about, but I wanted it running properly. Taylor was not particular about either.

Ted tossed me the keys while walking to the passenger side. "You drive first partner; I need to catch a few winks if the radio stays quiet long enough." It was a Tuesday night, not usually a busy time.

I put the car in drive and eased out of the alleyway. I would drive the first four hours and Ted would take the last four. I was thankful to drive first; in four hours I was afraid I would be comatose.

"I hear the new squads will have radios, A.M. only, but hey, we'll take what we can get." Ted mused.

"You got that right; I'm tired of hearing myself sing."

"I'm tired of hearing you sing, Jordan."

I stuck my tongue at him. We were comfortable working together, and I knew I would miss Ted when my training was complete and I would be assigned to ride with a permanent partner.

"Speaking of Loretta, her call came in yesterday afternoon. She may be dead by now. I don't know why she waits for us to come on duty," I said. Ever since I'd read the riot act to Dewey, Loretta treated me like her guardian angel.

Ted looked at me with one eyebrow cocked.

"Who are you kidding? She waits on us because you're her personal little cop-ette."

I rolled my eyes and tossed my hat at him instead of placing it behind the seat. He caught it and propped it alongside his between the front seat and the prisoner cage that separated us from the back.

"God almighty, Jordan, you're violent already. Okay, I know what you're thinking, let's ride by Miss Loretta's and make sure we don't smell blood. You won't be happy till we do."

He reached for the mike and advised the dispatcher 10-8. I eased the cruiser onto Main Street and headed toward our sector of the city. It's was amazing how the demographics changed once the sun went down and the daily influx of workers left the city and returned to their safe, quiet, bedroom communities.

The dark, empty streets were both serene and sinister. The city took on a different realm at night. After a heavy rain earlier, water stood on uneven sections of the road; the streetlights glared off shiny asphalt. As our tires splashed through the reflective pools, dirty water sprayed the side of the car, adding to the grime.

The dispatcher's voice interrupted the silence. "Fox 100, copy 10-21." Ted pulled the clipboard from the seat organizer and reached for the radio mike.

"Send it."

"233-9292. Loretta"

"FOX 100 copy, 10-4. There you go cop-ette"

I glared at him, but pulled up to a police call box on the next corner. Call boxes were installed in strategic areas so officers could easily make phone calls. Ted stepped around a puddle of water and inserted the phone key we all carried into the square metal box mounted on a light pole. His call was answered immediately and the conversation was brief and in a couple of minutes he was back in the car.

"Loretta says she's leaving, wants us to meet her at the apartment." I pulled from the curb and made a U-turn. "She's waiting at the phone booth on the corner down from the apartment house and she doesn't sound drunk."

"I hope she leaves, if not he will end up killing her," I said. Ted nodded in silent agreement. On our shift alone, we had responded numerous times to their drunken brawls. The last time we had to call an ambulance, when we found Loretta crumpled at the bottom of steep steps leading to the back yard. Remarkably, she only suffered a broken collarbone and a mild concussion. She was as drunk as Dewey.

She spent three days in the hospital charity ward but still refused to sign a complaint against Dewey, insisting she slipped and fell down the steps. While she was in the hospital, I visited her every day I was on duty. She was hooked up to an oxygen tank and was wheezing terribly. The nurse confirmed she'd been diagnosed with emphysema.

"Oh, it's just them damn cigarettes," Loretta told me. "They won't let me smoke in here and I'm goanna giv'em up when I get out. Liquor, too. I'm quittin."

The next day I volunteered to drive her home from the hospital and as soon as we pulled out of the hospital parking lot, she asked me to stop at the Corner Mart for some gum. When she came out, a pack of Salem was stuck in her shirt pocket and she was swigging on a paper-sack, hiding a tall Malt Liquor. She offered me a piece of Juicy Fruit but I declined. I knew it was useless, so I said nothing.

I sighed and drove on. Before we reached her apartment, I tried again to persuade her to press charges against Dewey or at least to leave. I told her Dewey would end up killing her faster than the cigarettes and liquor combined. It gave me some hope when she reached in her purse and handed me a piece of paper with her son's phone number in Texas.

"Okay," she said, "Go ahead and call him. I don't know if he'll have me." Not knowing if she would follow through, I called him immediately from headquarters.

Her son, Horace, worked on an oil rig in the Texas gulf. He was more than willing to give his mom a place to live *"as long as she didn't drink and didn't bring that piece of shit from South Carolina with her."*

CHAPTER 30

1975

It had been two days since Loretta was released and I had made the call to her son. As I pulled the car to the curb, Loretta was waiting by the phone. She looked stronger, not nearly as haggard and I didn't believe she'd been drinking so much. A social worker arranged to have her hair trimmed at the hospital before discharge. Loretta looked old for her 53 years but she was looking a little healthier. She told me was ready to catch a Texas-bound Greyhound, leaving at 1 A.M., an hour away. We gave her the official police escort to the crumbling old house, and entered the apartment for her to gather her few belongings.

All of her possessions fit into two old suitcases she had bought at the Salvation Army store. Anything else of value had been sold or pawned to buy wine. As we entered the apartment, Dewey, who was sleeping, began to wake up as we entered.

"What the hell?" He began, as he saw Loretta pulling her suitcases from under the bed. Then he noticed Ted and me standing by the door.

"Stay calm, Dewey. Loretta's finally leaving your sorry ass." Ted told him. "We will be here till she gets her belongings."

He shrugged and grunted, "Good, I don't give a good damn you Bitch! Fuck you and the horse you rode in on. Good riddance to you."

He was in the bed with the covers pulled up to his grizzled chin, looking much the same as when I first laid eyes on him months ago.

"That ole whore'll never get herself another man," he pointedly said to me. "You better make sure she keeps her hands off my stuff or I'm pressing charges."

"Dewy, she doesn't have a man now. Your stuff is as worthless as you are. Shut. Up." He just made me furious.

Loretta did not say a word and never looked at Dewey. She packed hurriedly and within a short time was ready to go. In forty-five minutes, Loretta was safely on a San Antonio-bound Greyhound. As the bus rolled out of the station, I smiled. There had been no drama, no heroic rescue with guns drawn like most people see on television, but just the same, we saved Loretta's life.

CHAPTER 31

Present

The persistent ringing of the telephone brought me out of ruminations. I placed my journal aside and followed the ringing searching for my constantly misplaced cordless phone. I glanced at the caller ID. *Momma.* Uncanny, since I was just having unpleasant thoughts of her.

"Hello?"

"Hello Darling. Are you coming over here today?"

I sighed. It was her third call of the day asking exactly the same question. I mentally reproached myself for mentioning too far in advance, that I would pick her up for lunch. When her mind became focused on one thing, although she couldn't keep the facts straight, she remembered enough to know something was supposed to happen. Her dementia was worsening.

"Tomorrow, Momma. I will be there

tomorrow, and we will go to lunch. I'll pick you up and we will go to a nice restaurant for lunch." I spoke slowly as if to a child. It was the only way she seemed to understand what I was saying.

"Oh, that will be good. Now what time will you be here?"

"I'll call you before I come. Don't worry, I'll remind you. You'll have plenty of time to get ready."

"All right, that sounds good. I want to go see Momma and Daddy. Can you carry me tomorrow?"

Another sigh, not quite so silent this time. It was a constant dilemma-knowing how much to tell someone when their memory was slowly disappearing. Some people say to gently remind her of circumstances, others said that it is simpler to go along with her illusions. I never knew how to handle it.

"Momma, remember Grandpa died in 1974 and Grandma died in 1981?"

"No they didn't." She was becoming agitated. "I don't know why you say such things. I haven't visited in so long I'm afraid they will be dead before I get to see them."

"Maybe I'm confused, let's talk about it tomorrow when I pick you up."

"You are confused, they're alive and I want to see them. I just can't remember where they live."

"Don't worry, we'll find them. It won't be long until your dinnertime, you rest, and I'll see you first thing in the morning."

"Alright darling. Now what time will you pick me up in the morning?"

"Around eleven, but I'll call first."

"Oh, that's good. And what are we going to do?"

"We are going out for lunch, Momma."

"Oh, that will be nice. I love you."

"I love you, too, Momma. Bye now."

As I hung up the phone I thought about the irony of the many phone calls, I received from my Momma. Because of my journaling, memories of past anguish with this woman flooded by mind. I sigh again, this time loudly.

Two weeks ago, I had taken her out for breakfast, and then to Garden Ridge to buy silk flowers and take them to the cemetery to arrange on both of my dads' graves. Momma enjoyed these outings and it was a beautiful day. She had forgotten she did not like Daddy.

As we pulled into Woodland Perpetual Gardens, she looked at me and said, "I sure hope we don't know anybody in this place."

"Momma, we are putting flowers on Harvey and Daddy's graves."

A wail rose up in her throat and sobbing erupted.

"Whaaaaat? Harvey's dead? Why didn't you tell me!?"

Oh merciful God. This was the first time she had forgotten Harvey was dead. The caregivers at the home said occasionally she would wander the halls looking for him, but a medication tweak had prevented that for the last several months.

With a sigh, I began to explain that Harvey died a few years before.

Momma had gotten where she had lost interest in her daily paper. The home where Momma resided, had informed me that they just piled up on her sofa, so I had stopped the subscription.

When her older sister died, I made the decision not to tell her. It would be too confusing. I received a panicked call from the director of the assisted living. Of all days she decided to look at a paper in the common dining room, and she saw a picture of Aunt Ruth, while someone at her table was reading the obituaries.

"That's my sister! That's my sister!"

She had become inconsolable, and I rushed over and took her out to lunch. That calmed her down. By the time we finished she was back to normal. At least, her normal. I dropped her off at the assisted living facility and she was to get her hair done, and I told her we would go to the mortuary and see Aunt Ruth. Her body would be ready for viewing by 3 that afternoon.

"I'm so glad you came; it's been so long since you came to see me." She told me, as I was helping her into the car later that afternoon.

"Momma, I was just here and we went to lunch."

"You were? Oh I forgot."

Never sure what she remembered, we headed out for what I knew would not be an easy afternoon.

As I pulled into the long drive leading to the mortuary parking lot, Momma seemed to recognize where we were. "I sure hope we aren't going there."

Merciful God

We parked and I decided to wait and tell her about Aunt Ruth once we were inside. They led us to a private room for viewing. We were alone in the room, and before we approached the casket, we sat down and once again I told Momma her older sister, Ruth, had passed away. She gasped and cried. After a few minutes, we walked to the casket and Momma cried and repeatedly told me that was her sister.

We pulled a couple of chairs up to the casket and sat for a while. I told her we were having her funeral right then. So, we prayed the Lord's Prayer, and she told her goodbye. By the time we arrived back at the assisted living, she had forgotten her sister.

CHAPTER 32

1977

Rotating shifts created scheduling chaos when officers tried to juggle court dates, family time, or to conduct business. My days seemed to speed by in a blur. I was barely aware that Thanksgiving was the week before and the start of the Christmas season was in full force.

As usual, the Solicitor's Office was trying to clear cases on the court docket before the end of year. I received subpoena after subpoena and found myself waiting half a day only for the case to be continued, or a plea accepted. When I returned the next morning, the waiting started again. Everyone was frustrated with delays but that was how the courts progressed or did not progress. The wheels of justice turned slowly, if at all.

It was the first week of December and Bart and I were at the courthouse waiting for a case we had made while working XRAY assignment. It was scheduled for that day's session. We made an assault charge against a good old boy from the mountains who ventured to Reedy View one night in search of female companionship. Alvin Ledbetter was 34-years-old, tall, and lanky but the deep lines that marred his face from working in the elements aged him considerably. He had lived all of his thirty-four years in the hills near the North Carolina border, north of Caesar's Head. When we did a background check on Alvin, he had only received one speeding ticket three years before, with no other record.

According to his background report, he was usually a quiet-spoken, shy man who still lived with his parents. He worked with his daddy and four brothers in the logging business. The paltry income generated did not amount to much after it was split five ways. Alvin apparently did not spend money on luxuries like dentists, barbers or a new suit from K-mart. They lived off the land and avoided town life as much as possible.

For his day in court date, Alvin had attempted to tame his unruly, white-blond hair with who knows what; it was greasy and parted off center. His momma brought a clean plaid shirt and ironed jeans for him to wear. She did not want her boy standing in front of the judge in the jail's orange jumpsuit. Alvin's lawyer would have made sure he had a presentable suit if he had been a paying client. However, as it was, the attorney was taking his turn as public defender, and this case was pro bono. He really didn't give a rat's ass how Alvin was dressed.

Alvin sat stiff as a board at the defense table, looking straight ahead like a soldier at attention. The process to choose a jury was about to begin.

Bart and I made the arrest of Alvin in July, when we responded to a fight in progress on Reedy View's lower Main Street. We arrived in time to observe the defendant methodically pummeling the face of one of the local prostitutes. The prostitute was screaming hysterically, her face contorted in anger and terror. Once we pulled Alvin away from the victim, and pieced the facts together, a clear picture began to emerge.

Alvin had driven into town and was roaming the streets where ladies-of-the-night habitually pedaled their wares. He thought he had lucked out when he picked up a tall, attractive black woman who promised anything he wanted for 20 dollars. She was wearing a short skirt and fishnet hose, with an off-the-shoulder, low-cut gypsy blouse that displayed ample cleavage. Alvin could not get her in the car fast enough.

"Roberta" was a regular on the streets of Reedy View, and all of us cops knew her well. Legally, Roberta's name was Robert Leroy Jackson but no one ever saw her/him even slightly resembling a male. Always dressed as a woman, he/she spoke in a soft, demure voice. Roberta wore thick false eyelashes and she/he applied makeup to perfection.

While assigned to the downtown beat, Roberta became an informant and was likable when I didn't have to arrest her or him. She kept me apprised about certain illegal activities in the business district. I knew many of the prostitutes and cross-dressers and most of the wino and addict population that hung out behind the downtown stores. Mostly, they were harmless. Occasionally one of the more desperate drunks would pull a robbery, but they were usually apprehended swiftly as they made their way to the nearest liquor store.

Working day in and out with these less-than-upstanding inhabitants of Reedy View led me to know them as individuals, each with their own particular traits, quirks, and personality. For the most part, we all got along harmoniously — until we didn't.

Life on the streets of Reedy View was akin to a stage play, all of us actors, some villains, others heroes, many bit players, yet all oddly connected, all earning a living or just living *on the street*. Some players were selling their bodies; some were slowly destroying their bodies. Meanwhile, the beat cop was trying to keep a balance in the bizarre theater. Occasionally the street opera became comedy when the Alvins of the world were faced with an anomalous twist to the plot like Roberta. Moreover, like most high comedy, there was an element of tragedy.

CHAPTER 33

1977

Alvin was in a murderous frenzy when we arrived. He was screaming at the top of his lungs, his voice quivering with righteous indignation. "You fucking queer, I'm gonna kill you!"

If Bart and I had not called on scene when we did, Alvin may have beat Roberta to death. Roberta, her make-up sullied by bloody smears and tears, was rushed to the emergency room by ambulance. It took 22 stitches to close the gashes Alvin had inflicted about Roberta's head and face.

Although she recovered, except for a few barely noticeable scars, Roberta never missed an opportunity when she saw me to point out and bemoan how Alvin disfigured her. Now, months after the incident, the case of Alvin and Roberta was going to trial.

Roberta was thoroughly enjoying her moment in court. Although a defendant many times, she had never been the state's star witness. Aside from pre-trial conferences with the prosecutor, she was basking in the notoriety from a recent newspaper article, "A Woman Trapped In Man's Body" with directs quotes from her. Roberta was taking great pleasure from the sudden interest in her lifestyle. I believe she would have endured the beating again to insure the same outcome.

She was dressed for her day in court in a beautiful, obviously expensive white wool suit with an artfully arranged red silk scarf draped at her neck. Six gold bangle bracelets clanked as she walked. Her outfit was completed by a wide-brimmed red hat with matching red shoes and handbag. She sashayed into the courthouse like a starlet walking the Red Carpet and even waved to a small gathering of adoring fans.

Before entering the courtroom, I held out my hand and she automatically handed me her red clutch, she smiled coyly and speaking in a voice that sounded so much like a woman it was hard to believe she was really a man.

"Baby, you know I don't have no gun or knife in there. But, Baby, you go ahead and take you a look anyway. I don't want you to get in no trouble. All you gonna see is 'Berta's Charles Of The Ritz compact and lipstick. You sure do look nice today, Baby, with your tie and dress uniform. Did you get all dressed up for little ole Roberta?" She pronounced it Roe-Buhta.

"Yep, sure did. But, it was for naught,

Roberta. You clearly outshine me." Roberta took back her handbag and smiled broadly at the compliment. An investigator working with the prosecutor motioned her to a seat directly behind the assistant solicitor prosecuting her case. Roberta had quite the crush on the young lawyer who was in his first year out of law school. He did not know how to take his flamboyant victim and stressed over the dilemma of how he would portray Robert/Roberta Jackson to the jury. Seating an unbiased panel of Roberta's peers in ultra-conservative Reedy View was going to be a challenge.

The strange circumstances of the case kept the young attorney requesting continuances for months, hoping the defense would take a plea bargain. But the defense attorney was in his second year of practicing law, and would not budge on a plea. So the assistant solicitor could put it off no longer. Now came the grueling task of picking the right jury. Obviously out of his comfort zone and looking uneasily around the court room, he seemed relieved when he spotted Bart and me walk through the heavy double doors of the courtroom. He motioned for us to join him at the prosecutor's table as we made our way through local winos, prostitutes and other assembled regulars who had gathered to provide Roberta moral support.

As Bart and I made our way to the front, there was a smattering of applause. Bart glared and I stifled a giggle. A few familiar faces wiggled their fingers at me in greeting, and I wiggled mine back. Bart then turned his glare toward me.

"This is a trial," he hissed, "Not a damn circus."

CHAPTER 34

1977

Seating a jury was no easy task, and both sides took their time questioning and deciding who to exclude and who to include. When that task was completed, the judge announced court would break for lunch and reconvene afterwards. The jurors filed out of the courtroom. Bart and I grabbed a hotdog and Coke from the downstairs canteen so we would not lose our parking place near the courthouse.

"Well, this thing has sure enough turned into a spectacle. I'm not sure who the jury will be sympathetic toward, Roberta or Alvin. I actually think they make a cute couple," I said before taking a big bite of my hotdog while trying to keep the mustard from dripping on my uniform. As I looked up at Bart, he was staring at me intently, with that crooked smile of his. He shook his head silently. I smiled back, feeling very comfortable with him. I also felt an odd rippling of excitement in my stomach as I looked into his eyes. It was the craziest time to be having such feelings. Something seemed to have changed in an instant. For a fleeting moment, we were not police partners, but a man and a woman, attracted to one another.

Lunch passed in a flash—too fast—and soon we were back in the packed courtroom. The bailiff led the jury from a side door to the jury box. When I was still in training, Ted coached me extensively about testifying and trial proceedings. He described court as a stage, with the prosecution and the defense performing for the jury. The goal was to present each side's perception of the truth to the jury-audience. If the judge allowed all evidence presented to the jury, then there was a good chance for true justice. However, what you must always remember, he emphasized, the award-a Guilty or Not Guilty-goes to the best performance. Although I had been in municipal and state courtrooms dozens of times already, I still got pre-trial jitters when I heard my name called to take the stand.

"Do you solemnly swear to tell the truth, the whole truth and nothing but the truth, so help you God?"

Hand on the Bible: "I do." Then I took my place in the witness box as the clerk of court replaced the Bible on the judge's bench. Judge Gentry was the presiding circuit judge. Officers and attorneys alike revered him as a fair, yet tough adjudicator. Many defendants and defense attorneys whose bad luck it was to draw him as the sitting judge had dubbed him the hanging judge. Judge Gentry possessed no tolerance for drug dealers, thieves, and liars; he sentenced more than one murderer to death. He never hesitated to give the maximum sentence when the crime was especially heinous. The police and prosecutors jockeyed to draw him as the judge in their cases.

This was my first time in Judge Gentry's courtroom but I was very aware of his no-nonsense reputation. I took my seat on the witness stand and looked at the solicitor with my best serious and professional expression, ready to do my duty.

"Well, Officer Jordan, are you one of those new-fangled police persons?" the judge leaned toward me from the bench and asked in a deep Southern accent. A rumble of laughter echoed through the courtroom. I tried to keep my face a blank, giving no hint of the dismay I felt. But I could feel the embarrassing flush spreading up my neck and face.

"Yes, Sir, I am." I replied.

"Proceed, Solicitor," the judge smiled broadly, as he looked toward the prosecutor.

"Yes, Sir," the young lawyer quickly jumped up, knocking papers onto the floor. It was a tense moment and almost comical, but he quickly recovered and approached the witness stand.

"Would you please state your name for the court?"

"Jessica Jordan"

"And where are you employed?" This sounded rather redundant since I was sitting there in dress uniform. But some facts were required to be read or stipulated in the court record., much like the childhood game "May I."

"I'm a police officer for the City of Reedy View."

"Officer Jordan, did you on the sixth day of July 1977, respond to a fight in the eight hundred block of South Main Street?"

"Yes."

"Is the eight hundred block of South Main Street inside the City of Reedy View?"

"Your honor, we will stipulate these fine officers were responding to a location inside their jurisdiction." The defense attorney interrupted and shook his head dramatically, implying the young prosecutor was wide of the mark in the arduous testimony. Of course, if the A.S. had not asked "may I" then the defense would be screaming for a dismissal.

The outburst seemed to rattle the assistant solicitor and he was silent. I held my breath half way expecting the judge to ask, "Cat got your tongue?" The A.S. finally recovered and continued.

"Officer Jordan, would you describe for the court what you observed as you arrived on the scene."

I related the facts of the case, which were brief and pretty much cut and dry.

"In your opinion, could the defendant have injured the victim, possibly fatally if you had not arrived when you did?"

"Objection Your Honor!" the defense interjected loudly, jumping to his feet. "This officer's not a doctor."

"I'll decide what is proper or improper in this court, sir, but your objection is sustained. Solicitor, stick to the facts and proceed."

I described what I had observed as we arrived on the scene. After a few functional questions to clarify a point, it was time for the defense to cross-examine.

"Officer Jordan, did Mr. Jackson have any weapons?"

"No, sir."

"Did you search Mr. Jackson to insure there were no weapons hidden under his disguise?"

"We…"

"Did you pat Mr. Jackson down, or did Officer Quinlan search him?"

"I …" I again tried to respond.

"Have you ever known Mr. Jackson to carry a weapon?"

I looked at the assistant solicitor, wondering if he was going to object to these rapidly fired questions by the defense. Apparently, he wasn't.

However, the judge did.

"You will wait for an answer to one question

at a time, can you do that, sir?"

"Yes, thank you your honor."

"You may precede, sir," Judge Gentry instructed.

"Uh, thank you, Your Honor. Uh, Officer Jordan, please answer the question."

"Which question do you want me to answer?" The court room burst into laughter.

CHAPTER 35

1977

For the first time, the defense looked bewildered, he read his notes for a brief time, then, obviously flustered stated, "No more questions." As I left the witness stand, I looked at the defense attorney and decided Judge Gentry rattled his composure as well as mine. I smiled congenially as I passed the defense table but I received a scowl.

Bart testified next, and then the victim, Robert/Roberta took the stand. The court seemed to inhale a collective breath as Roberta approached the witness stand pausing dramatically before she finally sat down. She took her oath as if reciting Shakespeare. As she answered questions, tears leaked from her eyes and she plaintively requested a drink of water.

I could have smacked her, I mean him. I could only imagine what the jurors were thinking when the defense attorney asked questions about the true gender of Roberta and if she had undergone any sex change surgeries. The cross examination was not as entailed as I feared, and after Roberta, there were only three other witnesses. The state's case was finally over and the prosecution rested just before four thirty in the afternoon.

The judge decided, due to the late hour, the defense case would wait until the following morning at 8:30.

Although the jury was not to be sequestered, Judge Gentry admonished them to not discuss the case, read the newspaper, or watch television.

Right, I thought. The hillbilly and he/she was yesterday's news. In fact, there was no media coverage of the trial that night; instead, reports of the Concorde's first flight from London to New York led both the local and national news.

Later, trying to read before bed, my thoughts kept drifting to Bart. I decided if Bart were interested in me other than as a fellow police officer, he would have shown it somehow. Yet I knew I was not imagining...what? A woman knows these things.

As quickly as I confessed the attraction, I chided myself thinking it capricious, and above all dangerous. The last thing I needed or wanted was to have more than a professional relationship with a married man. If he was still married.

Bart reportedly was back and forth with his wife. I purposefully avoided the subject and he would not discuss it. I decided the approaching holidays had me in a lonely nostalgic mood. Taking some extra days off after the first of the year would fix it. There was always a freeze on vacations during the holidays. While *normal* people took time off to visit family and friends, we worked longer hours. Holiday meant heavier traffic, more traffic accidents, more shopliftings, and increased burglaries and armed robberies, especially.

When court reconvened the next morning, the defense presented its case in short order and before noon, the jury was filing out to deliberate Alvin's fate. The judge gave the usual charge to the jury, explaining they could believe any or all of the testimony from any or all of the witnesses. When deliberating, they must find the defendant Not Guilty of the charged offense if there was any doubt he was, in fact, not guilty. The doubt must be a real doubt, which any prudent person would consider as doubt and not a whimsical doubt.... The judge's charge droned on and after finally giving the jurors a list of secondary counts they might also consider if they should find him Guilty but not of the more serious charge of Assault and Battery with Intent to Kill.

The jury was out less than an hour when the bailiff returned to announce there was a verdict. Court reconvened immediately before breaking for lunch. The jury had given up their lunch break to expedite the process. It was Friday, maybe they were thinking about Christmas shopping.

As they filed back into the jury box, I could only imagine their discussion of the strange set of circumstance that brought us into the courtroom. In addition, what did only forty-five minutes of deliberation mean? I could tell nothing from their expressions.

The jury foreman stood when asked and told the judge the verdict reached was unanimous. The clerk handed Judge Gentry the verdict, he read it and passed the sheet back to the clerk who returned it to the foreman. The judge asked the defendant to rise and face the jury. Alvin, stood ramrod straight, but I had decided he was scared stiff. He peered intensely at the twelve people who held his future in their hands. The jury foreman then began to read the verdict.

"As to the charge of 'Assault and Battery With Intent to Kill' we find the defendant Alvin Ledbetter Not Guilty." The courtroom began to erupt with gasps and shouts but the rapping of Judge Gentry's gavel silenced them. He threatened to remove anyone making another outburst. As soon as the courtroom calmed down the clerk continued. "As to the lesser charge of Assault and Battery High and Aggravated, we find the defendant Guilty."

There were again shouts of both anger and delight. The gavel banged again and the judge quickly called Alvin forward and sentenced him to ten years, suspended to time served and probation. As soon as the proper paperwork was completed, he would be free. Roberta collapsed weeping into the arms of her many supporters. I thought I might have to slap her yet.

With court finished, Bart and I returned to police headquarters where we retrieved our respective patrol cars and headed again for regular duty on Reedy View's streets. We agreed that both the verdict and Alvin's sentence were fair. We also believed that since *Roberta* had so obviously enjoyed the proceedings — her time in the limelight — even her final emotional collapse — everyone was as satisfied as it was possible to be.

CHAPTER 36

1977

Working the day shift in December was a nightmare. While traffic was never easy in Reedy View, it was a killer as Christmas approached. The mall was a madhouse, and if you were not directing traffic, you were in a foot chase or vehicle pursuit for a shoplifter or armed robber.

Holiday scheduling began in December and the lieutenant had us draw straws to see who would receive the coveted extra days off for four additional officers, leaving a skeleton crew for Christmas. Ted drew a long straw, meaning he would be working. Bart drew a short straw and he was delighted he would have Christmas morning off to spend with his son. When my turn came, I, too, drew a short straw. I was pleased, but on impulse I turned to Ted, handed it to him and smiled.

"Merry Christmas, Partner."

He looked so touched by my gesture; I thought I glimpsed his eyes welling. I had no children, so to me it was no big deal. Ted had a wife and kids. I actually preferred working Christmas than making the tiresome family rounds and listening to my mother complain.

Ted thanked me so much it was embarrassing. Then the other guys pretended to be hurt as they accused me of liking Ted more than them.

"What'd he promise you, huh Jess, huh, huh?" They ribbed me unmercifully, but I could tell they approved. We shared a strong bond, a camaraderie, and these guys had become my family. I wanted to be with them on Christmas Eve and Christmas Day.

Christmas morning dawned bright and beautiful. The forecast called for highs in the fifties and there was not a cloud in the sky. If anyone was disappointed at yet another thwarted white Christmas, joy replaced it as youngsters hit the streets on new bikes. The city was quiet and peaceful.

There was to be a rare full moon and I was glad I wouldn't be working the second shift. Full moons wrought havoc for most emergency personnel. I couldn't explain it.

Most businesses closed, but I managed to find a Dunkin Donuts open until noon. I went in and had a couple of warm corn muffins with strong black coffee. By the time I was finished, I felt energized enough to get through the day.

156

I answered a few calls regarding thefts of Christmas decorations, one stolen car, and a vehicle broken into at a local parking lot. Missing was a C.B. radio and small amount of cash left in the console. A Citizen Band radio was the item of choice for thieves during the 70's. I finished the reports and patrolled my usual streets. The day was progressing along at an easy pace.

By two o'clock, I was counting down until shift change. Historically, we were relieved early on Christmas Day, and I figured I would most likely be on my way home by three thirty at the latest. My brother's wife had roasted a turkey and made dressing with all the trimmings and my stomach was starting to rumble a bit. Those two corn muffins had not stuck with me. Thoughts of Christmas dinner with cookies and eggnog filled my head.

"Fox 100, unknown situation at four-one-three, Maine Place. Complainant states she thinks her husband may be injured."

"Fox 100 copy four-one-three, Maine Place." I was trying to remember why the address was familiar, and then it dawned on me it was the residence of the chief deputy for Pineville County. The City of Reedy View was the county seat for Pineville and Woodrow Watson had been with the Sheriff's Department for nearly 40 years. Chief Deputy Watson was highly respected in Reedy View. Many residents had expected him to run for the top job against Sheriff Owens when a former sheriff retired, but he decided not to put his hat in the ring. The chief deputy was described by those in the know as an *old school law man*. A policeman's policeman who hated the politics involved with the Sheriff's office.

His philosophy was there should not be Republicans versus Democrats when it came to law enforcement but simply, *good guys versus the bad guys*.

Law enforcement officials from across the state held Woodrow Watson in high esteem. He was a big man with a strong, rugged countenance and deep voice that drawled his South Carolina roots. He handled public relation commentaries and any release to the media. He was also a close friend of Sheriff Owens. The first order Owens had given when elected fifteen years earlier was to promote then Captain Watson to chief deputy. It had been a bold move by the newly elected Sheriff — others had historically *cleaned house* to surround themselves with members of the same political party and loyal cronies in all staff positions. Appointing Watson second in command in Pineville County was a move that almost everyone on the political spectrum and law enforcement applauded. He had retained that position and done an exemplary job since.

Chief Deputy Watson was practically a folk hero among the police officers of RVPD. I had heard his name ever since I was a young girl, long before I ever thought about going into law enforcement.

Just the year before, the chief deputy had suffered a heart attack. He spent five days in the Cardiac Intensive Care Unit. He had returned to full duty in September.

I pulled into the driveway of the white two-story residence on Maine Place, and my apprehension was building not knowing what I might find. Had the Chief Deputy suffered another heart attack? Dispatch already had an ambulance on the way, since the nature of the emergency was unknown. It was not clear why the caller had not given more information. Dispatch stated that the complainant was Mrs. Watson, and I assumed she was the wife. I had never met any of his family. Dispatch advised the line was now busy.

"Fox 100 on scene, four, one, three, Maine Place." I exited the vehicle and scanned the area around me. All was quiet. I could not see a soul up or down the block. This was an older historical neighborhood, only a few blocks from the central business district.

I approached the door and listened for movement or noises within. Hearing nothing, I rang the doorbell. Immediately, I heard someone fumbling with the lock on the door, a deadbolt. I heard an elderly woman, presumably Mrs. Watson, mumbling in a shaky voice, *was she talking to herself?*

"I've got to open the door; I don't know what he's done...Uh umm...I'm trying to get the door open, I've got to. The door will not open. Oh, Woodrow, I don't know what you've done…what have you done Woodrow?"

She sounded disoriented and her speech was agitated and slurred.

I turned the knob but it was still locked. She continued to fumble with the lock and mutter to herself. Much of what she was saying was garbled.

I called through the door and asked her to unlock the door.

"I need someone to come quick," she answered. "Woodrow won't come out and he won't open the door." Was she talking to me or was she on the phone? She was obviously distressed and confused.

"Mrs. Watson, I need you to calm down and unlock the door now!" I tried to get her to listen to me. She continued to mumble and grapple, then I finally heard the tumblers click and the door swung open.

Geneva Watson was disheveled and confused. She persisted in reminding me that Woodrow was in the bedroom as if I knew that already.

"He's still in there you know, I told you, I don't know what he's done."

Mrs. Watson, like her husband, was in her late sixties but looked much older than he did. Her gray hair may have originally been coiffed in a French twist, but was now hanging in loose tendrils about her face. I took in her appearance briefly, as I made my way across the front living room to a closed door, apparently leading to a bedroom. She had partially peeled red polish from her fingernails. She wore a faded apron covered in grease spots. I was shocked and little appalled at her unkempt appearance. The Chief Deputy always looked as neatly turned out as a four-star general. Never did you see a spot on his uniform or a hair out of place, even when he wore his regulation Smoky the Bear hat. At all times, his trousers were sharply creased and his shirt neatly ironed and tucked.

Suddenly the pungent odor of alcohol along with body odor and urine hit me head on, as I walked past her. The living room was overheated and stuffy. She kept pointing toward the closed door.

"Mrs. Watson? What is wrong?" I asked, as I approached the door. She stood motionless at the front door and started to whimper incoherently. I knew that whatever else was wrong; was compounded by her being intoxicated.

"Chief Deputy?" I tapped loudly on the door. There was no answer.

I dreaded opening the door and briefly wondered if I should wait for backup. However, the thought that he needed immediate assistance quickly took over as I placed one hand on the butt of my revolver and with the other hand turned the doorknob. The door was unlocked and opened easily.

The scene unfolded before me in tunnel

vision. A figure lay on a double bed directly opposite the door. First impression he was asleep. But, his mouth was opened in an abnormal angle and as I got closer, I could hear shallow breathing. His right hand hung from the bedside and a .32 caliber pistol was on the floor directly below his unmoving hand. There was a gaping red-black hole in his right temple, an exit wound on his left temple. Tiny droplets of blood splattered the pillowcase and wall. There was tattooing from the gun on his right temple and traces of blow back from the wound on his right hand and arm.

The bullet had probably lodged in the wall beyond. I backed out of the room in a state of shock and mounting grief. For the first time on the job, I thought I might be physically ill. I briefly wondered why he was still breathing.

CHAPTER 37

1977

"Mrs. Watson, do not come in. Wait by the front door for the ambulance. The deputy chief is hurt; we must get the paramedics in here.

I radioed for EMS to step it up, I'm sure my voice was frantic and I also requested a supervisor on scene. I asked that Sheriff Owens be contacted to respond immediately.

"The Sheriff? On Christmas Day? Can you advise?" the whiney dispatcher questioned my request. I was in no mood to deal with her.

"Notify Sheriff Owens and have him respond ASAP." I repeated emphatically. I knew the strain and irritation was overriding my professionalism.

"Fox 100, what you got over there?" the sergeant inquired. Since it was a holiday, there was only one sergeant on duty. He knew from my voice this was not a routine call. I told him I could not advise over the radio. Within minutes, he walked through the door, with paramedics following. Sergeant McIntyre had been on the police department almost as long as the chief deputy had been with the Sheriff's Department. He stepped to the door of the bedroom and looked in, with horror registering on his face just as I had done minutes earlier.

"Sweet Jesus..." he whispered as he too backed out of the room. He turned his attention to Mrs. Watson, and then questioningly looked back at me. I raised my eyebrows and silently shrugged.

Those in the profession of law enforcement, regardless of the department, became extended family. A team-like spirit, also embraces the emergency medical personnel, including first responders and emergency room personnel. We all become intertwined during intense, acute, situations, where too many included injury or death.

It was surreal to be standing in the home of a man that I had known from afar and respected as a leader and role model since I had joined the police force. It was not the first suicide I had responded to, but he was one of our own. The atmosphere grew even more solemn when Sheriff Owens arrived. He drove up in his county car just as the EMTs were preparing to transport the chief deputy. The Sheriff paled; I thought he might become sick. He looked helplessly from me to Sergeant McIntyre, then to Mrs. Watson. He walked into the kitchen, I assumed to be alone for a moment as medical personnel began to put the chief deputy on a stretcher. No one said a word. Mrs. Watson was still whimpering and babbling nonsense. I was not sure she realized what had actually happened. Suddenly we heard the ambulance leaving with all of its emergency equipment activated.

We all knew it was for naught. Word had spread quickly that the victim was Chief Deputy Watson, and city officers were blocking the intersections and standing at attention as the ambulance went screaming by toward the Emergency Room, giving one last salute to a great lawman. No one yet knew this transport was futile and that when his heart finally stopped, it would be by his own hand. He was still breathing, but he had for all practical purposes, given himself a lobotomy and would not survive much longer. He had committed suicide on this Christmas Day, in the year of our Lord nineteen hundred and seventy-seven.

CHAPTER 38

1977

Before leaving for the hospital, I walked back through the house. The sheriff had arranged for someone to take charge of Mrs. Watson after the forensic team conducted a gunshot residue test. She had not fired the weapon. He saw her obvious state of intoxication and neither he nor I spoke a word. A deep sadness began inside me as the reality unfolded as to what life must have been like in this house.

I walked into the small kitchen and saw a beautifully browned turkey sitting in a roasting pan not carved and cold. Next to it was a large baked ham, waiting to be sliced and served for Christmas dinner. Grief overcame me as I realized no one had arrived to share Christmas with this sad and lonely couple. Had they prepared this meal in expectation of someone joining them? Why had no children embraced their parents on this day when families customarily gathered? *The Season of Peace, Joy and Love.*

What a crock of shit. As the overwhelming sadness washed over me, I willed back the tears that threatened to flood my eyes. I did not cry on duty. What a terrible waste of a man who had dedicated his life to serving his community. What brought him to this point? What depth of sorrow could be so unbearable that he chose death over life?

My mind churned with unanswerable questions. I felt nauseated from sorrow and disbelief. I suddenly understood why so many cops became cynical about life. *No Virginia, there is no fucking Santa Claus.*

Sheriff Owens stood looking out a bay window in the adjacent breakfast nook. From the window, there was a full view of the expansive front yard. Gardening had been the chief deputy's passion and refuge. He loved tending the banks of azaleas that hugged the front of the house and pruning the tall Crepe Myrtles that lined the rear of his lot. Now they were fittingly barren and bleak.

Nevertheless, even in December, there were camellias budding and pansies planted in ceramic pots along the small porch. The lawn was neatly trimmed and without weeds.

The sheriff sensed my presence and turned, but I wasn't sure he saw me. He was battling to keep his emotions intact. His blue eyes looked tired and shimmered from the unshed tears. For the first time, I noticed the deep wrinkles around his eyes.

"Son of a bitch!" he suddenly exploded. His fist hit the dining table so hard that the Christmas centerpiece, a Styrofoam angel, fell, and I jumped.

"I can't believe this. I should have known. I should have done something, said something. Why the hell didn't I see...?" His question hung in the air, unanswerable. I said nothing.

Then he looked directly into my eyes and spoke quietly about his friend of so many years. "Woody and Margaret, this was a second marriage for both of them. They married 20 or 25 years ago but none of their children ever accepted it. Damn rotten kids, so high and mighty they practically disowned their parents. Woody had two girls, both married with kids living down in Atlanta. Margaret has a son who lives in Charleston, I think. Woody never got over how those girls just cut him off. It was a rancorous divorce and their mother turned them against him. That is what he always thought.

"If anyone killed Woody, it was them ungrateful kids of his. Both he and Margaret used to enjoy a drink now and then but Woody gave it up several years ago. I guess Margaret couldn't...or wouldn't. There wasn't much left for her. He told me her drinking was bad in the last few years, after it was pretty clear they weren't ever going to untangle the family mess. Margaret has grandkids she has never seen...and let me tell you, it wasn't because she didn't try. She used to be a right pretty woman. When they met, she was married to an asshole that ran around with other women all over town. He was a lawyer and they lived over in Chanticleer. Woody hadn't been happy for years—it was one of those situations where they got married right out of high school and never should have married in the first place. Woody and Margaret met when she worked a temporary job at the courthouse. Saw each other on the side for a while and then they both got divorces. That asshole lawyer Margaret was married got her for adultery—you know the laws in this state. She ended up with nothing. Same with Woody. He paid through the nose. But, still, they decided life was too short and they loved each other, so they got married and thought they'd eventually work things out with the kids. It never happened. Woody told me he saw his girls about once a year, never for long, and it was always tense. When—I should say if --he got a Father's Day card from one of 'em he was so proud. Always propped it on his desk and showed everyone."

Suddenly he fell silent and dabbed at his eyes. Then he continued, "Every year they sent out open invitations to the kids to come over for Christmas dinner. Woody said that Margaret would start cooking early, she always thought there was a chance they would stop by. They put presents under the tree for the grandkids. Oh, they probably knew it wasn't going to happen but they still went through the motions. 'I can't cook for just two people for Christmas dinner', she always told Woody. She would make enough food to feed the whole bunch. I know Woody tried going behind her back and asking her son to try to visit. He always had an excuse. When dinner was almost complete, Margaret would hit the Bourbon and be drunk by the time she got the food on the table. It happened year after year. Woody and I were good friends...he told me these things. Maybe it just got to be too much this year. He's had such a rough year anyway."

Sheriff Owens continued talking in a quiet monotone while starring out the window. "He told me before he came back to work after his heart problems that he should've just got it over with. I thought it was just the depression talking...you know that people usually go through after they have a heart attack. I didn't take him seriously. He was always such a strong, reliable, resilient man.... Those damn spoiled kids will now show up, howling and carrying on, posturing for the cameras at the funeral, makes me sick to think about it." He was silent then; he nodded in my direction, abruptly turned, and left the room. I watched him get into his car and drive away.

I fervently wished there was some way to keep it from the media that the chief deputy had committed suicide but I knew it was hopeless. Tomorrow it would be on the front page and probably the headline story on RVTV-News.

Later, as I finished writing my report—being very careful as to how I worded the afternoon's events—and in a terrible funk—I mulled over the previous year, the highs, and the lows. My days and nights came and went now without much notice. The schedule I followed had become almost humdrum. I had dinner at Momma's house now and then when I was working days, but mostly my life was work and home, work and home. My social life was non-existent.

On one hand, my first two years as a cop had flown by, yet I could not remember how it felt not to be one. I had tucked away my past life in a nice mental compartment, and opened it rarely.

It had been a rotten year. Elvis had died on August 16. That affected me more than I admitted. Everyone was shocked and upset over Elvis's sudden death. Everyone, that is, except Bart. I would frown when he disparaged Elvis. Who doesn't like Elvis? His over the top rancor sent another red flag and I ignored it. Chief Deputy Watson. That scene, his death had been the most real. All this sort of muddled around in my mind and made my head throb.

The year would soon be over, nineteen seventy-eight was only a week away. I yearned for someone to share my melancholy mood. But, there was no one who would understand, no one I could talk to about this lousy Christmas. Confidentiality was part of the code. No one but another cop would understand.

I don't remember making a conscious decision to dial Barton's home number. When he answered the phone, I was almost shocked, yet I felt at ease and welcomed the outlet of passing on the news of the last call I'd taken. We were, after all, friends.

He acted like my phone call was natural and he asked about the specifics. I think he sensed my need to talk about the details. I had never called him at home before, yet, it seemed the only possible choice. After talking a while, I felt much better and suddenly realized it would be dark soon, the others on my shift long off duty.

As I drove home I thought back over the day and ended thinking about my phone call to Bart. I knew it was more than calling a fellow officer, or a partner. I had phoned Mark many times when we first joined the force. Why hadn't I called Mark? I felt this strange sense of…could it be guilt? That is ridiculous I told myself. We all worked together and passing on information was natural, we did it all the time. I still had a nagging feeling I refused to bring into the light, I refused to acknowledge it, and therefore it didn't exist, as long as I kept it in the shadow. Paradoxically, living in the shadow would become my existence.

CHAPTER 39

1978

January dawned cold and dreary; winter had arrived in a big way. Our section of the South received only the occasional snowstorm, but that year twelve inches fell in a two-week period. By the end of February, temps climbed into the upper fifties on a few days, offering a slight promise of spring.

On one unseasonably warm morning, I had just made a fresh pot of coffee and walked outside to the porch overlooking the wooded area behind The Quarters. I surveyed the damage done by ice and began mentally noting what I needed for spring planting. I had inherited my grandmother's love of flowers and looked forward to getting my hands in the dirt. Spring could not get here fast enough for me.

Feeling somewhat melancholy, I stopped short of admitting I was lonely. I was thinking about calling Casey to see if she wanted to meet for brunch when I heard my doorbell. Puzzled at who could be visiting so early, I peeked out the peephole before opening the door. I was shocked to see Bart standing at my door holding his little boy by the hand.

"Hey! What are you doing out this early, and this must be Matthew!" I threw open the door. The little guy had beautiful blonde hair and huge brown eyes, alert and bright as the morning sky. A big grin covered his face and I automatically held out my arms. Without hesitation, he put his small arms around my neck and gave me a hug. I was immediately smitten.

If I look back now at a single split second forever frozen in time, and recognize a defining moment that occurred in my life, it was when Matthew first gave me that little-boy hug. For three years I had eaten, breathed and slept police work. It was my life's blood. There was no room for anything if it interfered with my job—until that bright, clear February morning when I gazed for the first time at a small, chubby angel. From somewhere deep inside, my maternal instinct burst instantaneously into full flower. For a moment, I forgot how strange it was that Bart was even there at all. As I regained my senses and my voice, I asked, "Are you both all right? Is anything wrong?'

"Oh, no. We were just out for the morning, and I wanted you to see my boy! He's a big one isn't he Jess?"

"He's precious is what he is. Matthew would be how old now?"

"He'll be two in June."

"Well, come on in, how about some coffee, I've just made a fresh pot."

"Exactly what I need, thanks."

This was the first time Bart had been to my home off duty. I was still a little puzzled as to why he was there. Yet, if I were honest, I thought I knew, or at least hoped I knew. There was a connection on a level beyond the job, which I refused to acknowledge. So, as we sat at the kitchen bar companionably drinking coffee while his little boy played happily on the carpet with a few toys Bart had pulled from his diaper bag, I somehow felt I had found the missing part of a puzzle. I wanted this Norman Rockwell scene to never end.

CHAPTER 40

1978

"Hmmm. He never precisely said why he came by?" Casey pondered later that same evening as she tossed a salad. As soon as Bart and Matthew had left, I'd been on the phone to Casey, asking her what she thought it meant, and we decided to make supper together.

Casey was one of the strongest women I had ever known. She never looked back once at Jack Morris after that night I had found her so badly beaten. Jack Morris had eventually been fired from the RVPD, and was found deceased from an overdose the following year.

Casey had lived with me for almost a year before getting her own place. I still missed her, but we both liked our privacy.

"Nada. He just said they were out and about and he wanted me to meet his little boy. Matthew is so precious; I just fell in love with him."

"The question is…have you fallen in love with his dad?" Casey deadpanned as she turned and stared at me.

"What? We work together, that's all. I work with thirty or forty guys just like you do. Stop looking at me! That's enough garlic salt."

"No, it's not. Sooo…what is it? Maybe? Uh-huh. That's what I thought!" Casey teased me as she gave her full attention to the salad she was concocting, adding more garlic and several dashes of onion salt.

"What's uh-huh? And if you put any more salt in that salad you know I'll be drinking water and peeing all night. My sleep will be disturbed."

"Uh-huh. But I don't think it'll be going to the bathroom that'll be disturbing your sleep, girlfriend. I think you're getting it bad. I have to remind you, Jess, it's common knowledge that Bart's constantly going back and forth with his wife. Some of the guys say the baby was the only reason he tried again with her."

"And how exactly is that related to me?" I asked matter-of-factly.

"At least be honest with me, Jessica Jordan. You can pretend with the brass, with everyone else, even with Bart, but I know you."

"You got me. But, can you imagine the assumptions and talk if we ever did decide to see each other outside the department? They say women gossip but those guys…."

"Jess, do you hear yourself? We work with the

largest number of male whores in the world, male cops for God's sake. Most of 'em will screw a snake if somebody holds the head. I can think of only a few who are not messing around on their wives or girlfriends. I can name a few who are screwing around on both the wife and girlfriend. C'mon, girl, this is Casey talking. I've got personal experience!"

"Casey, it's not that common."

"You working on Mars? In Reedy View, they're *screwing* around."

"I admit there are a few—okay, more than a few, but Bart is just so far removed from the typical cop. I've worked with the guy, and you get to know a person pretty damn good when you work together, as you well know. He is just different..."

"If there is anything different about him, it's that he's moodier than most. I don't think he likes me."

"Not so, Case! He just thinks you are fickle."

"Fickle?! What the hell is that supposed to mean?"

"Oh, never mind, he mentioned it once, that's all."

"Anyway, it's none of his business what I am. He does not have a clue what I am. All I know is he gives me weird looks and he is not friendly. He's strange." Casey gave me one last knowing look, and finished tossing the salad.

As we sat down to eat, I tried to keep my

thoughts on other things, but they kept going back to Bart and his little boy. No doubt about it, my mind was stuck like a record, Bart and Matthew, Bart and Matthew. Matthew and Bart. Was I becoming obsessed? I couldn't shake the strong hope that Bart and Little Matty, as he called him, would drop by again.

CHAPTER 41

1978

By early spring Bart and I were spending more and more of our days off together. Matthew was always with him, which thrilled me. I could hardly wait until they arrived each week. I baked chocolate chip cookies or brownies and I supplied my spare bedroom with toys. It was so much fun picking out books and toys that I thought Matthew would like. He seemed to have taken to me wholeheartedly, and each time they walked in the door, he came running and would literally jump in my arms. My heart continued to melt each time, and I grew to love him more and more.

Most had shortened my name to Jess and some of the guys and Bart would occasionally shorten it to J.G, since all reports are signed with the officer's initials and then last name. Matty's version came out Jay Gee. I practically glowed every time he ran across the room calling out Jay

Gee! Jay Gee! I woke up one morning and realized my life revolved around this wonderful child. Bart would watch us silently and just smile. Matthew made me happy and so did Bart. Did Bart make me happy?

Matthew was always such a precocious, inquisitive happy child. When I had Matthew, there seemed to be completeness to my life that I'd never before felt. I continued to have an internal dialogue telling myself this was not real; he was not my child. I was captivated with someone else's child.

Bart one day just blurted out, "you know in all probability, I love you." I smiled, but all I thought was, that made Matthew mine. My mind knew better, but my heart refused to believe it. God help me.

When I asked Bart about his wife, he shrugged off the inquiry and would just say, "It's over." On the few occasions I tried to delve further into the subject, he became angry and refused to talk. One day, I asked what Matty's mom thought about their visits, and did she know. He stood up without saying a word, picked up Matthew and walked out the door. I was stunned. Then the fear set in, my heart felt like it would explode. I had grown to love both of them so much. As soon as I figured he had had enough time to reach his parent's home, I called.

Even though I thought he was the one who owed an explanation for his behavior, I apologized. "I'm so sorry, Bart. I don't know why I got carried away with the inquisition. I know what it sounded like. I'm sorry."

He was silent for a time, and would just say something to Matthew just to let me know he hadn't hung up the phone.

"Matthew is begging to talk, hold on…"

"Hey Jay Gee!" My heart soared as I heard his voice. "I want to come see you."

"And I want you to come see me!" I answered, fear still gnawing at me that they might not return. Bart and I had never actually said we were a couple. We more or less started showing up at the same time and place for platoon activities, softball games, choir practices after work. We would mostly keep to ourselves, talking, but mostly it was me listening to Bart's memories of his youth and, on rare occasions, his military experience.

Eventually the other guys started asking, are you two going to be at the choir practice tonight? One day—it's hard to say when—we were automatically a couple, and it seemed it had always been so. By late fall of 1978, we were discussing moving in together. After all, it was the seventies; suddenly everyone was doing it, no commitments necessary. In our profession, any given day could be our last. Any call could be fatal. Although it was not constantly on our minds, we lived with that truth. In reality, many officers would never even draw or fire their weapon except on the range qualifying.

CHOICES

Before Bart and I took the next step in our relationship, we decided to take a few days of general leave and headed for the coast of North Carolina. Wilmington. We were meeting his sister and her family for a few days. Mary Ellen lived in Fayetteville but Bart had a love-hate relationship for Fort Bragg and he did not want to be that close. He'd gone through his training for the Special Forces there, but he seldom talked about the Army, 'Nam or his wounds. Physically or mentally.

"Why would I want to be anywhere near a place I barely survived?" was all he said when I asked why we weren't going to Fayetteville.

Mary Ellen was vivacious, an animal lover after my own heart, and a wonderful mother. She lived with her husband and three kids, two dogs and one cat. She and her husband had opened their own CPA firm the year before.

We got along immediately. I had been somewhat apprehensive about meeting her but she welcomed me warmly and it was obvious she loved her brother.

"Call me Mare, that's what Brian and everybody else calls me. Big Brother and the folks can't get away from both names, a southern thing, I suppose." She gave me a welcoming hug, then the same for Bart.

Mare was down-to-earth and outspoken, yet even-tempered with her three active preschoolers. She was the exact opposite of Bart, who was prone

183

to show annoyance at the little ones' loud shouts and tireless activity. Brian was as fun loving and gracious as his wife. The children, twin girls aged three and a boy, one, were adorable, non-stop bundles of energy. I could not understand why we had not brought Matthew. He would have absolutely loved playing with his cousins.

"Why didn't we bring Matt?" I innocently asked Bart, while sitting on the beach watching the children play in the surf. Bart ignored my question and scowled. I should have become accustomed to these sudden silences brought on by imagined insults that he felt were aimed at him—but I had not. It always set off a gnawing in the pit of my stomach. What have I done now? Why was he so easily offended, and especially over a comment about Matthew?

The justifications began in my mind. He was probably just tired from the drive. It was hurtful mentioning Matthew because he missed him. If so, we should have brought him. Maybe he just wanted us to have some time alone. We were not alone.

Looking back on the almost surreal relationship with Bart, it was never about the sex. Bart's attitude toward sex was apathetic at best. He never initiated it. I use the word, sex, because making love was never part of our relationship. If I try to recall those intimate times between us, my memory is blank. I used the very act of sex as a safety net when the fear he would leave overwhelmed me and I panicked. I used sex as barter and it always seemed to end with me feeling indecent and unfulfilled, as if I had committed a sin. It left me only fleetingly secure and never once satisfied. This is difficult to admit to myself, even now.

"You always want to do some hanky panky," he would tease but I came to realize, he wasn't really joking. Intuitively, I knew he thought my sex drive was somehow unnatural and dirty. When Bart admonished my attempts at intimacy, I inevitably heard Momma's angry voice from my teenage years, "you better be a good girl, you hear me? You know what I mean." I wasn't always sure what she meant in those early teen years. Momma never had a conversation with me about the *birds and the bees*. In the fifth grade, the girls were sent to the Home Economics room of the high school and the teacher explained what would happen to our bodies and that babies would grow inside us, but no explanation on how the baby would get there.

When I got home the day of that awful unveiling of what would happen to me, Momma told me to let her know if I had any questions, and that was it. I learned the real birds and bees story from my older cousins.

As for Bart, I would never quite understand his prudishness about sex. I began to view myself as inadequate and unattractive. When I tried to kiss or caress him, he would often pull away and scoffed a few times that I was oversexed. That stung terribly. Was I? I half believed him and resolved to better control myself. During all the years we were together, although I know there was some sex, we never once made love.

The only time I ever remember him initiating sex was the day that I left him. Bart was an enigma, a large, complex jigsaw puzzle with many missing pieces.

CHAPTER 42

1978

"I suppose three toddlers is quite a challenge?" I asked Mary Ellen, as I scrubbed potatoes. We were cooking in the condo rental that evening.

"Let me tell you, Jess, I don't even remember that first year. Changing diapers was like a production line." Just then she heard squabbling and was off to quell the latest sibling rivalry.

Bart was reading the paper behind me at the kitchen table. I turned suddenly, leaned over and gave Bart a kiss on the cheek and then resumed peeling potatoes. I didn't want anything to mar this time. It was the first time we had actually taken a trip or spent any time together away from Reedy View. I was still waiting for something to happen between us to define our relationship.

"You like it here, Jess?" Bart seemed to have let the Matthew comment go.

"I've always loved it anywhere on the coast, but I've always liked Wilmington. Mare is great by the way. I see why you love her. It's good to finally meet her."

"Call her Mary Ellen, that's her real name. I didn't know you had ever been here before. When were you here?"

"I've been a couple of times. When we were kids we always went to Myrtle Beach on vacations, but I've been to Wilmington a couple of times when I went to Fort Bragg. A lifetime ago."

"You were here with your mom and dad?"

"No, I was 18, and came with my first husband, his cousin and his wife. We rented a house at Fort Bragg. Not sure how that came about, it was a lifetime ago. He was in the National Guard, and we tagged along for their summer training or something. Lord, we were such children." I laughed.

I turned from putting the potatoes in the oven, smiling at Bart. His expression had turned dark and he glared at me.

I blinked, with thoughts racing through my mind. What had I said? Was it because I had been to Wilmington and Fort Bragg before? When would I learn! It was just natural to share my life, but the sudden outrage would come on so suddenly, all I could feel was dismay and regret for opening my mouth.

My past was seen as transgressions, and his anger at anything or anyone from my past would frequently be seen as a depravity throughout our time together. I had to always be on guard, because I never knew when something I said would offend him or conjure up that green monster that lived inside him. I eventually became adept at constant self-censoring. In other words, as I look back, I began to lose myself, my identity, on that first trip we took together.

"So what, you just came down here for a little hanky panky with your husband?" He asked as he started out of the kitchen. His tone was accusatory and always scathing.

"What do you mean?" I glared at him. "I came with my former husband. Why? You asked. Did you not ever bring your ex-wife down here?"

He didn't answer. I figured the last words I slung at him had gone too far. He ignored me, stalked out of the kitchen onto the deck with his brother-in-law. They began talking sports. I wandered back into the kitchen, at a loss in understanding what had just happened.

When Mary Ellen returned, we talked companionably while we finished dinner. I was uneasy, but tried to push the incident away, and soon I forgot about it. Then at dinner, I was reminded when Bart pointedly ignored me. I could feel my face burning and I thought my chest would explode with the need to cry or scream. An otherwise delicious steak dinner was tasteless, and I'm sure that Mare, I mean Mary Ellen (I had to remember her real name) and Brian were aware that something was wrong.

Bart fell asleep without speaking. Tears dampened my pillow as I silently cried, trying to figure out what I had done wrong, what had I said that had angered Bart so. I desperately wanted things to be right between us. I wanted a family. I envied Mary Ellen with her husband and three happy children. Maybe that was the problem, Bart wanted a woman that acted like a woman, not a cop. Would I give up the career I loved so much for this?

Maybe.

CHAPTER 43

1978

The next morning Bart was up long before me. I had no idea what time I had finally fallen into a restless sleep but it had been a short night. My face attested to my distress; my face and eyes were such a mess I had to drench my eyes with cold water until the redness and swelling diminished. With mascara and a touch of lip-gloss, I felt almost presentable.

When I finally entered the kitchen, Bart and Mary Ellen were drinking coffee and happily chatting. Bart shot me a derisive look and rather than saying good morning gave his full attention to his sister. Good hostess that she was, Mary Ellen jumped up to get me a cup of coffee and cinnamon roll. She seemed oblivious to the strain between Bart and me. I realized his attitude was childish and cruel, yet it was so off-hand, I wondered if I were being paranoid. Finally, he greeted me.

"Morning, sleepyhead." He said this only after Mary Ellen had given me a hug and handed me a steaming mug of coffee. She was obviously enjoying the visit with her brother.

"Good morning." I replied and smiled sheepishly at both of them. He moved over to make room for me on a dark-stained wooden bench I slipped in beside him and gratefully sipped the coffee.

"Cream or sugar, Jess?" Mary Ellen placed some butter on the table in case I wanted it on my cinnamon roll. The kitchen smelled delicious.

"No, thank you, black is good. These rolls look yummy."

"She likes her coffee as much as I do, Sis."

"I can see that you two complement each other," Mary Ellen remarked with a smile. Bart reached over and sort of hugged me to him. Suddenly a feeling of relief flooded my body, pushing away the dark anxiety from the night before. I felt warm and safe. It was okay, he wasn't mad. Maybe I was just too sensitive. I hugged him back and kissed his cheek. "What an adorable couple you two make," beamed Mary Ellen.

The rest of the day was wonderful. We spent the morning on the beach and napped in the afternoon. After fresh seafood and a favorite local spot, we headed back for an early night.

The next day we left for home, we had to be back at work the following night. Bart pulled into a service station for gas. After filling up, Bart went to make a call at the payphone. I assumed he was calling his mom to check on Matthew. As he hung up, I walked up behind him and reached for the receiver.

"Who are you calling?"

"I thought I would check in with my mom, just let her know we're safe and on our way home." I smiled as I continued to reach for the phone, but he blocked me and frowned.

"We need to get on the road."

"Bart, it won't take but a minute." I again reached for the receiver.

"No, let's go, you don't need to call your Mommy." His words had ended in mocking sarcasm. I was too stunned to reply and just turned silently and returned to the car. We were driving my newly purchased 1976 Ford Thunderbird. It was a great buy with only ten thousand miles on it. It was yellow with a sun roof and was the nicest car I had ever owned. Bart refused to own anything other than junk. He continuously worked on his 1957 Impala—which was constantly breaking down. Neither of us wanted to risk the drive in his unreliable heap. But, it brought back memories of his high school in the '60s. I had begun to realize that the only things Bart seemed to get excited about were his experiences in high school, his glory days as the football star, and that damn rattletrap car.

We drove a few miles in silence, pressure

slowly building until I could stand it no longer. "What the hell is wrong with you?" I demanded. "What was the big deal about me calling my mom? You called yours!"

"I was checking on my son," he replied angrily. "You think I shouldn't call to see how my son is doing just because you and I are on a trip?"

"Of course you should call to check on Matthew. I just don't understand why I couldn't call my folks? I wanted Matthew to come with us for God's sake."

What in God's name was going on here? We had for the most part had a pleasant visit, almost. I couldn't understand the dissent Bart seemed determined to create. Why was he angry and why did I allow his irrational behavior?

It was crazy. I was crazy—and I suddenly made the decision to break off the relationship as soon as we got home. I could not let myself be held hostage to this kind of mistreatment only because I so desperately loved his little boy. I certainly did not want to move in with him. Our so-called romantic interlude had not once included sex.

"So, you need to call your Momma instead of being happy with me?"

"No. One doesn't have anything to do with the other." I was so frustrated I wanted to hit something, but instead I sat quietly seething for most of the trip home. When we arrived back at my place, he didn't even offer to help me with my luggage. Instead, he grabbed his small duffle and threw it into the trunk of his piece of shit Impala, and without so much as a "bye, see you later," was gone.

I stood there long after he was out of sight, trying to figure out what in the hell had transpired. Was I upset or relieved? When I thought about not being allowed to make a phone call, I knew I had been reduced to a child asking permission. I cringed with shame when I thought about my whining, *but you called yours.* Did I want that for the rest of my life? *The rest of my life?* No, I did not.

That man has some major issues, I told myself. *I do not need this. Walk away now.* My intuition seemed to be screaming at me. Casey was right, he was strange. No, he was more than strange. I was an adult woman, a police officer, a professional for God's sake! I continued to chastise myself as I busily put away clothes from the trip. I placed my lotions and creams back into their proper places in my bathroom while troubled thoughts coursed through my head. My sensible, rational self was doing battle with my needy, domesticated self— neither were winning.

When I thought of beautiful little Matthew, I became distraught to think that I might never see him again. Anything was preferable to that. Everyone commented on how attached he was to me already. Moreover, my attachment to him was my sustenance. I loved that child with every fiber of my being.

Thoughts of a real home and Matthew became the essence of my existence. I began to think of him as my child. Part of me had become a mother and I could not bear to think about life without Matthew.

The phone rang bringing me out of my mental tug of war. It was Bart. My stomach twisted.

"Matthew wants to tell you goodnight," he said in a curt voice. Then just as suddenly as my stomach had sank, my heart began to sing when I heard Matt's precious little voice, "Night, night, Jay Gee. I love you."

For the first time in three nights, I fell into a deep and peaceful sleep.

CHAPTER 44

1978

Duty called the next night and I was grateful my time off was over. That spoke volumes, or should have. All day I left the telephone receiver off the hook to avoid any negativity from Bart. Then, no sooner had I placed the receiver back in the cradle, the phone rang.

"Bout time you got moving, girl." Bart's voice was bright and chipper. He claimed he had been trying to call for an hour.

"Sorry. I had a lot to do and I wanted to take a nap. I was tired."

"Tired from what? You just had a vacation." He acted as if there had never been a cross word between us. I was always perplexed at his swift mood changes. We chatted for a few minutes and he said he would see me at roll call.

First order was coffee. It was 9 pm but I had to get myself back in graveyard shift mode. The coffee was making progress but not fast enough, so I did my fast exchange of cup for carafe and let the glorious liquid drip directly into my stone mug. The newspaper was still folded on the table where I'd thrown it that morning. I removed the Lifetime section and went directly to Dear Abby and the comics. Escape was what I wanted and not another thought of him.

* * * *

The muster room was noisy with conversation as I made my way to an empty seat. Greetings exchanged, some joking, some trying to wake up or stay awake. I settled in next to Larry Redman. Larry had been on the force for about a year and was well-liked by everyone.

"Welcome back, Jess. I worked your beat last few nights. All is quiet on the western front." We both laughed. Larry was a military history buff.

"Lord, Larry, give world war two a break."

"I just watched the movie Patton again tonight." I rolled my eyes laughing as the door swung open again and Bart entered. My smile froze. His eyes were on me and had gone steely. A well-aimed dart so fleeting no one else noticed. He turned and began talking to Ted, laughing with an unnatural joviality and totally ignoring me. Just before seating himself next to Ted, his eyes knifed again into mine, but so brief I could have almost imagined it. Nevertheless, I had not. He had seen me talking with Larry. Stupid.

I was working solo that night and determined

to let Bart stew in his own jealous juices. I didn't need this crap. I had done absolutely nothing wrong. My earlier resolve returned in full force. I would break it off. Bart was just too moody. And odd.

I made sure I was first to get my shotgun and radio in the arsenal, and was out the door to my patrol car in record time. Within a few minutes I had completed the vehicle check and called in-service.

Light drizzle began to fall and I groaned as I pulled out of the alleyway onto Reedy View's Main Street. I slowly drove past the closed businesses, making sure I caught the reflection of my patrol car in all the plate glass windows. When I was a rookie, Ted and I both had missed a plate glass window completely removed in one piece, obviously a professional job. The business was a pawnshop. The burglars disarmed the alarm and proceeded to haul out over 300 guns. While I was not solely to blame, I was in training, I still felt I had failed and most of the guns were still on the street. A lesson learned the hard way.

I made a U-turn at the top of Main and drove back down repeating my patrol of the opposite side of the street. At the end of the block, I pulled into a local all-night café, the Koffee Klatch and got my usual BC powder, a coke and a black coffee to go. The Koffee Klatch was a small diner and bakery opened twenty four seven and the close proximity to police headquarters made it a favorite for the officers.

"I'll be back when this stops working," I told Peggy the night manager. She cackled as she flipped bacon on a large flat grill behind the counter. I crawled back in my patrol car, arranged my survival kit, and once again began patrolling. I knew it was going to be a long night. First night back on graveyard always was. Not a single car had moved down Main Street since I came on duty. Dispatch had given out a few calls and I knew Bart was working a traffic accident on his beat. I chuckled, glad he was probably miserable. He detested working traffic accidents.

I flipped the switch to turn off the brake lights and the headlights. I glided like a phantom through the dark, drizzly night. Some departments called patrol cars prowl cars. Prowling was more fitting when I was checking buildings to insure the criminal element wasn't also on the prowl. I would equally divide my time between alleyways and main streets. When a shift was busy, you could easily miss a burglary of a business. It was always better when the beat cop discovered the break-in. Better yet, if you caught the burglar in the building red handed.

As I glided past a local backstreet bar, I immediately saw the glitter of glass on the sidewalk. The front door window was shattered. Damn! I glided on out of sight and immediately called for backup, giving my location and the bar's location.

"10-85, possibly in progress." I turned down the volume on my walkie talkie, and walked back around the corner waiting for the nearest car to advise when it was in a position in the alley behind the bar.

"Delta on scene in the rear."

"Delta on scene, all units, emergency traffic only until Fox and Delta can advise."

I crept slowly toward the doorway. The front plate glass windows were painted over to create a better atmosphere inside during the day. I heard muffled banging as I neared the door. I could tell it was coming from the rear of the establishment. I radioed my position and within a second, Ben Davis pulled his patrol car to the curb and approached the business from the opposite direction. He heard the banging as well and we didn't have to speak. I motioned for him to go to the right when inside and I went to the left. With guns drawn we slowly made our way inside clearing the front part of the establishment as we went. A small office was located in the back behind the bar. A small glow of light could be seen and the loud banging never let up. We made little noise but the perpetrator couldn't have heard us if we yelled.

Ben and I stepped slowly inside the doorway and observed a lone white male hammering steadily on a locked fire safe with a hammer and a chisel. The man couldn't have been much over five feet five and he was as wide as he was tall.

"Police! Don't move," I shouted. He immediately dropped the tools as he raised his hands and began to turn.

"Don't move and don't turn around. Lace your fingers behind your head, do it now." He followed our instructions.

"Drop to your knees, do not turn around, do it now!" When he was in the position we wanted, I holstered my weapon and Ben covered me as I patted him down and secured his hands with cuffs.

I pulled the perpetrator to his feet and read him his rights, advising he was under arrest. The sergeant had arrived and my back-up in the alleyway was instructed to stand by for the owner. As I started to lead the rotund burglar out I noticed a large wet spot where he was standing on the rough wooden floor of the bar. "Damn! Who wants to transport this guy?" I asked.

Ben gave me a puzzled look. He followed my eyes and noticed the puddle and then the dark wet spot on the guy's pants. "Not me! He's your collar; I wouldn't dare try to horn in on this arrest." He was laughing so hard I thought he might wet his own pants.

"Gee, thanks," I moaned as I led him out. I prayed it was only pee staining his pants.

We were all laughing after I placed him in the back of my car. As I took off my hat and got behind the wheel, I looked up and saw Bart slowly riding by. He glared as he saw the camaraderie and banter taking place.

Well, screw you too, I muttered under my breath. But just as quickly thoughts of Matthew popped into my head, cold, hard fear surged through my body.

By the time our next days off arrived, Bart was his old self, and arrived at my apartment with Matthew, and I was lost to that little boy and being a mother. So when Bart brought up us moving in together, I said yes.

CHAPTER 45

1979

"You will fire twelve rounds in thirty seconds in sequence, double tap. Ready on the left, ready on the right, all-ready on the firing line."

The range sergeant barked out instructions over a loud speaker, as he stood halfway down the line of twenty officers with our weapons holstered. The double tap was two to the heart portion of the target and one to the head, in case the person trying to kill you was wearing a vest.

A blast of the range sergeant's whistle signaled we could begin firing at will. I slowed my breathing as I squeezed off six rounds, emptied the cartridges on the ground, then using the speed loader loaded six more bullets and continued firing. As I pulled the trigger for the last round the whistle blew.

"All clear on the firing line, holster your weapons, police up your brass, and bring your targets to the range house!" The range sergeant was headed inside to begin scoring the targets.

Each platoon is divided into squads, and my assigned squad had been scheduled for the required monthly firearms qualifications. It was second shift and the summer heat was almost intolerable. I already felt like I needed another shower. Our uniform pants were a wool blend even in summer. Add a dark navy shirt and black tee shirt over a bullet proof vest, and you could actually simmer in three layers. With the temps hovering around 96 degrees for the entire week, I wondered if a bullet might be quicker than heat stroke. August in South Carolina is brutal, and the forecast was calling for triple digits.

Our squad would receive an abridged edition of roll call, and then go on duty from the range. We were all drinking iced cokes, hot, sweaty, yet trying to make the best of it with humor as usual.

"The following vehicle was taken sometime between 01:00 hours this date and 07:00 Hours. A silver Datsun 280 Z."

"I think Ben is a good suspect." Mark leaned over and said loud enough for Ben to hear. One of the things I loved about my fellow officers, was the joking and camaraderie, even as we headed out to the unknown on the streets. It made the job easier and often got us through the tough calls.

"Damn, wish I'd seen it first, my dream car!" Ben agreed, and we all laughed. The Sergeant frowned and we immediately wiped the grins off our faces.

"Okay, as you were." Ted made a weak attempt to be gruff but was still smiling. I still found it hard to call Ted, Sergeant Evans, so I opted for 'Sarge'. Ted was an awesome leader. If we talked informally, he insisted I still call him Ted, but the majority of the time he was sergeant.

Just two months ago Ted was promoted and Bart had been surprisingly agreeable to a celebratory cookout for Ted and his family. We even bought him a small gift, a daily organizer. Not much, but for families on a police salary it was the thought that counted and Ted seemed delighted.

Matthew had been wild with delight at playing with Ted and Linda's two boys. One was three years older and one a year younger than Matthew. It was a welcome change for me also.

Although I loved to entertain, we seldom had people over, and Matt delighted in the company of other children.

Rollcall was winding down, Ted had a few other BOLOs (Be On the Look Out), and then we were all filing out to our patrol cars. I hung back and waited on Bart. He had helped with the target grading and I had not seen him enter the range classroom.

"You thought that was funny, huh Jess?" He looked at me with apparent disgust.

"Thought what was funny?" He sneered, and I frowned, perplexed.

"I guess you want a fancy car like a 280Z." It wasn't a question, and I had learned just to keep my mouth shut when Bart made such comments. However, the usual tightness in my gut was instant, whenever there was something new with his petty jealousies.

"I see you looking with those shifty eyes. You've got shifty eyes, Jessica. You think I don't see but I do. So now you can go ride around with your boyfriend, but sorry, it's not a fancy sport car."

He looked at me with contempt and walked away. I stood there with my stomach in my throat. It could almost be comical, the ridiculous situations that would set him off. But it was merely pathetic. A few chuckles, the usual banter as always before shift began. The hurt and humiliation I felt for allowing Bart to control me was unbearable. Yet I allowed it to continue. At moments like this, I despised him, and was torn between my disgust for Bart and my love for Matthew. Another officer walked up to Bart and as they began talking, Bart's signature quirky smile appeared. It wasn't cute any longer. I wanted to slap it off his hateful face.

CHAPTER 46

1979

Mark Carlton and I had been partners for almost a year. He was one of my best friends since the academy and our first night in roll call.

"Earth to Jordan, you with us?" Mark asked good-naturedly.

"Oh, sorry Mark, yeah, I'm here."

"Could've fooled me," he replied. I took the shotgun from the trunk and placed it in rack in the front of the patrol car. As I climbed into the passenger side of the patrol car, Mark asked if I wanted to drive first half or second.

"You go ahead, Mark." He looked at me questioningly. "It's all right, don't ask."

"You know Jess, it's none of my business, but for someone who is supposed to be in love, you sure seem unhappy." I felt the anger ignite.

"You're right, Mark, it's none of your business," I snapped. Then I immediately regretted my comeback.

"Sorry Mark, it's just the heat. It makes me crazy."

"Yeah, the heat... The heat can be a killer all right." As I turned to look at him, he was staring at me intently.

"Let's roll, partner." I tried to muster up enthusiasm. No use taking my resentment at Bart out on Mark. I picked up the mike and told dispatch we were in service and available for calls.

"I sure hope we're busy. I don't think I can handle just riding around, I want to get into something," I said. Mark nodded in agreement. For the past year that we had been partners, we had made good cases. We had heard the scuttlebutt that we were being considered for The Detective Division or Vice and Narcotic Division. Mark wanted to work vice so bad he could taste it. If one of us was off, the other worked solo, but we were a good team. We both enjoyed the job and proactively looked for wrongdoing to keep busy. A few of the other cops thought we were too gung-ho.

We were idealistic. *"Damn hotdog rookies,"* is how older veterans referred to us. Although we were four years on the force, to some we would always be rookies.

We eagerly awaited the next dispatch, hoping it was an armed robbery, a fight in progress, even a domestic. Our abysmal yearnings were justified by believing these things would occur nevertheless, and we might as well be the responding officers. We worked well together and instinctively knew what the other was thinking, so we seldom had to speak when we arrived on a scene.

We were also brutal with our humor. Mark was a good cop, a funny and loyal partner and a great friend. Although it was never directly stated to me, I was aware that certain other officers hesitated to partner with a female. Mark always came to my defense against such attitudes. We made an exceptional team. I was going to miss working with a partner, and that went tenfold with Mark, if the department followed through on the plan to put more solo patrol cars on the street. Some cockeyed consultant had done a study that decided one-manned cars would bring higher police visibility and therefore would deter crime. Those of us that did the actual job didn't believe it.

Over the coming years as crime and suspects grew increasingly more violent, I became even more convinced that riding solo was not the most effective way to fight crime, and certainly not the safest. Regardless of training and requiring bullet proof vests on all officers, safety first was only a state of mind.

It came first, if it suited the brass, the mayor and council. Men and women who wore the uniform and risked their lives every day had their safety decided too often by budget allocations. We all believed there should be no argument over money when it came to officer safety. But no one wanted our opinions.

I knew Bart would be happier if I worked solo. Screw safety, he didn't want me in the car with another male officer. Stupid as it was, I found this somewhat touching. It was his way of showing love. Wasn't it? To me, family came first and that included Matthew and Bart. In spite of misgivings, I felt Bart and I would be married soon. He never would commit to a date but I was sure I would be planning a wedding before long. Bart was the kind of old-fashioned man I wanted for a husband. I was finding motherhood with Matthew much more appealing than locking up drunks and breaking up brawls at beer joints.

CHAPTER 47

1979

Bart frequently made snide remarks about how I looked in my uniform.

"Don't you get tired of trying to look like a man? You should apply for that opening at the credit union, that's a woman's job."

A police officer is who I am I thought. It defines me. How could he ask me to leave it? Why is he now trying to change who I am?

I loved who I was when I was in uniform. My love for the job and my love of motherhood was a constant battle. My internal dialogue about quitting the department often left me literally sick. I felt if I quit then Bart would marry me. Would I give up my career for Bart? No. Would I for Matthew? The real conflict was over Matthew. Matthew was my life. *Matthew was my life.*

These thoughts thundered through my mind daily. When I allowed myself to look at the situation objectively, I admitted Matthew was not my child. I had no say about his discipline or support. His birth mother was alive and well and a good mother, and I had come to realize this despite the limited comments Bart made about her. Being objective when it came to Matthew was nearly impossible for me.

I remembered an incident just a few months prior. Matthew was afraid of the dark. I wanted to leave a night light on but Bart absolutely refused. Matthew screamed for a long, long time, calling out for me.

"Jay Gee! Jay Gee!" he had sobbed.

"Bart, what can a night light hurt, he's just a little boy, three years old. He's still a baby."

"He's my boy, not yours, and he doesn't need a night light." His cold words put me in my place and he then went into the bedroom and spanked him. I felt bitter hatred boil for this ass-hole. I went into the bathroom and cried. Not the first time I had done that. In fact, it was becoming more and more frequent. I asked myself what I was doing with this man. Then I would look into the eyes of Matthew or lift him up when he ran giggling into my arms and I knew that sweet little boy was my true heart and spirit.

I had myself convinced that once we were married things would be different. I would finally be an *honest woman* and that would change everything. Bart was insecure. Marriage would make things better. The unhappiness I felt with

Bart was more than offset by the pure joy Matthew brought into my life. I was sure that Bart loved me. After all, didn't he always say, "I wouldn't be here if I didn't."

CHAPTER 48

1979

"Officer Jordan," Ted smiled as I sat down across from his desk. He had gone from being my assigned training officer, to a good friend, and now my sergeant. I smiled back. It was time for my yearly review and hopefully a raise.

"Don't you look like you are somebody, Sergeant Ted." At six feet two and over two hundred pounds he was an imposing figure. I always teased him when he was my training officer, saying that we looked like a 'Mutt and Jeff' team.

"I clean up pretty good if I do say so myself." He laughed, as he shuffled through the evaluation forms for the nine-man, one-woman squad assigned to him. He went through the evaluation and when he finished with all the accolades regarding me doing a great job, I was beaming with pride. It felt good to know I was making the grade in this *man's world*. Ted closed the folder with my name on it and folded his hands on top. His face grew serious.

"Uh-oh..." I quipped.

"Jess, how are things going for you on the job?"

"Great Ted, just great. The platoon couldn't be more supportive; I have no gripes whatsoever."

"How are things at home? With Bart?" I was somewhat taken aback with this question. Although we lived together and were a couple off duty, no one really mentioned our relationship at work. Neither Bart nor I wanted to draw attention to it, although our relationship was no secret. I was always a little surprised the brass had not separated us, but general orders did not address our particular situation. Although it would in the near future, for the time being, we worked the same shift.

"Things are fine, Ted. Matthew is three and a half, and growing like a weed. I hate to leave him with his mother or grandmother when we're working."

"He is a beautiful little boy, Jess, and it's obvious how much you love him." He was silent for a moment. Then he continued, "A lot of the guys who came on after you and Bart got together, they think Matthew actually belongs to you, that he's your birth child. For one thing, you are obviously devoted to him."

I smiled, pleased. I was mostly alone with

Matthew when we went to the mall and invariably we would see other cops either on duty or working off duty side jobs as mall security. I was secretly thrilled that they assumed that Matthew was mine.

I started to rise from my chair, thinking he was finished. But Ted continued. "Jessica," he began. I sat back down. *Whoops, Jessica.* Using my full name, which he seldom did, meant something serious was coming.

"The chief has been asking what the situation is with you and Bart. Females on the department are breaking new ground, even though you've been on over four years now. He always gets ideas when he goes off to these Chief of Police conferences." He chuckled but I knew he was trying to soften what was coming. "He has observed a personality change in you."

"What? Me?" I felt my face flushing. I was a little alarmed that the chief had been discussing me with my sergeant.

"He mentioned to me how any time he sees you, you're standing around looking like a, well you know how he is with his down-home metaphors."

"You mean like when he comes over the radio asking if we caught the peckerwood yet?" We both laughed, but it was a bit forced. I was waiting for Ted to continue. The Chief of Police, a man well past 60, was a lawman of the old school and retained a strict code when it came to law enforcement. I was more than a little curious and apprehensive to know what the chief had said regarding me.

"What did he say, Ted, and don't leave out anything."

Ted remained quiet for a minute as if carefully considering his words. This made me all the more nervous. Then he blurted out, "He thinks you look like a whipped dog standing out in the hallway waiting around on Bart, like you're afraid to speak to anyone. He said you seem like a different person. Afraid to talk and less friendly."

I blanched and then felt the hairs on my arms prickling. Was I? Did others see me as different now? I knew it was true. If I was my normal bubbly self or even minimally sociable with fellow officers, Bart saw it as flirting. I never knew when it would send him into one of his black moods. Sometimes he would become so enraged that he would stalk out the door and disappear for hours or even days.

"That really pisses me off, Ted. Why is it the chief's business who I talk to or who I don't? As long as I do my job and do it well, which you just said I did."

"Calm down now, Jess, don't get all crotchety on me, I just wanted to pass along the talk that's going on. It's not only the chief noticing things. I also wanted to let you know if you ever need to talk about anything, anything at all, I'm a friend first, then your sergeant."

For some god-awful reason, I felt tears threatening and cleared my throat quickly. I would not cry in uniform, especially here in the sergeant's office. But his concern touched me and also made me realize how much I would really like to talk with him about Bart. But couldn't. He and Bart were friends and had been partners the majority of time before Ted's promotion. In some ways he was the last person I should talk to about my situation with Bart.

"Jess, I love Bart like a brother. He is a good guy, I would trust him with my life, hell, I would trust him with my wife and boys' lives. He's a solid man of integrity. Having said that, I also know he has a few chinks in his armor.

"You have changed, Jess, and not for the better since you've been with Bart. I'm telling you this as your friend, not Bart's. He would probably take my head off if he heard me talking to you about this. I'm speaking here as both your supervisor and as a friend who cares. As your supervisor, I can tell you that the brass is concerned. Your name came up for a detective opening a couple of months back. But they passed you by because of this thing with Bart. It's not so much that you're living together. Half the damn world is living together. It's the change in you and the talk that you might be leaving."

He grew quiet and looked at me intently, waiting for my reply. I also had heard the rumors that I was being considered for detective. But I had no idea there had been talk among the higher ups about Bart and me. I suddenly felt stung with regret and humiliation. For if, I was honest, I knew there had to be talk. The guys talked about everything and everyone, why would I be any different?

The truth was that there had been changes all around. The other cops who had once joked and teased with me had become reluctant to do so, especially when Bart was nearby. Before Bart, we would all horse around, maybe even shoving each other playfully, nothing but friendly camaraderie. Inevitably, there were sexual jokes tossed about but never anything the slightest bit serious or disrespectful to me. Bart had even been a part of this banter until we became a couple.

The first time it happened afterwards, he told me I could forget about him if all I wanted to do was play grab ass with the guys. Yes, things had changed, but, it further angered me because no matter what the guys did off duty—or on—it never seems to affect their careers or promotions. The more I dwelled on it, the madder I got.

"What about Newhouse?" I was almost yelling now. "He can screw a dispatcher in the backseat of his car in the frigging parking lot, Ted, and you know it's true! Did he even get a written reprimand? No. He made detective! And what about Scarborough and that little incident with the streetwalker? I believe he made sergeant afterwards. And Captain Muller? I'm sure you've

220

heard the rumors about him. But because I don't talk as much as I used to, or because I don't have a dick—I guess that's what I can insinuate that means, I'm overlooked for a promotion? That's fucking bullshit!"

"Oh, come on Jess, you know you break out in the hives when you get mad." He shrugged. "I don't know, Jess, you know I'm not saying I agree with it, I just wanted you to know what it's looking like to the chief and others. I like you too much and you are too good of a cop to let this hurt your career."

"Well, maybe I've had enough of this fucking job. Maybe I should walk into the Chief's office right now and throw my badge on his desk."

"Your face is getting red, Jess, and before you quit this job make sure you line up another one." Although pay for cops was not great, it was good pay for a woman and more than I could make anywhere. That also enraged me.

"Don't go off the deep end here; just keep what we've talked about in mind and keep it to yourself, please." Ted looked at me pointedly and I knew he was asking me not to tell Bart. Well, little did he know that I wouldn't dare, there was no need to ask. That was the last thing I'd do.

All I could think was how unexpected and unfair it all was. What was I going to do about it? If I stood up to Bart, I would lose Matthew. I couldn't think about that.

Because I was quieter than I used to be,

because I refused to kiss ass and had quit acting like an adolescent boy in a locker room, and maybe, just maybe because I acted like a woman, I would not get a promotion. The old double standard was alive and well in the Reedy View Police Department.

Before I left Ted's office, it became evident he had something else he wanted to say. I waited, not speaking. Finally, he looked up, "Jess, you know how much I admire Bart, but it's not any greater than my admiration for you.

"Matthew is a wonderful, sweet little boy, a beautiful child. But, you can't give up your life and your career for Matthew. He is not yours, Jess. Bart will never change Jess. I've probably gone too far, I just..."

"No, no you haven't gone too far, Ted. I suppose deep down inside I know that is exactly what is slowly destroying me. As for Bart...I do not know. I can't be any more faithful to him than I am. He imagines and makes up things to worry and get mad about. He doesn't trust me but I've never given him a reason not to. He says he'll take Matt away...." The tears were threatening more heavily now and I cleared my throat and swallowed hard. I walked to the window and back trying with all my strength to maintain composure.

How indeed could I ever leave my child? Although not from my womb, he was from my heart. I felt the tears overflow and couldn't stop them. Ted reached in his desk and handed me a tissue.

"Lord, now isn't this great. How often do you hand out Kleenex when doing evaluations with the guys?" I took a deep breath and sat silently for a moment trying to clear my head and decide what to say.

All I could think was cops aren't supposed to cry.

"If I ever left Matthew, it would be like cutting out my heart. How can I cut out my heart, Ted?" I turned and walked out of his office.

CHAPTER 49

1981

At first you cry. The deliberate wounding, the crushing hurt brought on by the person who is supposed to love you. It's a mind numbing pain that aches deep within. Then the panic and a consuming fear. What if he leaves and takes what you hold most dear, the child? The fear of losing a child is worse than that of losing your life, your breath, your soul.

But, this is the way of the abuser. Sometimes, far worse than any physical pain is the slow, insidious way the abuser suffocates the joy in your life. Let him glimpse your happiness, that which is part of your heart, and the abuser finds a way to snatch it away. Gone in a flash, slicing a piece of your heart, beating you down, daring you to smile.

Like the building of a dangerous storm, what began as a beautiful spring day, the sky begins to darken. The dark cloud builds, consuming the once blue sky. The wind becomes stronger. Then the funnel is suddenly upon you, on the ground, wreaking havoc, chaos, and near destruction.

Hopefully, at last, a burning anger will begin to grow and then comes indignation. It's a survival anger, slowly awakening you from exhausted barrenness searching for a righteous rebirth. The anger becomes its own violent storm that cleanses the earth fresh and new, but only after it leaves near devastation.

After the turmoil comes realization that for all the endeavors to achieve a dream there was no dream. It shattered, if it ever existed.

An indignation inside you lingers, a rage to be free from a hell where there is no foundation for a future. A realization that the abuser will never change. An infestation has slowly eaten away any foothold and the whole has finally crumbled. No hope of saving it. Surprisingly, you do not want to save it. I was lucky. After the storm, beyond the anger, I was still alive and I was still me.

Maybe if we could have kept the world at bay, if no one else existed but the three of us, we would have been fine. But, as soon as we returned to the world, to work, there would always be some atrocity I committed. I would laugh too much, too loud or too quickly. I did not mean to make Bart angry, I tried not to upset him, but I never knew the rules. His rules.

Gradually I stopped talking to Mark around Headquarters and even Ted would make sure Bart wasn't around if he wanted to talk freely and not offend the man he still called his good friend. Once, before rollcall, Bart and I had walked down to the canteen to get some snacks before we went out on patrol. Ted was perusing the drink machine and looked up to greet us, then went back to studying his options.

"How about this, they must be trying to keep us healthy and slim. They are now stocking bottles of V-8." He slapped his own head, like the television commercial and said, "I could've had a V-8!"

All three of us laughed. Ted left with his Dr. Pepper and Snickers bar and I pulled a bag of chocolate-coated pretzels out of the machine. Then I noticed the scowl on Bart's face.

"Everything's so funny to you, isn't it, Jessica." He said in that mocking and accusatory voice I'd grown to despise.

"I thought we all laughed. So what? It was funny."

"Uh-huh, you think you're sly, you with your shifty eyes. I guess you wish you were still partners with ol' Ted, huh?"

"Please, Bart, don't be ridiculous, Ted is your friend and I consider him my friend as well. What did I do?"

He didn't answer, just popped open his coke and walked out with me following. As we walked into the alley, Ted was there but avoided looking at me. He immediately started talking with Bart.

226

Outside of work, my life had slowly settled into a bizarre parody of normal. I had a son whom I adored and we were always doing fun things together on my days off. Sometimes we would go to the park, or I'd strap him into the child carrier on my bike and we'd ride around the neighborhood. I delighted in cooking for him. He had such a delightful imagination that I was constantly entertained by his new discoveries about nature, life and the world in general. In fact, it seemed that I was rediscovering the world through Matthew's eyes. I had never been happier than when I was with that child.

It was bittersweet when on the first day of July, the Chief announced Bart had been promoted and would be assigned to another division. Bart was full of pride about the promotion but distraught that we would be separated. I pretended to be distraught, but actually I had mixed emotions.

* * * * *

"It's the Fourth of July, Matthew! Get up! Today we are going to cook hotdogs and hamburgers at Grandpa and Grandma's house!"

"Yeah!" Matt yelled as he sat straight up in bed, smiling his wonderful smile. "What is the four?" He wanted to know, his interest kindled.

"It's the Fourth, and it's when our nation celebrates our independence from England."

"What is impend...ant?"

"Yes, Matthew, I want to hear Jessie explain

that." Bart stood in the doorway smiling.

"I guess I better keep it simple, huh?" I laughed.

"Matthew, it's like this. Our country had a big war and ran all the bad guys out and we now celebrate our country's independence on the Fourth of July," Bart explained.

"Bad guys like Darth Vader?" he asked with a serious look on his face.

"Yep, just like Darth Vader," I added. Bart and I both laughed at this bright precocious child whose eyes were shining with excitement.

We had a great time at my folks' house and returned home before dark. Matthew was excited about the fireworks display Bart had promised. We planned to go to the festival downtown after dinner. However, once home, Bart changed his mind and said he was going to bed early. I was disappointed and knew Matthew would be, also.

Some of my fondest memories were of the times Momma Alex made the simplest occasions special. I remember when I was a small child, she announced we were going on a picnic. She wrapped cold fried chicken in foil and put deviled eggs on a paper plate. Bread and butter sandwiches were placed in wax paper sacks. Then she put sweet tea and ice in a jar. I was given the duty of making sure the tea didn't spill as we made our way through the woods to a little creek behind her house. The distance was probably no more than several hundred yards but it was as exciting as if we'd hiked for miles. Momma Alex spread the food upon a quilt and we ate our feast along the creek bank. It was the most wonderful picnic I ever had.

I decided I would not let Bart spoil our fun.

"When are we going to see the firelights, Jesse?" Matthew asked.

"Fireworks, honey, and it won't be too much longer. I have a great idea. We can take a blanket and sit out on the sidewalk with our treats and milk and watch the fireworks. It will be so much fun, especially since it will be dark."

"Yeah!" Matthew jumped up and down. It gave me great pleasure that he was so easily excited. There was no way I was going to let him miss the fireworks!

I got out graham crackers, marshmallows, chocolate chips, and flipped on the oven. In no time, I had makeshift S' mores dripping with melted chocolate. Then I put ice cold milk in a thermos. I spread a blanket out on the sidewalk in front of The Quarters and brought out a tray with the warm s'mores on it.

Matthew's eyes shined with happiness as we sat Indian style eating our sweets and drinking our milk. The paper had said the fireworks display would begin at 10 pm and it was just about time as we reached for the last cookie. Right on schedule the night sky began to burst with lights and color. Both of us ooed, ahhed and clapped at the beautiful lights. When it was over, Matt turned to me full of awe, "Do it again, Jessie!"

"We will have to wait until next year, Matty."

"Why?"

"Why, why, why," I laughed as I tickled him. He laughed as well, a laugh that seemed to start somewhere down in his toes until it filled his tummy and bubbled into his throat. His laugh made my heart swell with so much love I thought it might burst.

"Here, lay down and look up." I showed him as I stretched out on the quilt and peered at the sky. He followed my lead. We watched the twinkling stars and moon in silence.

"Let's look real hard and see if we can see the man in the moon, Matthew."

He stared intently, his small eyes a study in concentration. "I do see him, I do!" he replied excitedly. "There's the man in the moon!"

So we lay there on the still warm sidewalk and gazed at the man in the moon as I softly sang a lullaby I had heard in an old Doris Day film. I loved the song so much, I memorized it.

"Twinkle, twinkle stars up in the sky…."

Matt's eyes grew heavy and I thought he would fall asleep there on the quilt. Just before he closed his eyes, he murmured, "I love you Jessie."

"I love you more," I whispered, then kissed him, lifted him in my arms and took him inside to bed.

Chapter 50

One day in early spring, I came home from work and Bart was arranging plants on the screened porch. As I entered he actually smiled and asked how my day had gone.

"I love that Spider Plant, and the Wandering Jew is so pretty," I said.

"I have a little bit of a green thumb," he said. "By the way, Mrs. O'Reilly from the neighborhood association came by wanting us to sign a petition to put up a sign for no outside solicitation."

"Well, I hope they get enough signatures." Door-to-door solicitation was especially annoying when we worked the night shift.

"Yep, I signed it but when I answered the door she wanted to know if I was Mr. Jordan."

I blanched and looked at him, but he wasn't angry, just amused.

"I think we need to get married, Jessica. I

don't want to be called Mr. Jordan again."

I was dumbfounded. Even though I had assumed it would eventually happen—a wave of fear suddenly gripped me. But, just as quickly I shook it off. Wasn't this exactly what I wanted...to be a wife and mother?

Yes. I wanted that more than anything. Marriage would make us a real family. I was convinced it would ease all of Bart's insecurities.

Bart and I picked out simple wedding bands at a jewelry store at the mall and decided to go to one of the magistrates at the Law Enforcement Center. There would be no frills, no celebration, no wedding guests, no church, no preacher.

We had been living together for a few years now-*in sin*- according to my Baptist relatives, and we both just wanted the legalities taken care of as quickly and simply as possible. As soon as we announced that we had tied the knot, however, our families insisted upon hosting a reception. It was a nice, not-too-elaborate occasion, and Bart was not too overwhelmed.

Matthew enjoyed the party more than anyone and told everybody over and over that he had gotten married. He ate so much cake I was afraid he would be sick. More than anything, I enjoyed the day because Matthew got such a big kick out of it.

After a three-day week-end with Matthew, Bart and I returned to work. I got the expected congratulations but I couldn't help but notice a look of sympathy from most of the guys. They just couldn't hide it. They were my family and you would have thought someone died instead of getting married.

As I walked with Ben and Mark after the shift was over, Mark asked. "So you really did it? You got married?"

"I did, Mark, we are very happy."

"Let's go get drunk, Mark." Ben quipped, only half-joking.

Mark shrugged. "Sounds like the only thing left to do."

"Stop it, guys! Be happy for me, won't you?"

"We'll try, but when are you going to be happy again?"

Bam! He had me, deadpan. I was mute.

Mark had a way of going straight for the jugular. He was as close a friend as I had next to Casey, and he notoriously pulled no punches.

As my relationship with Bart had progressed, he and his wife, Shelby, had been cut from my life and for the most part, so had Ted and Linda.

Suddenly I felt ashamed that I had allowed myself to be cut off from these guys. I was regretful but said nothing. Did nothing.

Bart and Matthew were my life now. They were everything I needed. I was happy...wasn't I?

Of course I was happy! I kept repeating the

Bj King

words to myself. Happy, happy, very happy!
The words echoed with a barren hollowness.

CHAPTER 51

1981

"Wham! Wham!"

The sudden wallops on the side of my patrol car gave me such a start I almost jumped out of my seat. A middle-aged black woman banged frantically on the passenger side window just as I had pulled from a stop sign. It was a few minutes before 2300 hours (11 pm) and I was glad the end of shift was near. I had just cleared from a domestic call near the train depot and headed back to Headquarters. I suspected this was another domestic. The woman was frantic and crying as I hit the brakes.

"Ma'am, what's wrong?"

She opened the passenger door and climbed in, her face a mask of fear.

"Ma'am, get out of the car and tell me what's wrong." I said more sternly. She opened the door and reluctantly got out, clearly traumatized. I exited the car and walked to where she stood shaking, her eyes darting up and down the street. I also scanned the street but could see nothing. I tried to quickly size up the situation and determine danger, if any. Was she crazy, drunk, hurt, fleeing? I saw no sign of injuries but she was clearly hysterical.

"We's got to get out of here, come on, let's get outta here. My brother's gawn kill me." She pointed behind us.

I turned and this time, about a block away, I saw a huge black man under the street light. He was advancing toward us at a slow, steady pace. Tucked under his right arm and hanging down to his knees was what appeared to be a rifle.

"Who is that?" I asked

"Leroy, my brother. He be crazy! We gots to get out of here."

I picked up the radio and called for assistance. "Man with a long gun, walking down third block of Boysenberry! Officer needs help!" I quickly pushed the frantic woman behind some shrubbery and told her to stay out of sight. I pulled my shotgun from its rack in between the seats flipped off the safety and racked a round into the chamber. I put the patrol car's engine block between me and the man advancing. By this time, I could hear the persistent clip, clop of his heavy boots and see the menacing expression on his face. "Drop the gun!" I shouted as I raised the shotgun to my shoulder. I would learn that his real name was Leroy Brown. He was big, bad Leroy Brown quite literally. He continued to advance, but did not raise his gun.

"Drop the fucking gun! Now!"

I stepped slightly into the glow of the street light, my shotgun now at eye level, pushed against my shoulder, my finger on the trigger. He kept advancing. God, he was big. I could feel sweat trickling down my armpits and the thump, thump, thump of my heart.

"Drop the fucking the gun!" I yelled.

At this point, it finally seemed to register with him that I had the sights of my shotgun aimed straight at his chest. He abruptly turned his back raised the gun above his head, and started ejecting the rounds from a bolt-action rifle and walked the opposite direction as he did. He had gotten close enough that I could hear the metallic clink as the rounds hit the asphalt. He began retracing his steps, back in the direction he'd come, moving at the same steady pace.

At just that moment, I heard tires squealing as my backup unit turned on to the street from the opposite direction with blue lights flashing and siren screaming. Leroy was halfway between us. He suddenly stopped, then threw the rifle down and started walking toward the approaching patrol car with his hands in the air. The backup officer jumped from his car as I ran in their direction, my shotgun lowered. Together we took the huge man down, cuffed him and placed him in the patrol car. I secured his gun, which turned out to be a seven millimeter Japanese rifle.

I returned to my car and called out for the sister. She was gone, not to be found. I didn't know where she lived or what her name was. As it turned out, my prisoner had been paroled two months prior. He had been serving a life sentence for murder.

A life sentence that was meaningless with our state's overcrowded prison system. Twenty years earlier, Leroy had become disturbed when a neighbor began cutting down a tree with a chain saw one morning. He'd calmly gotten out of bed, walked out onto his porch and had blown the neighbor's brains out. Since being paroled, he had stopped taking his medication and when his sister disturbed his bedtime, he tried to kill her.

He was a violent paranoid schizophrenic but some parole board in Columbia had seen fit to put him back on the street. In addition, thanks to former President Jimmy Carter, the mental health system was practically non-existent.

Even though the sister refused to testify, Leroy went back to prison. He was a convicted felon in possession of a weapon and was returned to serve out his lifetime in prison, if Reedy View was lucky.

After facing down big bad Leroy Brown, my knees were wobbly and I was shaken but relieved that the situation had ended without shots being fired. When I got home that night, still a bit rattled but proud of the way I'd handled a potentially dangerous situation, I started telling Bart about the incident.

"I don't want to hear it," he snapped. "Ted already called. You think you're a hero or something? You were a damn fool, is what you were."

The next morning was no different. He acted as if I had committed a crime for putting myself in such a precarious situation. "I'm a cop, Bart! What the hell was I supposed to do? Scream like a little girl and run away?" He only glared at me. So I pushed the incident to the back of my mind and refused to say anything more. He knew and I knew that I'd followed procedure.

We were pitiful. Marriage hadn't changed a damn thing, just made it worse. We shared nothing but Matthew. I fleetingly wondered at the damage that seven millimeter rifle could do to a person...

Chapter 52

1982

In the years Bart and I were together Christmas season was the best. I was almost happy with Bart at Christmas time. The magic of the season was inescapable with Matthew in my life. Sharing the holiday with Matthew brought joy I hadn't experienced since I was a child.

Bart also loved Christmas. He loved everything about it, the food, the music, the decorations, colorfully wrapped presents. Although he seldom acknowledged other occasions with gifts, at Christmas Bart went overboard.

One year he bought me new dishes and matching glasses; the next year I received an elaborate stereo and speakers. Those were things we really couldn't afford, but I accepted them graciously. Such nice presents meant he loved me, right?

But even in the season of Peace and Goodwill, Bart's dark side never entirely vanished. It was always lurking, materializing out of nowhere to douse the happiness in our charade as a family. It was our second Christmas as a married couple and I still yearned for a perfect union.

* * * * *

"Jess, I've got to go to the other end of the mall to get something." Bart grinned, and it was obvious he had my gift to pick up.

"All right, but I get to inspect all packages." I teased in return.

"Not until Christmas morning. No peeking." He was in a good mood and I was happy to be shopping with him. We were at the entrance to Belk's Department Store and I was beginning to run out of steam. We had been shopping since noon.

"Let's meet back here and we'll go across to Chicago Pizza and grab a bite before we head home." He disappeared into the crowd as I meandered into the department store, checking my list to see what else I needed to purchase.

'Only 16 shopping days left', the warning was plastered in the paper, on television and on radio. Pressure was building to finish our shopping list so I could relax and enjoy the season. There were only a few things left to buy. I looked forward to the wrapping and baking, sitting in front of a fire and listening to Christmas carols.

We had struggled to the attic with all of

Matt's Santa, hidden away until Christmas Eve. I had listened intently as Matthew sat on Santa's knee two weeks before and clearly articulated exactly what he wanted. He explained patiently which Spider Man he wanted, the Star War figure and the electric police motorcycle. He made sure Santa understood just who Yoda was. He desperately wanted Yoda that year and apparently so did all the other children in Reedy View. I had finally found it at a mall in Anderson, and had driven there the week before, weak with relief.

Bart and I both went a little crazy when buying Christmas for Matthew. But what the heck. Christmas is all about kids and Matt was the center of our universe. He'd solemnly assured Santa what a good boy he'd been....and he had. There was as much joy watching Matt on Christmas morning as there was joy for him seeing his new toys.

I was thrilled with the wool sweater I found on sale for Bart's sister. A pale peach silk blouse would go perfectly with the wool slacks I had found for Momma. I was making progress as I made my way to the register. I winced at the long double line for the checkout. I could see the entrance from my place in line, but I could not see Bart anywhere. Hopefully, I'd finish before he returned. He hated to wait and I continued to be overly conscientious of anything I did which might upset him. As the line inched its way toward the checkout, I was lost in thoughts of what still needed to be done before Christmas. I was tired and hungry and a little flustered by the crowds.

"Jess Jordan!" I turned at the sound of my name.

"Dave!" We hugged each other. I had known David Carter since first grade but hadn't seen him since Johnny and I divorced. We had been close in high school and he was also a good friend of my ex-husband. Dave and his girlfriend, at the time, would often double date with Johnny and me. He was a frequent visitor once we married. But since Johnny and I split, we hadn't seen each other.

Dave had joined the Air Force and we had lost contact. As I continued in line, he stood beside me and we chatted about old times. He filled me in on some of the antics of the old gang. Meredeth had a new baby. Becky now lived in Charlotte. Danny had married the nerd he teased all through high school.

"The one with those horrible black framed cat glasses?"

"Well, you should see her now!"

He was amazed that I was a cop. It wasn't news to him, he said, after all I'd been all over the papers and TV there for a while. His mother had cut out all the articles and sent them to him in Germany.

We were laughing and talking. It was as if all the years we hadn't seen each other disappeared in an instant. We talked about old friends, new jobs, all that had happened in the years since we'd last seen each other.

Then suddenly I thought of Bart and realized he would never understand a reunion with old high school chums. Where was he? Was he near? My eyes shifted nervously.

"You looking for someone?" Dave asked.

"I was supposed to meet my husband...." This was ridiculous. Why was I suddenly so nervous? If I had been with anyone but Bart, I would have invited Dave and his wife over for a meal, but I instinctively knew it would never fly with Bart. Socializing with someone I'd known when I was married to Johnny was a definite no-no. Not only was it a major ordeal for me to see Casey, but now even Ted and Mark and their wives.

Finally, it was my turn at the register. Dave and I said our goodbyes as I jostled the bags and finally headed for the mall entrance to wait on Bart. I threw a goodbye over my shoulder as I walked away. It had been great seeing Dave again. I was pleased and happy with my purchases.

As I looked toward the entrance again, I saw Bart and lifted a bag to wave. A cold dread grabbed me and I felt the trepidation build in my stomach as I noticed the flinty-eyed stare he was giving me. The closer I got, I saw the fury in his eyes.

Why had I hugged Dave? Oh my God. It meant nothing, but Bart had seen, no doubt. My heart was pounding and my stomach was knotted.

As I got closer I forced a big smile and reached up to kiss his cheek. He pushed me away. "You," he hissed, "can forget Christmas." He turned around and walked hurriedly toward the exit, leaving me to trot behind like a wounded dog.

"Bart, wait, what is wrong?" Of course, I knew. I was panic-stricken that I had completely ruined Christmas, yet angry because his reasoning was preposterous and unfair. I dared not express my anger for fear of putting the final nail in my coffin. I felt a chill to the bone. What was that old saying about *a rabbit running over my grave?*

The thought of not being with Matthew Christmas distressed me so deeply that I was physically ill. Tears welled in my eyes and I remembered the old tensions I painfully remembered from childhood. Such feelings had returned with a vengeance over the last several years. The bouts were now accompanied by throbbing headaches and I always had trouble sleeping. What in the hell was I doing? I was having a private battle within myself just to keep the anger from raging out of control. The realization that I'd been reduced to a sniveling, begging, wretched weakling left me self-loathing and ashamed. There is a fine line between love and hate. Did I love Bart? Even if I didn't, why did I stay? There was only one answer, Matthew.

I refused to admit this, even to myself. I didn't always like Bart but I couldn't deny my feelings were turning to hate. I felt the resentment,

Bj King

the same as I had years ago, along with the panic when I first realized I hated my mother. I knew all too well you could love and hate at the same time.

CHAPTER 53

1959

The Fourth of July holiday was fast approaching. My Weekly Reader had a picture of the new flag scheduled to fly for the first time on the Fourth, with 49 stars for the new state of Alaska. It would fly for only one year. Hawaii would become a state in 1960.

Charlie and I were always so excited when it was time for vacation. We vowed not to sleep a wink until it was time to pull out of our driveway, which was always in the wee hours of morning. We never questioned why we left in the middle of the night for our annual trek to the beach. We didn't have an air conditioned car or house; so didn't grasp we were literally racing the sun to the coast.

The only time we experienced air-conditioning was at the Carolina Inn, our yearly destination in Myrtle Beach. Noisy window unit apparatuses dripped water inside and outside. The air it blew into the room seemed not right to us...like it had taken the wonderful, hot summer air and turned it into something cold and weird. The air always smelled funny and we would shiver changing from wet swimsuits into regular clothes.

The window units looked foreign, poking out of almost every window of what had once been a beautiful mansion. There had been a time when huge live oaks were enough to keep the sun at bay.

But that was long ago. As the Grand Strand exploded with growth, year after year, more and more trees were leveled and concrete poured in abundance. Most of the trees at the Carolina Inn had been taken down in the mid-fifties to expand the parking lot. Only one majestic tree remained, its branches draped with Spanish moss.

Each year, the sun had started its climb by the time we reached the Horry (pronounced Oar-ree) County seat of Conway. On the rare occasions it rained, we studied the sky attentively and scrutinized the slightest break in the clouds. When the sun did make an appearance we would clap and cheer like we were at a football game. Momma would glare from the front seat. But thankfully, she was wedged in between Daddy and Harvey, so she couldn't really do anything.

Our first stop when our trek started, was always in downtown Columbia where we had milk and a donut at an all-night donut shop. After a compulsory bathroom break, our journey resumed toward the sea.

Charlie and I would stare open-mouthed as we passed the State Mental Hospital, our eyes peeled in search of a wild maniac or axe murderer. As we glided past the darkened facility located on Bull Street, we never saw a soul in all those years we traveled the route through downtown Columbia. Then it was on to Conway and our final stop for a real breakfast before our highly anticipated first view of the ocean.

In Conway before we crossed the intra-coastal waterway to the Grand Strand, our yearly stop was at The Live Oak Café, a small family owned restaurant located just before the bridge, and was our final stop before driving into Myrtle Beach.

Breakfast at the Live Oak had become a tradition and I looked forward to the steaming plates of grits, eggs and country ham. There were pancakes and waffles on the menu, and I could never make up my mind which I would have. Eating breakfast in a restaurant was almost as big a treat as the beach. Our yearly vacation was the only time we ever went out for breakfast. We slid into a booth, our legs in Bermuda shorts sticking to the red vinyl seats. Johnny Horton was singing about the battle of New Orleans, followed by a dreamboat by the name of Paul Anka, singing "Lonely Boy." We were ecstatic and talking nonstop. I even remember Daddy smiling a few times. I think.

In May, Daddy had driven a blue and silver 1959 Chevrolet Impala home. We could hardly believe our eyes. We whooped and hollered and clamored for a ride in the front seat. Momma kept telling us they would hear us all the way over on Main Street if we didn't shut our mouths. But she was just as excited.

In the end, Daddy said he would take Charlie and me for ice cream at Tab's Dairy Bar. Before we could get in the car, Charlie and I ended up in a yelling, slapping, spitting fight over who would ride next to the window until Daddy assured us we could both ride in the front seat, me next to the window first and Charlie by the window on the way back. That seemed fair until we started home and I realized Charlie would get the window last. So I pouted, but it was still the most exciting thing I could remember. A new car!

Now it was time for the annual beach trip and we were going in the new car. The only chink was that Daddy's friend, Harvey Farrow, was going with us again. Harvey had become a constant visitor at our house. He was always referred to as *daddy's friend,* although they never seemed to talk or do things together. For some reason, it made my stomach hurt when Harvey came around.

Somehow, I got the impression that Daddy didn't really like Harvey. So I didn't understand why he was always at our house or going places with us. His presence left me feeling a bit anxious.

CHOICES

It was obvious to Charlie and me that Momma
was the one who was really friends with Harvey.
We thought maybe she liked him too much. When
they were together they would laugh a lot. With
Momma, that didn't seem quite right.

Yet, we still liked Harvey. He was always
smiling and joking and never got mad. I secretly
felt guilty that I liked Harvey when I sensed that
Daddy didn't. Part of me wanted Harvey to never
come to our house again, and part of me was
afraid he wouldn't. One thing we liked about
Harvey was that he always drove his car fast. If
there was a bump in the road, he'd speed up
instead of slowing down like Daddy always did.
His tall tales could entertain us for hours.

Daddy and Momma acted exactly opposite
around Harvey. Daddy became quieter than usual
and Momma got more animated. I noticed that
when Harvey came Momma took extra care with
her hair and makeup. She was like a different
person around him. Although she'd never paid
much attention to me and Charlie, it was even
worse when Harvey was around. The good thing
was that she always cooked special stuff when he
visited. Things like lemon icebox pie and Sara Lee
coffee cakes and buttered popcorn. For dinner,
she'd make pot roast instead of beans and franks.
Sometimes, Charlie and me would just enjoy our
good fortune and let it go at that.

At the beach we irritated Momma even more
than we did at home. No matter what we wanted

to do, it exasperated her. "Can't y'all go on and play by yourselves?" she always asked. Usually, that was fine with us, as we could get away with more when she wasn't around.

Momma's idea of fun at the beach was to take long walks alone, or to sit on a lounge chair by the swimming pool or on the beach. Charlie and I often asked to accompany her on her walks but that wasn't allowed. She didn't want Daddy going either, she said that vacation was her time to get away from everybody and be by herself. We never knew where she went even though we'd try to watch as she walked along the sand. Pretty soon she'd disappear among the sunbathers and would be gone for hours.

Sometimes she would lazily thumb through a magazine while also getting a suntan. She never seemed to get through more than a page or two, and always ended up burned to a crisp. I inherited Momma's fair skin, and summer sunburn pain was a frequent malady.

It wasn't that we really wanted to go with Momma when she disappeared, more than anything else we just wanted to know where she went. It was also peculiar, or maybe not, that when Momma went on her long walks, Harvey decided to go somewhere, also. He said he had an old high school buddy who worked at one of the golf courses, so he'd borrow the car to go see him and maybe get a free round of golf with loaner clubs. Daddy was never invited because he didn't play golf. I strongly felt something was going on with Momma and Harvey. Not knowing kept my stomach in knots.

Daddy was an acquiescent man, clearly to a fault, as I looked back on those days. He loved the beach as much as Charlie and I. Looking back, I realized that when momma and Harvey disappeared, Daddy would rent rafts from the lifeguard and we could catch waves and ride them in onto the beach. Kind of like surfing I guess, but you never saw anyone surfing on the Atlantic coast. So Daddy, Charlie and I romped in the surf, Momma took her long walks, and Harvey played golf with his old high school buddy.

CHAPTER 54

1959

As I watched the waves roll in and wash over the sand, pondering where Momma might be, I thought about when we were home, on weekends and Harvey came over. I would be sick with worry then, also.

It was weird the way the three adults sat lined up on the sofa watching Maverick or Bonanza on our black and white Motorola. Momma would sit between Daddy and Harvey, while Charlie and I would lay on the area rug spread out over the hardwood floors. When I asked Momma why Harvey didn't have a wife, she said it wasn't any of my business. I figured he was probably too old for a girlfriend. We would all sit in front of the television—Charlie, Daddy, Momma, me and *Daddy's friend*, Harvey—a strange parody of a family.

Hear no evil. See no Evil. Speak no Evil.

Momma with her perfectly applied 'Cherries In the Snow' lipstick that she never used until Saturday afternoon. Momma with her hair perfectly coiffed. She always kept it twisted with bobby pins during the week. However, without fail, on Saturday she looked like a movie star. Everybody always talked about how pretty Momma was, but for some reason, I didn't think so. All the time I would watch her. I watched and I waited. I knew something not good was happening and the trepidation twisted my gut.

Momma and Daddy bought a secondhand upright piano so I could take piano lessons. After a couple of years, I grew tired of practicing and staying after school for lessons when everyone else was outside playing. For a few months a teacher came to the house on Saturdays, but when Momma realized I was no longer interested, the lessons stopped. She never offered for Charlie to take lessons, just one of many inequalities she showed between the two of us over the years.

My guilt over Charlie always being on the short end of the stick still haunts me. I would try to teach Charlie how to play what I knew but he was only interested in loud, cacophonous banging until it brought Momma running. Faye's fury we called it.

One Saturday evening, to our amazement, Harvey sat down at the piano. He could play by ear, he said, whatever that meant. Momma called him a natural musician. We were delighted when he began banging out familiar tunes like Boomerang Romance and Anytime. He even knew how to play Chop Sticks. As we listened, I realized Daddy had quietly left the room. I promptly joined Daddy watching an old western on TV. Almost immediately, the other three joined us, and Momma went to the kitchen to finish making supper. Daddy did not look at Momma, and she did not look at him. Even as a child, I noticed these nuances and their deeper meanings.

Daddy usually ignored Harvey, he just kept watching television. Harvey sat down on the sofa and watched along with him. The awful churning in my stomach would be a permanent pain for years to come. So, I watched and worried and waited. Mostly I prayed nothing bad would happen. I was the family sentry, the little fixer. I knew everybody's most subtle temperament, what a certain look meant, the way they held their mouths just so when they were furious but trying not to show it.

I was the expert interpreter of each vein that throbbed or lips that tightened in a grim line. Somehow, I felt it rested upon my shoulders to make it better.

I could always make one and all laugh by imitating Red Skelton and all his crazy faces, for example. I would do my antics often; Momma would laugh, then get tired and scold me. That well-taught beginning would lead me through a life plagued with worry, always waiting for the next lurking tragedy. In addition, the guilt. Always the guilt.

What I failed to realize then was that tragedy was taking place every single day. Our family unit was being destroyed. The laughter, love and joy were gone. Maybe it never existed.

That summer vacation of 1959 would forever change my life by confirming all of my intuitions. The whole kit and caboodle, that I wanted to be my imagination was suddenly irrefutable.

The guest rooms at the inn had two doors for each room. One was the standard full door on the inside, but on the outside was a louvered swinging door hinged about two feet from the top and bottom of the door frame, café doors. These allowed increased ventilation.

Harvey always took a room near ours. I bounded up the steps one afternoon to ask permission for some excursion or other, while Momma and Daddy and Harvey were dressing for dinner. As I neared Harvey's room, I could hear whispering. My stomach instantly cramped and right away I knew Momma was in there with him. With my heart pounding hard, I silently crept up to the swinging door, squatted down, and peered underneath the louver. The loud hum of the air-conditioner kept my movements from being discovered. Momma was lying languidly across the bed and Harvey stretched out beside her. They were both clothed, but it was still indecent and sordid to my nine-year-old eyes. She was gingerly toying with a lock of his hair using one of her long red fingernails. He turned his head and kissed her on her ear, whispering again. She smiled. As I watched the intimacy between them, any remaining facade of their relationship fell away.

It also confirmed my suspicions of the nights back home when Daddy was working graveyard, and as we prepared for bed Momma would take the bobby pins from her hair and put on lipstick. Then she would turn on soft lights in the living room that we seldom used. In my darkened back bedroom, I'd lay motionless, straining to listen, trying to hear the slightest sound, yet afraid to get up and look out the window for fear I would see something. As long as I didn't see them, there was a chance it wasn't really happening.

But on that hot summer afternoon in 1959 in Myrtle Beach, reality slammed into my gut with such force my life changed forever. I peered, surreptitiously, through the louvers, and thought I might vomit. My ears were ringing and I could no longer hear the humming of the air-conditioner.

In a place that previously held such joy, excitement and laughter, a place we dreamed about all winter, dreams of frolicking in the ocean and our bare feet burning in the sand...in that special place, my childhood ended.

I didn't understand how so many terrible things could happen in one year. My hero, Superman, shot himself in Hollywood. A singer named Buddy Holly died in a plane crash along with the Big Bopper. They said it was the day the music died. But, for me the music died July 4, 1959, the day I realized I hated my mother.

CHAPTER 55

1982-1983

Christmas was bittersweet. After the shopping excursion blow-up, Bart disappeared for two days with no idea where he was. I was crazy with worry that he wouldn't come back and at the same time afraid that he would. One thing was clear. Barton would never change. His black moods were an integral part of him. His darkness was beginning to envelope both of us.

Unhappy as I was, I did not want Christmas spoiled for Matthew. The third day after he had left, Bart suddenly reappeared. He simply walked in the door holding Matthew's hand. Matt ran to me excitedly holding up a beautiful ornament he and Bart purchased on the way home. It was two silver doves holding a wreath around a house with flecks of snow and the words "HOME FOR CHRISTMAS 1982" etched underneath.

Tears sprang to my eyes as I hugged Matthew

tightly and thanked him for the lovely ornament. Together we took it to the already decorated tree and carefully placed it in a prominent place.

Bart acted as if everything was wonderful. He joined Matthew and me at the tree and put his arms around us, the perfect little family unit. He mistook my emotion as tears of joy. I cringed inside when he touched me. Matthew, however, was full of happiness and I was determined not to spoil Christmas.

The three of us stood together admiring the beautiful, shiny new ornament. I was optimistic Bart had chosen the ornament as a symbolic avowal of a new beginning. However, I was doubtful. Still, it was the closest thing to an apology he could muster.

Please, I prayed silently, let me find the strength to get over this so we can become a real family. It wasn't only Matthew who concerned me. I wanted Bart to be free from his doubts and rages, simply enjoy the life we were trying to build. *No, the life I was trying to build.*

All through the holidays, Bart showed an atypical amount of attention toward me. It was as though he could read my mind and was determined to prove that everything was right with our world. As usual, he went overboard with Christmas gifts. His generosity was touching but the animation on my face that I knew he expected was forced.

On the outside, it appeared we were happy,

happy. Then suddenly a crushing, wounding pain would wipe out my joy. I felt his unpredictable moodiness hovering unseen but still there. Impossible to forget.

Matthew was thrilled when Christmas morning finally arrived. My folks spent the night at our house so they could see Matthew wake up Christmas morning. With flashbulbs flashing, squeals of laughter and delight with each new toy, I lost myself in Matthew's happiness. He couldn't decide what to play with first. After the final gift was opened, I went to make coffee and began the traditional waffles and bacon. It was a wonderful Christmas morning and I would remember Matthew's precious face for the rest of my life.

CHAPTER 56

1983

Matt soon returned to his birth mother to travel and celebrate the season with her family in Tennessee. I reported to duty on New Year's Eve and welcomed in 1983 breaking up a bar fight. From there I went to a domestic dispute caused when the husband burned the ham intended for New Year's Day. His wife threw it at him and burned his chin with the hot grease. Their weeping teenage daughter called in the complaint. Both mom and dad were drunk. Why they were baking a ham at one in the morning was anyone's guess.

After several traffic accidents, a loud noise complaint and a drunken driving arrest—my shift finally ended. By the time I made it home and to bed, I was exhausted. Bart was working the day shift, so his tour would be fairly quiet. I wouldn't even see him until I woke in the late afternoon. We were settling back into our routine.

Christmas had gone so smoothly; I was filled with hope that maybe things would work out after all. Bart was affectionate and even-tempered.

The black mood and days of silence had not appeared since the shopping trip in early December. If anything, he was being extra nice and solicitous. After all, he was a new sergeant with new respect and responsibility. I was as proud of his accomplishment as he was. Yes, maybe we would be fine.

* * * * *

Casey phoned the second week of January to remind me I had promised to speak at a seminar. I mentioned it to Bart, feigning misery at having to make a public presentation. I didn't tell him, however, that Casey was the facilitator. A lie, I suppose, by omission. I avoided mentioning Casey's name whenever possible. I also didn't disclose the seminar topic.

I had written my speech on the subject weeks earlier and felt comfortable with it. The seminar would take place in a conference room at the Reedy Hotel downtown. The grand old hotel was built at the turn of the century and had recently been refurbished. The restaurant was wonderful, and Casey insisted on treating me to dinner before the program.

"Remember, you wanted me in uniform, Case, I'll stick out like a sore thumb in such a highfalutin' place." I said this only partly in jest.

Barton had managed to make me feel conspicuous and unattractive when I was in uniform, but especially off duty. I felt so ill at ease in my blues that I'd drive home and change rather than go into a Seven-Eleven to buy a carton of milk while in uniform. The only time I felt comfortable in uniform was when I was on duty.

"What the hell is wrong with you?" she asked, exasperated. "I also wore the same uniform—proudly, I might add. You look damn good in uniform, Jess. Forget Barton Quinlan's shit." I flinched at the stinging remark, but let it pass.

"Sorry." She momentarily appeared abashed, but added. "It makes me so angry when you constantly put yourself down. You are a bright, intelligent, professional police officer, who does a great job. And everyone is excited about you being one of the speakers, by the way."

"All right, I just...oh, never mind. I'll be there and I'm ordering the most expensive thing on the menu."

"Good, so am I. The Solicitor is paying so if they have prime filet with béarnaise, that's what I'm getting. That is, if I can control my pre-game jitters. My fingers are crossed this thing turns out successful. Meet me in the hotel dining room, say sixish?"

"I'll be there." As I hung up the phone, I could feel the nervous excitement beginning. This would be a welcome change in my everyday routine.

On the evening of the presentation, I arrived shortly before 6 pm and sat in the lobby awaiting Casey. The furnishings were elegantly Victorian and soft classical music floated from an unseen piano. Near the center of the room a large placard stood on an easel: *Welcome to First Annual Reedy View Seminar on Domestic Violence. The Magnolia Room.*

Casey finally arrived and we hugged, glad to see each other. I realized how much I missed her even though we worked and lived in the same town. I hadn't seen her since before Christmas when she arrived with a black Lab puppy for Matthew. Bart was furious; Matthew was ecstatic and named him Darth Vader, which was shortened to Vader.

By the time dessert arrived we had caught up on news. She had spent the holidays with her family in Florida. She claimed to be a basket case about the seminar that night, although she looked and acted completely at ease. The idea for the seminar was hers. When she approached the Solicitor with her plan, he'd been surprisingly enthusiastic, and offered a reasonable budget to organize and conduct it. The Thirteenth Circuit Solicitor, who was Casey's superior, recently promoted her to Chief Counsel of the new Special Victims Division, which would include Criminal Domestic Violence and Sex Crimes and Crimes against Children, along with victim witness counseling for the three counties they served. Two other attorneys, a full time counselor and volunteers all worked under Casey.

It sounded impressive, but when one looked at the caseload, then the attorneys assigned to the unit, it was understaffed before she ever started.

She handed me the final copy of the program and I winced. She had listed my name as Jordan, not Quinlan. Changing my name at the department was still a sore point between Bart and me. I was slowly getting that done, although legally it was changed in all other matters. It was just too confusing around the department, and I still appeared on the work rosters as Jordan. Maybe, subconsciously, I was holding on to the last vestige of the real me.

Casey brushed off the misnomer as a typo, but I doubted it. She claimed she meant to hyphenate Jordan with Quinlan but the printer made a mistake. I smiled, jokingly threatened to kill her, and prayed that Barton never saw the program.

Casey was passionate about the mission of her new office.

"Right now we could keep two or three attorneys busy full time on sex crimes and domestic violence. When the new CDV law goes into effect, it will change how the police respond to domestics and how we prosecute them. It needs to become a specialized division with specific training and expertise in Criminal Domestic Violence," she explained. She was animated when she got on her soapbox. And who could blame her? Casey knew all about the plight of the victim. Casey worked as a uniformed police officer for four years.

With what she learned on the streets, she finally made up her mind to tackle law school. Her parents were thrilled and financed her schooling and she was immediately offered a job by the Solicitor's office. She loved her job and was vital in the prosecution of domestic violence cases.

"You never stop, Casey. I'm so proud of you. I think you should consider running for Solicitor," I said. Her eyes twinkled mischievously and I realized she was already thinking about that.

"Well, not for four more years, anyway," she smiled, then continued, "I like the sound of Special. I think we need a specialized team within the police department to respond to domestics and that's what I've been lobbying for. Some of the larger cities already have such teams. There is usually a male and female partnered. It would be huge a step forward for Reedy View. Some of the guys have horrendous attitudes when they go out on these calls. We have to make changes."

"Tell me about it," I agreed. "I've been on too many calls where the male officer blames the victim. Some woman has the shit beat of her and all some cops want to know is why they stayed or came back or didn't leave before it happened. No sensitivity to the psychology involved whatsoever."

Casey shook her head as she tasted her crème

Brule. She could eat more than any man and yet remained pencil thin.

"Thanks, I knew you would be supportive," she continued between mouthfuls. "I think they should call it the Domestic Violence Response Team. DVRT. Has a ring to it, don't you agree?"

"Making me Sergeant or Lieutenant Jordan in charge of the unit has a better ring," I answered. We both laughed but Casey's eyes twinkled again. "What?" I asked. Then realized I used Jordan instead of Quinlan. We both broke into laughter. It felt good to share a laugh with my best friend again.

CHAPTER 57

1983

After dinner, we went to the third floor where the seminar was being held. Although it was still early, several attendees were already milling about, some sampling the coffee, tea and pastries the hotel provided. It already looked like a success.

Participants consisted mostly of professionals in the mental health, medical and legal communities. I hoped perhaps a few battered women, longing for help or answers would attend. It was free to the public, limited to one hundred. All of the reservations filled within a week of the seminar's announcement in the newspaper. As the speakers assembled, I was impressed with the expertise Casey managed to assemble.

I was to speak first since the police are usually first on the scene of a domestic disturbance. After myself was the director of the new women's shelter, then several mental health professionals. Casey would speak last as the Prosecutor of cases that reached the court system.

I thought my stomach might fly out of my mouth as I walked toward the podium. Casey introduced me as Reedy View's first female patrol officer and I got a standing ovation. I was proud, yes…but I really did hate this sort of thing.

"Hello, I'm Jessica Jordan and I've been a police officer with the Reedy View Police Department since 1975," I began.

As I finished my own short introduction, I finally got into the flow of the topic and felt myself relax as I related stories of the calls I had responded to over the years, interjecting a little humor here and there, and pointing out that domestic calls are one of the most dangerous, as well as the most frequent, calls that police officers respond to.

"Assistant Solicitor Demarches will explain later in detail a new law. This law will literally untie the hands of police officers across the state of South Carolina." There was more applause.

"From the time I was a rookie in 1975, domestic calls were often frustrating when trying to make an arrest. Until Governor Dick Riley signed the Criminal Domestic Violence Act into law, we would leave homes knowing assaults were occurring, but unless the victim signed a warrant or we witnessed them, we could not make an arrest. Often victims have been too intimidated because they know that the next beating will be worse if they act. The Criminal Domestic Violence or CDV Law will allow officers to make an arrest based on probable cause that violence has taken place." I continued, occasionally taking a sip of water "I'll share one call in particular, to which I responded. This is indicative of the tragedies when victims and their abusers refuse to get help or when the victim remains in the abusive relationship.

"The woman suffered silently for years at the hand of her abusive husband, a husband she loved. However, when intoxicated, he became violent. He had previously put her in the hospital twice and had injured her numerous other times. It was always an accident, she told her family and doctors. She called the police for help but then refused to press charges. She claimed to have fallen or walked into a door. Always some freak accident."

I gave an abbreviated version of the case story, and of course revealed no names, but it was a case I would never forget. At the time I was partnered with Ted.

We were responding to a possible domestic disturbance in one of the city's upscale predominately black communities. We pulled to the curb of a red brick house with a beautiful flower garden and shrubbery. We were working the second shift on a steamy hot August night in 1975.

272

As we entered the house, we noted that it was furnished tastefully and perfectly kept. We were met by a middle-aged lady, who introduced herself as Mrs. Taylor, the complainant. She showed us into a lovely formal living room where we saw many professional photographs of smiling children. On another wall were framed pictures of President John F. Kennedy and the Rev. Martin Luther King. Mrs. Taylor led us to a burgundy velvet sofa and she sat across from us in a matching chair. She was dressed in a neat pantsuit with a coordinating scarf.

She spoke softly in a mild-mannered and melodious southern cadence. Ted was already reaching for a .22 caliber revolver — what we call a Saturday night special — we were shocked to see resting on the coffee table. She pointed to it as she sat and then smiled at us.

"I'm Mrs. Anita Taylor," she again told us. Of course I didn't use her name as I related the story to my audience. She pointed to the gun.

"Please take it." she said.

Ted quickly secured the weapon, and we looked at Mrs. Taylor quite perplexed. Then she nodded toward the bedroom and stated.

"I just killed my husband." The tears were now sliding down her face in sheets, but she showed little other emotion.

We were startled to find a middle-aged man lying on his back with a small hole in his forehead. There was very little blood, which probably meant he died almost instantly. Later I would learn the .22 contributed to the lack of blood, since there is seldom an exit wound, instead it does all its damage inside. We were stunned as we quickly tried to process the circumstances. Mr. Taylor was obviously dead.

That was my first homicide and I'll admit to you it was not what I envisioned a murder scene to be. The victim looked as if he just returned from church, suit and tie. We requested an ambulance only because emergency technicians have to notify the corner, another one of those cat and mouse games. In turn, the coroner could officially pronounce him dead.

I stepped back into the foyer with our suspect, Anita. She'd told the dispatcher she needed to speak with a police officer about a disagreement with her husband. The dispatcher nearly gasped over the radio when we called for an ambulance and coroner relating to a gunshot victim who appeared to be deceased. Mrs. Taylor lost her calm demeanor and began to visibly shake. I was afraid she was going into shock. We led her back to the living room away from the body and started questioning her. Although she was shaking, she remained stoic.

We read her rights and she nodded assent. She declined an attorney. With the tears still flowing, and speaking barely above a whisper, she said she'd just killed the only man she'd ever loved, the father of her children.

They had been married for forty-two years. She explained that she loved her husband and he loved her, but that when he drank *the devil took him over*. Of course, there is so much more to this story, so many sad details, I just tried to relate the essentials. Her husband, she said, was an alcoholic and since his retirement, the drinking had escalated. When drunk he could easily become mean and violent. She had sustained many injuries over the years, broken ribs, a broken arm and she had even lost partial sight in one eye due to a beating. However, her husband had never been arrested. The Taylors were well known in the community as upstanding and respectable citizens. They were active in their church and Mr. Taylor was an Elder. She refused to let anyone know the truth, until that hot August night in 1975.

When her husband was sober, she told us, he would cry and promise it would never happen again. He was always remorseful. But he refused to seek help or go to AA. She knew she should have left the marriage when the violence first began, but she made many excuses to herself. She couldn't take his children away, he couldn't get along on his own, she loved him and he loved her, and where would she go?

There was always an excuse. She thought each violent episode would be the last. The previous week, she learned she had breast cancer and surgery was already scheduled. Her husband reacted to the news by upping his alcohol intake. On that evening they'd gotten into an argument about his drinking and he reacted in his usual way.

His moods made her more frightened than ever before, and she had secretly purchased a small handgun for protection. He didn't know. She took the gun from its hiding place and when he burst through the bedroom door, which she'd locked, the pistol was in her pocket. He knocked her onto the bed, and told her he was going to teach her a lesson. At that point she withdrew the gun, and told him, "Not tonight, not tonight you won't."

When he took another step toward her she shot him point blank in the head.

We arrested her. I broke protocol and led her to the patrol car without handcuffs. The ambulance arrived and they were waiting for the coroner. Another patrol car stood by until the scene was processed. I asked that the broken bedroom door be photographed from all angles. The husband was a large man and his wife was not much over five feet. I knew the size difference and the damage to the door would go a long way toward a self-defense plea.

At her trial, her children testified they witnessed physical abuse on many occasions. What their mother thought was hidden from them, was not. Shame and fear kept it a family secret. It was a secret that ended in the worst kind

276

of tragedy. Although she was eventually found Not Guilty due to self-defense, the tragedy will follow Mrs. Taylor and her children as long as they live. The point is—it didn't have to happen. The Taylors were caught in a vicious cycle and thought there was no solution.

As I finished the abbreviated version of my story that night, the audience actually applauded when they heard Anita been found Not Guilty. I saw a few wiping their eyes.

"It's important to point out," I continued, "that shooting the abuser was not the answer to this tragic circumstance. The husband should have been arrested the first time he hit his wife. He should have been court-ordered to seek counseling. The whole family should have gotten help. We failed Anita Taylor and we failed her husband and her children. With the new Criminal Domestic Violence Act, and new methods of Law Enforcement in place, hopefully, similar tragedies can be prevented."

Unfortunately, that was not to be. South Carolina would remain the leader in the country, for men who killed their wives or girlfriends, into the twenty first century.

CHAPTER 58

1983

The audience applauded enthusiastically, completely captivated by the story. Some heated discussions followed and the question was, "At what point is deadly self-defense justified?" That was a direction I had not intended the discussion to go, but it was valid.

I then added to my talk by telling the story of a Michigan woman who was charged in 1977 with the murder of her husband. She burned him to death as he lay sleeping. He abused her for years and although she divorced him and left numerous times, she could not escape. A new age dawned for victims of marital abuse when Ms. Francine Hughes was acquitted of the charges. One of the cases that gave birth to the "Battered Woman" legal defense. Francine Hughes was legally divorced yet living with her abuser at the time she killed him. A book and movie followed, THE

BURNING BED.

I summed up my presentation by reiterating how dangerous domestic calls were for police officers. Situations charged with passion and anger could quickly escalate to an explosive point and go from abuse to murder before the perpetrator thought about it clearly. This was compounded when alcohol or drugs were part of the equation.

The next speaker was the director of Reedy View's new shelter for abused spouses. She gave an interesting talk on why so many women stay in abusive relationships, the primary reason being that they think they have nowhere else to go.

"We are finally trying to do something about that unfortunate reality," she explained.

As I listened to the other presentations, I became absorbed by the stories and statistics given. When a psychiatrist, Dr. Eileen Powell, walked to the podium, she spoke about verbal and emotional abuse and how it was often the precursor to physical violence.

"The abuser constantly belittles, chipping away at the victim's self-esteem, thereby defeating her. Verbal abuse can cause uncontrollable pain and anguish. Yet, so many women will stay for a variety of reasons. Economic, they can't support themselves. Parental, they have concerns for their children's support, and last, but certainly not least, for overwhelming psychological reasons.

The abuser treats the abused as an object, an

extension of himself. The abuser looks at the victim as property. The victim becomes more and more isolated from family and friends because the abuser sees others as a threat. The abuser accomplishes this by intimidation, cajoling, threats and eventually physical violence to control his victim."

As I listened, my face grew hot. I forced myself to take deep, slow breaths to subdue the emotions I feared were showing on my face. She was describing my life. I slowly looked around to see if anyone was staring at me. Did they know? But all eyes were on the speaker. I was shaken to my core. This is ridiculous, I told myself. Barton would never hurt me. He never laid a hand on me.

My entire being suddenly went still; I was actually holding my breath. Except for that one time...well...two times? He was leaving one of the many times during a black mood. I ran up and tried to grab him as he went out the door. All I could do was pound his shoulders in frustration. He suddenly turned and grasped my throat. His hands grew tighter and I thought I would pass out; I had begun to see stars, when he suddenly let me drop to the floor. I gasped and clutched at my throat, but literally could not speak.

"Don't you ever grab me again," he sneered. Then he walked away, not caring if I was hurt. He stayed gone for a week that time. I had trouble swallowing for days afterwards and finally went to the doctor fearing my throat was damaged. Yet for some reason I was afraid to let Bart know I was injured. How in God's name did I forget? How did I put it out of my mind...until now...?

My face flushed again as I remembered the doctor checking me and frowning. I assured him it was an accident.

"Was the accident, a choking accident?" he asked.

"Yes." I almost whispered.

"It will take a few more weeks, but there isn't any permanent damage, this time." He went into detail about muscles bruised and elasticity stretched, but there was no permanent damage. I never told Bart I sought medical help. I was a cop, for God's sake. I never saw the doctor again; I was too embarrassed. I convinced myself it was my fault.

I tuned back into the speaker as she ended her lecture with the signs of an abused spouse. "One more thing," she added. "The victim will often think the abuse is her fault."

My mind was spiraling out of control and the reality of my life was undeniable and overwhelming. What would I do? When the audience applause signaled the seminar was over and Casey invited everyone to please enjoy the refreshments, I was more than relieved.

"You were wonderful, thank you so much for doing this." Casey gave me a hug. She was obviously excited at the success of the seminar. "I plan to continue these presentations in different parts of the county," she continued. "I want to reach as many women as I can. Tonight the audience is largely professional. But they and I will carry the message to the women in lower income areas, government housing, and the suburbs. I want to reach the victims who are caught in this awful cycle. Would you be willing to speak again?"

"Oh, absolutely, I think it serves a much needed purpose," my voice caught.

"Are you all right, Jess?" She gave me an inquisitive look.

"What? Oh yes, just tired suddenly. I've got to run; I'll talk with you tomorrow." I could almost feel her dumbfounding stare as I left the room. I had to get out of there.

Was I an abused woman?

By the time I arrived home I felt violently ill. I barely made it to the bathroom. I vomited until my stomach was empty. I began to feel better. I wanted to blame my nausea on the rich food we'd eaten but I knew better. I went straight to bed, thankful that Bart was working. It was a long time before sleep finally came.

The next morning, I tried to process my situation objectively. It was incredibly difficult to think rationally about myself. I wondered what others thought. Even Ted, one of Bart's dearest friends, could not break through the black mood when it descended upon Bart. I knew how Ted felt about Bart and me. There was no doubt how

Casey felt.

Tension began to tighten my stomach. Indecisiveness overwhelmed me. The transformation I hoped marriage would bring about had not happened. Bart's black moods continued. There were respites but…they always returned.

I dreaded spending time with Bart. I was afraid he would begin to see the change in me. *Change?* For the first time in almost five years there was outright discontent and unrest. The acknowledgement threw me into a cauldron of guilt. I must fight this. Bart was a good man, and I could not imagine a life without Matthew yet I knew I did not love Bart.

CHAPTER 59

1983

My life at work improved since Bart was promoted and reassigned to a different platoon. I began to enjoy work again. I began to socialize with the other officers again and found myself smiling more often. There was no more looking over my shoulder to make sure I wasn't being watched.

Ted was still my sergeant and he even remarked how good it was to see me smile. It felt good to smile again. Of course, if Bart was home when I got off duty, the glum state of my life returned. Because we worked opposite shifts, we rarely saw each other. On our days off, we had Matthew. Matthew and I often went to movies, the park or the zoo. Bart rarely accompanied us, preferring instead to watch sports on television, obsess over the untidy house or tinker with his piece of shit car.

Rotating shifts and caring for a young child on my days off left little time for household chores. I was tired! But cooking and cleaning were wholly the wife's responsibility according to Bart. He never offered to help, just criticized what he saw as my inadequacies as a housewife. Needless to say, I preferred work to home.

When the day-in, day-out existence with Barton ended after his promotion and transfer, I felt like I had escaped a prison. I began to make new friends with some of the officers I'd previously been afraid to speak to. I saw Casey more often. We met often for lunch or drinks after work when I was on the day shift. Bart frowned on social drinking. On the days that Bart was home, when I left for work, I realized it was an escape and I felt only relief.

I now worked a solo beat, but according to the type of call, backup was a constant. I am not sure of the first time I noticed Caleb Larson or had a conversation with him. I thought he had a great smile. He was handsome with dark hair and hazel eyes and an Oklahoma drawl. He worked an adjoining beat, so we found ourselves often responding to the same calls. We would talk endlessly about cases, police politics, and life in general. I began to consider him a good friend.

"Don't you have a son, Jess? How old is he?"

"He's six, just started first grade."

Caleb and I were about to clear a domestic call, where three young children were all traumatized and crying after their parent's argument turned into a dish-throwing brawl. Both mom and dad had to be transported to the Emergency Room. Two of the children were boys near Matt's age and I calmed them down by talking about Star Wars, while we waited for their aunt to take custody for the night. The Social Service caseworker was willing to prevent further trauma by placing them with relatives. The husband and wife each adamantly refused to prosecute each other. We made a decision to let DSS get involved.

I suppose Cal, as most of us called him, was reflecting on the three kids as they drove away, prompting him to ask about Matthew. "I hate it when kids get caught in these lousy situations," he muttered, obviously affected. He was full of compassion for children. We often talked about domestic laws and what we could do to help families stuck in cycles of violence.

I finally received another call and left, but not before realizing, I had grown to have warm feelings when I talked with Cal Larson. He was a kind, professional officer and a first-rate cop. He was not a skirt chaser as so many of the guys were. Everyone knew there were women who relentlessly pursued police officers. Too many marriages ended when officers strayed with the cop groupies.

A few weeks later, I was involved in a minor traffic mishap while on duty. A young mentally challenged man, 22-years-old, rode his bicycle out of a driveway and shot onto the street just as I was executing a right turn. His bike rammed the front right fender and he went flying across the hood of my patrol car. I was frantic that he might be dead or injured as I jumped from my car to give aid. He appeared uninjured and wanted to leave on his bike. I wouldn't let him until EMS arrived and they insisted he be transported to the emergency room. I requested a supervisor and another officer to write the report. The first on scene was Cal. It was a Saturday and the traffic division was off duty, meaning the beat officers investigated all traffic accidents. I was relieved that Cal was there, he was one of the best at accident investigations. He had been a military policeman for five years, taking advanced accident reconstruction among a myriad of other training while with the U.S. Army.

I was in the ambulance writing down the victim's information and reassuring him that I would secure his bike until he could return home. Just as I stepped down from the ambulance, another officer, Andrew Saxon, arrived stating he was assigned to investigate the accident.

Cal closed his clipboard and said, "I'll leave it to you then."

"No, I want you to work this," I insisted. Since I was the senior officer, it was my call. The other officer was relieved to get out of an accident report.

Cal smiled. For a split second we held each other's gaze, then, I looked away, flustered. I handed him the registration for the patrol car and my driver's license.

I wasn't sure what transpired, but I was befuddled and I started rattling on like a complete idiot. "Uh, I know you're probably wondering why I wanted you working the accident but, uh, to tell the truth, I want a thorough, professional investigation. Saxon—I like him and all, but—well, he can be a little ditsy on occasion." I bit my lip, wishing I could take it back.

But the fact remained, if Saxon was female, they would have fired him. It was a subject Casey and I discussed more than once. Bless his heart he was one of the best-looking officers in the department, downright pretty. However, his elevator did not always make it to the top.

Two months prior, Andrew responded to an armed robbery at a convenience store. The suspect ran from the store and almost ran into Andrew. Instead of resorting to protocol and training, he pulls out his flashlight and hits the guy over the head. It worked, knocked him out cold, but really?

"I wasn't wondering and I don't mind," Cal smiled. "It's pretty obvious the guy plowed right into you, no way to avoid it."

I waited in my vehicle while he recorded the information and took pictures of the patrol car and bicycle. He gave me the case number and stated he felt this would be the end of it. The guy's bike wasn't even damaged and you could hardly see the dent in the patrol car.

From that day on, I found myself surreptitiously watching the door for Cal to arrive at work. It seemed each day he walked into roll call his gaze found mine. I would feel my face flush and my heart beat a little faster. I began taking extra care with my appearance and thinking about him while I was off duty.

I knew my feelings were dangerous. Just thinking about Cal made me happy. At the same time, I was horrified at what I was thinking. I would never, could never, be unfaithful to Barton. It was a harmless little crush. Even though I told no one, I could imagine Casey laughing and telling me that just because I was married didn't mean I was dead.

CHAPTER 60

1983

There was no harm in looking. Yet my attraction to Cal grew. My emotions so scrambled with the repugnant memories of Momma's deceitfulness and the repulsion for even thinking I could ever become my mother. The thought alone made my blood run cold and my stomach churn.

The humiliating fact was Bart and I seldom had sex. We were no more than roommates who didn't even like each other.

I convinced myself that my infatuation was harmless because I never talked with Cal about anything other than police business. And I never would. If, for no other reason, I would never give Barton the satisfaction of thinking he was right about me. For years he'd been accusing me of being on the hunt for other guys.

God! I was now talking to myself so much I was making my own self crazy. So, the days came and went and Matthew was my only constant. He was my anchor. On my days off, we always did something special. My devotion to Matt was the only thing that had Bart's approval. One afternoon, Matt and I went the mall in search of the latest Star Wars replica. After making our purchase, we were sitting outside Baskin Robbins, enjoying our ice cream cones, when I heard someone call my name.

I looked up and there was Cal. He was in uniform, so I knew he was working a side job at one of the department stores. My heart jumped at the sight of him and I thought it would leap right out of my chest.

"Hey, that ice cream sure looks good, young man," He smiled down at Matthew.

"It is, want some?" He held the dripping cone up toward Cal. "No thanks, I'm too full right now," Cal patted his stomach, and Matt continued licking. Then, the joy at seeing Cal turned to fear. It began to build inside me until it was almost overwhelming. I abruptly stood, telling Matthew we needed to leave. What if Matthew talked about the policeman he talked with?

He loved police officers and never seemed to correlate that his dad and I were officers. I was seized with such trepidation I was almost in a panic.

"No, Mommy, I want to finish my ice cream."

"Well, hurry, we have to get home."

Cal must have sensed my discomfort. He

quickly made an excuse to leave.

"I've still got a couple more hours to work. Take care, little man." He smiled. "You know, Jess," he said. "He has your eyes." Then with a wave, he was gone.

I realized he did not know Matthew was not my child by birth. It was a common misconception, especially with the newer officers. I knew I should have immediately explained to Cal, but I let it drop. I secretly loved it when people thought Matthew looked like me. I desperately wished Matthew was my birth child. If he were, I would take him and leave Barton in a heartbeat.

The realization was startling, yet I knew it was true, I was filled with remorse and dread. Remorse, Matthew was not my birth son. Dread, because I was going home to a husband I had grown to hate.

CHAPTER 61

1983

Working the graveyard shift during January was grueling. There could be snow and ice to deal with, which was not that common for the upstate of South Carolina. But when it did fall, it brought everything to a standstill. Burglaries were way up since the first of the year. The unusual heavy snowfall made it difficult to maneuver the patrol car through alleyways not cleared by public works road scrapers. I was often on foot around businesses in burglary prone areas.

One dark night I was checking the rear of a pawn shop to insure the back door was secure. As I made my way back to the patrol car, my feet suddenly went out from under me and I landed flat on my back. I was cussing out loud, mad, freezing cold, and covered with snow. Just as I reached my car, I noticed another patrol car pulling through the lot. It was Cal.

"Hey, saw the cruiser here with no one in it, just checking on you."

"You should have been three minutes sooner and you could have witnessed me busting my ass."

I brushed furiously at the damp snow covering my backside. Cal broke out laughing and there was nothing left for me to do but laugh with him.

"I think you need a hot cup of coffee, my treat," he said.

"Coffee sounds great but I'll treat myself. Thanks."

We drove to an all-night donut shop and parked just as another officer was leaving. We claimed a couple of bar stools and ordered coffee and donuts. "I need this donut like I need a hole in my head," I said, sinking my teeth into the sugary treat. It was warm and delicious.

"You're beautiful; you don't need to worry about donuts." Cal took a bite of his and I froze in mid bite. He didn't seem to notice my discomfort and continued eating. I finished my coffee just as the server came by with refills.

"So, how long have you and Quinlan been married?"

"Just about a year, but we've been together for over four. Actually, Matthew is Barton's child from a former marriage. But I love him like my own."

"Hmm." His face was blank.

"What does hmm mean?" I finally asked.

"Oh, nothing. You just seem sad sometimes. I was just wondering what could make such a nice lady like you sad." He turned and looked directly at me then, with thoughtful, penetrating eyes. My heart quickened and I thought I might fall off the stool. Instead, I reached into my pocket, pulled out some bills and plopped them down on the counter.

"How can you do this job for any length of time and not be sad on occasion?" I replied, standing up to leave.

"I heard that. We see some bad stuff all right. The domestics get to me the worst, you know. There are so many of them. Women with kids who are married to sons of bitches who treat them like shit."

"Well, that's part of the job; you just have to leave it when you go home. You have to forget." My face was burning. I knew he was not talking about the job. I needed to get out of there; I was too embarrassed and too frightened to continue the discussion. I would not discuss my personal life or admit there were problems. I was beginning to feel as if everyone knew how Bart treated me. Did they talk behind my back? I knew good and well there was always gossip around headquarters. Secrets did not remain mysteries for long. I left without looking back, but could feel his eyes on me as I walked out the door.

CHAPTER 62

1983

As I continued patrolling my sector, I began to doubt myself. Cal probably wasn't talking about me at all. I was just feeling self-conscious because of the seminar. I'd been thinking about it too much. Cal probably thought I was acting crazy.

"Fox 100 to Fox 200," I called his unit.

"Fox 200, go ahead Fox 100."

"10-19 in front of City Hall?"

"En route."

We arrived about the same time and with no cars on the street, we pulled as most cops most do, driver side to driver side and talked through the window.

"I was thinking…" I stuttered. "I mean, you mentioned domestic calls and my best friend, Casey, she was a former officer before she went to law school.

"Yeah, she's an assistant solicitor, right?"

"Yes, and she recently implemented a program, a presentation for the community focusing on domestic violence. She uses various professionals and always needs an officer to speak. I, uh, just thought if you're interested...?"

"Yeah, I would be, most definitely. Will you also be speaking?"

"Uh, no, not if you are. I mean, she only wants one officer at each seminar and I, well, I've already done it. But I won't always be available and she asked me to find other officers who are interested."

I was telling a bald faced lie about Casey wanting other speakers. I would have to call her and fill her in as soon as she was awake.

"If you're not there, I wouldn't be so interested."

"What?"

"I said no, if you're not there."

"But...why? What difference does it make? I mean..."

He started laughing and assured me he was just teasing. I laughed as well, but this was beginning to get a little strange, so I was relieved when the dispatcher sent me on a call. A burglar alarm activated across town and the beat area car was busy.

"Duty calls see you later." And I was off.
Grateful for the call but also a little disappointed. This Cal thing was becoming bizarre. And dangerous, yet I couldn't get his face out of my head.

CHAPTER 63

1983

I welcomed the end of third shift. My time with Matthew was always limited when I worked midnights. With three days off, I promised Matthew we would picnic at the park if it wasn't too cold. Bart agreed to go, so once again I was back to hoping we might work things out as a family. The most important thing in my life was to make it work for Matthew's sake.

The day we chose for the park outing was cool, bright and perfect. I made deviled egg sandwiches and packed chips and cheese and sodas. Matthew was ecstatic and asked over and over when it would be time to leave. I packed everything into the car and went in search of Bart. He was watching television in the den.

"All ready for our adventure," I chirped.

He continued to stare at the TV and didn't speak. I suddenly felt the old fear grip my stomach. What now?

"Barton, are you ready?" I asked again walking toward him.

"I'm not going. Call your friend Casey to go, why don't you?" He still didn't look at me and his voice was a snarl.

"What are you talking about? Matthew is counting on you."

"Why didn't you tell me this domestic speech you gave was all arranged by your little slut friend?"

Suddenly I was filled with anger. "She is not a slut and it was arranged by the solicitor's office."

"Well, suit yourself. I'm not going to the park."

"I'm not disappointing Matthew." I turned to leave but his next words stopped me cold.

"Matthew is my son, not yours, and I say neither of us are going to the park. You can go by yourself."

"Please, Bart." My eyes filled with tears. "I'm sorry I didn't mention Casey was in charge of the seminar. Maybe I didn't want what is happening right now to happen."

"What else have you lied about Jessica? You're two faced, that's what you are."

"I didn't lie to you Bart, I just…"

"You just didn't tell me the truth. That's a lie. You should have known better. Don't ever let that happen again."

"I won't, I'm sorry." The tears finally spilled

over. He continued to look at the TV. Although he never once raised his voice or looked at me, I felt like I had been physically struck. I was reduced to a child being scolded and I hated it. I hated him, yet I continued on with my life. What was wrong with me?

"Fine, then. I guess Matthew would be disappointed so he should go to the park. But I'm not going." His voice was cold and full of contempt. All I could think was a reprieve! I wanted to shout thank you, oh lord and master, but I knew to keep my mouth shut.

I dried my tears and tried not to let Matthew see how upset I was. "Why isn't Daddy coming?" he kept asking. My mind replayed Bart's words, "Matthew should go to the park." He never thought about my feelings, he never hinted he even loved me. It appeared he just owned me, controlled me. *Property.*

Abusive, controlling men treated their partners and considered their partners as property. Property they owned. I recalled those words from the psychiatrist at the seminar. I then remembered the argument we had a few weeks ago, after I had gone for a haircut.

"You know I don't like your hair that short. Don't ever cut it that short again," He had sneered. It was not short at all, chin length yet off the collar. Who the hell was he to tell me how to cut my hair?

Worse, it seemed, he was ashamed of me. He

hated that I was a cop. I suspected he disliked all females who worked in law enforcement. Worse, I suspected he hated women.

"Daddy's tired, sweetie, so it's just you and me."

"That's okay, Mommy. We will have more fun without him."

I looked at him, wondering whether he understood and meant what he was saying. Matthew was right...we would have more fun without Bart.

CHAPTER 64

1983

Most of my time away from work was spent with Matthew. My life solely revolved around Matthew and protecting him from his unstable father. The fact that I admitted I thought Bart was unstable was sobering. However, no one else seemed to realize that. At work he was quiet, slow talking and officers respected him. He was practically idolized because of his military service in Vietnam. So I would just enjoy each day rediscovering the world through Matthew's eyes and being there for him. Keeping him safe.

While I knew that Barton loved his son, he was a harsh disciplinarian who thought little boys should never cry. He did not want Matthew to bake cookies with me, or to play anything remotely girlish. Bart was already teaching his son to play football. He wanted Matt to be the man Bart wanted him to be. If Matt hurt himself while learning to tackle, he got yelled at along with a hard swat on the butt. I could hardly stand to see such a tiny boy treated so harshly. I became so frustrated and angry that I wanted to scream but I knew if I said anything, it would only make matters worse. Bart already accused me of trying to make Matt into a little pansy.

Bart was not fair in the way he disciplined Matthew. It almost broke my heart one day when Bart spanked Matthew because he wanted to stop playing football.

"I'm tired, Daddy, can I have some juice?"

Before I realized what was happening, Bart jerked him up and spanked his bottom two or three times, hard. "You will not be a lazy football player!" he screamed. Matthew cried and reached for me. This angered Bart even more, but I didn't care. I grabbed Matthew and pulled him into me.

"He's tired for God's sake, Bart!"

"He's not your son, Jessica." But he turned and stalked into the house. He always threw the fact that I wasn't Matt's real mother in my face when I dared to speak up. Those words shot me down worse than anything I could hear and he knew it. *He's not your son, Jessica.* Damn it, my head knew that but my heart told me differently.

In quiet moments I admitted to myself there was no hope for my marriage. *Love is patient and kind.* There was no other way I could prove myself to Bart. I had tried to say all the right words, made idyllic promises, performed how I thought he wanted. Yet he continued to treat me as if I were a liar and a cheat. Or, at the very least, as if deception was my true nature and that I was always scheming to accomplish this.

I was tired and weary and in quiet moments, I faced the truth that my only happiness was Matthew and my job.

Chapter 65

1983

The week after he refused to go to the park, Bart announced we were going to a basketball game. Ted's oldest son was playing in a church league and Matthew thought 10-year-old Jason hung the moon. We stopped to get hamburgers before the game and, as usual, were running late. The teenagers working the counter were disorganized and there was a line of customers waiting. When one of the kids tried to give our order to a couple who just walked up, I spoke.

"Hey, I think those are ours?" I wasn't rude and was actually smiling at the young man, who was obviously flustered.

Bart hissed at me to shut up and at the same time kicked my shin. The pain was unexpected and sharp, but I struggled to act as if it hadn't happened. Tears from the hurt and humiliation threatened to overflow, and I battled to stay controlled. Bart was so introverted; he was almost awkward in a social setting. I was amazed he could function on the job.

"Oops, right, you're number 23." The teenager plopped the tray in front of us and we made our way to a table. Matthew was oblivious to what had transpired and Bart refused to look at me. I couldn't eat a bite. As we sat down, I feigned an urgent need to use the facilities and hurried into the bathroom.

Trying to collect myself, I checked my leg where a large, blue knot was already forming and the skin was broken and bleeding.

Surely Bart didn't realize how hard he kicked me or that he hurt me. He probably meant to kick at my foot. He was so easily embarrassed. Calling Bart an introvert was an understatement. I often wondered how he managed to be a good police officer. Officer Jekyll and Sergeant Hyde.

I returned to the table and forced myself to take a few bites. Before we ordered I was starving, now the hamburger tasted like cardboard. Bart wolfed his burger down. He suddenly stood and declared if we didn't leave we'd be late.

"No problem, I'll just take mine with me." I started to gather my purse and the bag.

"You should have eaten with us." He gathered all the bags and drinks onto the plastic tray and dumped everything in the garbage. He was punishing me for not finishing my meal. I cowered in silence, afraid that people were looking at us. I plastered a smile on my face and told Matthew to hurry so we could see Jason play basketball. I hoped he hadn't picked up on the tension between Bart and me. I knew all too well the paralyzing fear a child has when parents yell and curse at each other. I knew how devastating it was to wonder why your Momma and Daddy hated each other. But, we didn't yell and cuss. His weapon was silence, but tonight it had escalated to a kick.

As we drove to the game, I tried looking at Barton, but all I could see was Momma. Her voice came back to me so clearly belittling Daddy, belittling Charlie, belittling me. Her mean, twisted mouth harping continuously about some infraction or other she often misconstrued. The nausea and feeling of helplessness so familiar as a child, returned full force like a war flashback. My empty stomach cramped and churned.

"Stop the car, I'm going to throw up," I yelled. Bart pulled over and I barely made it out of the car. The tears came then and I tried to catch my breath and will the crying to stop.

"Mommy, are you sick?" Matthew asked, obviously alarmed.

"You want me to take you home?" Bart asked coldly, not can I do anything or are you all right, not should we all go home. His glare was conveying how fucking long are you going to hold us up with this inconvenience. There wasn't a caring, nurturing bone in his body. I was a thing he controlled and when that failed, he became sullen and angry.

I remembered three years earlier, when I was awakened from sleep, in the middle of the day with an abscessed tooth. The first toothache I'd ever had. We had both worked the midnight shift and had been asleep for about three hours. The pain was almost unbearable and I was sick. I woke him after I had called my dentist.

"Bart, can you drive me to the dentist? My tooth is killing me and Dr. Brown can work me in if I get there in the next half hour."

I'll never forget how he glared at me, furious that I had awakened him.

"Well, go then," he snarled.

I was often angry with myself for continuing to allow such treatment. But like so many abused women, I considered myself a mother, a mother with a child whom I loved more than I loved myself.

"No I'm okay. I must have gotten too hot." I crawled back into the car with Bart scowling and looking at his watch. I rode silently to the church, overwhelmed with sadness. Matthew's small hand softly patted my shoulder, "You'll be okay, Mommy." I wanted to take that sweet little boy into my arms and make the world go away.

"Quit that." Bart snapped, pushing Matthew's hand away.

I clenched my jaw in hurt and loneliness but also, there was beginning a slow building anger.

CHOICES

How long would it be, I wondered, before Matthew learned from his father how not to show love and compassion, how not to care? That you treated your wife as property.

CHAPTER 66

1983

When a platoon ended a tour on midnights, we were rewarded with a 32-hour break before reporting for a month of second shift duty. It was customary to have a party somewhere, according to the time of year. If it was summer it might be at someone's lake house, but in cooler weather we usually gathered at the Police Club, owned by the officers, and maintained by officers.

It was a huge open room building, complete with a restaurant-style kitchen on one end and a television and comfortable sofas on the other. There were plenty of folding tables and chairs, allowing for large groups. There would be beer and booze, if you wanted, in addition to tea, soft drinks and snacks.

Bart and I attended several gatherings over the years, and as long as I didn't appear to enjoy myself, he was okay. The upcoming party would be the first choir he practice had hinted he would attend since his promotion and transfer.

After long hours on graveyard shift followed by sleepless days, choir practice was a welcome break. I told Bart it was to be held at the Police Club. I chattered on as if our attending were a sure thing.

When my shift ended, I went home and slept four hours, then did a few long overdue housekeeping chores. Hell would freeze over before Bart would lift a finger

The fact I did the same job he did at work meant nothing to him. He hated what I did and felt I shouldn't be there in the first place. He conveniently forgot my salary paid the mortgage. The mortgage and my car payment were my debts before we married, therefore mine to pay. Bart liked to think he was debt free.

But we always seemed to drive my car, because his second piece of shit car was now a 1970 Dodge Charger and a cash cow, and always in need of repair.

I never complained about the child support even though Matthew lived with us the majority of the time. Anything for Matthew was fine with me. Bart's only household responsibility was the utilities. Almost everything else, including groceries, came from my salary. I knew he squirreled away a nice chunk of change in a savings account each month, and I had no idea how much.

Of course, a person never enters police work for the money, but together we made a decent income. We could have lived a lot more comfortably. Bart refused to discuss finances, savings, or business where a meeting with a banker, lawyer or accountant was required. Once the uniform came off, his personality was taciturn at best and reclusive at the worst.

In our early days together, I blamed his moodiness on Vietnam. I cut him slack and thought that my love, patience and nurturing would eventually heal those old wounds. But as time progressed, I suspected there was something in his angry psyche more deeply rooted than the war. He grew up on Army bases across the world. Rather than the erudite adult I thought such an upbringing would produce, he was instead painfully shy, reclusive and obsessive-compulsive and, if evaluated, probably bi-polar.

From what Bart shared about childhood, it was painful. His father had been an abusive alcoholic. Barton Quinlan Sr. was a career military officer who commanded his family in much the same manner as he did his soldiers. It was humiliating when, as the oldest, it fell upon Bart to fetch his father from the Officer's Club, his momma waiting in the car.

His mother finally divorced his father, but the damage was done. His father eventually died before I ever got a chance to meet him. Bart would only give glimpses of the pain from his childhood

312

and I came to partly blame his father when the black moods descended.

Was he transported back to a jungle in Vietnam, or was he a young teenager dragging the colonel home from a bar, so drunk he couldn't stand. I would never know the answer.

By the time Bart came home, the house was in good shape. I showered and put on jeans with a cotton sweater. Everyone dressed casually for these gatherings. I hadn't even bothered with makeup, just a little pink lipstick. I was looking forward to a beer with friends and a hamburger I didn't have to cook.

As soon as Bart walked in the door, I could see the dark scowl. God, what now? My heart automatically dropped, my mind racing to remember anything that would annoy him. I could think of nothing.

"Hi, how was your day?" I piped up, pretending to ignore his mood. He glowered at me without answering and went to change his clothes. When he came out, I winced when I saw him dressed in his ragged work jeans and an equally worn flannel shirt.

"The guys are eating at the club between six and seven, what time do you want to leave?" I held my breath waiting for his response.

"Don't you get enough of the guys at work, Jessica? Do you think you have to be up their ass when you're off as well?"

"They are your friends, also, Bart, in fact more

your friends than mine. You said you wanted to go." I was beginning to fight the tears as I felt my emotions building.

"Well, I've decided I don't want to go."

"Fine, then. What to do you want for dinner? I haven't planned anything."

"That's your speed, Jessica. I work hard all day and there's nothing to eat."

"There's plenty to eat Bart, I just didn't thaw anything out because I thought we were going to Choir Practice."

"It will take forever, forget it."

"It wouldn't with a microwave." I snapped back.

"You always want something, don't you, Miss High and Mighty." He sneered. "Well, we aren't getting a microwave and I'm going to Mother's for supper." He grabbed his keys and walked out the door.

CHAPTER 67

1983

I just stood there, dumfounded. But instead of tears, I felt rage surging through my body. I wanted to throw or hit something. If my situation had not been so pathetic, my next thought might have been humorous. I thought about Matthew's superheroes and silently wished I could morph into The Incredible Hulk for just five minutes. It would feel so good to beat the pure-tee shit out of Barton Quinlan.

Instead, I slumped to the sofa and gave into tears. I cried for so long that my eyes were swollen and I was ashamed even to go to a fast food drive-thru. I finally scrambled some eggs and when Bart still wasn't home at 10 o'clock, I went to bed exhausted. Surprisingly, I fell asleep almost immediately. When I awoke the next morning I felt only relief that Barton had not come home.

I was having my second cup of coffee when

the phone rang. It was Bart calling from his mother's house. "I worked on Mother's washing machine until late last night. I have to go buy parts and finish up. Aren't you off tonight?"

"Yes, I have three days off. I was leaving to go pickup Matthew."

"Y'all come on over here then, Mother's cooking dinner for us tonight."

I shook my head as I listened to him. It was as though the night before never happened. I wondered, if I wasn't in the picture, how often he would get Matthew. While I knew he loved him, he treated him like a possession, solely for his pleasure and always at his convenience. Much as he did me.

"Isn't he a big boy? Won't he be a monster on the football field? Built just like his Daddy huh?" Over and over, he stressed what he wanted his son to be and do as he got older. If Matthew were a girl, I seriously doubt Barton would want anything to do with his child. How did I end up married to such a narrow minded, cruel, selfish prick like Barton Quinlan?

CHAPTER 68

1983

After high school Charlie escaped to the North Carolina mountains for college. During those years he became an avid skier. Until I met Barton, I usually joined him on the slopes at least once a year. When he and Ally married, they tried to ski two or three times during the season. It was a tradition for several years to spend the week before Christmas in Gatlinburg, Tennessee. It was a time to relax and do last minute shopping in the quaint shops in the tourist town. It had been five years since we had gone skiing together.

This year Barton still wouldn't go to Gatlinburg before Christmas but he did agree the three of us would join my brother and sister-in-law in March for a long weekend.

Barton didn't like Charlie. We hadn't been together since Christmas and I missed the family gatherings. Charlie was an engineer with a construction company and had been transferred to Charlotte a few years before and the drive took only an hour or so, but I could never get Bart to make the trip.

"Charlie and his snobby wife just want to show off their fancy house," he always said.

"That's not true," I insisted. "Ally is one of the most gracious and sweetest people I know. She reminds me of your sister."

"Then you go." It would end there, so I was thrilled when he agreed to meet Charlie in Gatlinburg.

Matthew was excited about the ski trip and could talk of nothing else. This would be his first time on skis. Reservations had been prearranged for a few lessons on the 'bunny slope'. My brother rented a chalet with four bedrooms upstairs and an open great room below. I could hardly wait to get away. This would be the last chance to ski before spring and I knew Charlie was excited as well.

The week-end before our trip, I took Matthew shopping and we purchased a snowsuit and warm gloves and hat. We would rent skis at the lodge. We planned to leave on a Thursday and return on Sunday. On the Monday before I left to work the second shift, I got two suitcases from the attic and began to pack a few things for Barton and myself. Barton was off work for the entire week, citing a need to replace a water pump in his piece of shit car. Whatever, I thought, exasperated with the time and money he poured into the thing. He

318

could afford a better car, but he refused to discuss it or shop for one.

"What are you doing?" He startled me.

"Gosh, you scared me. I was getting a head start packing so we won't be so rushed Thursday. " I turned and smiled at him. His face was a mask and his mood unknown. So I continued with my chatter.

"I'll leave your suitcase in Matthew's room and you can put in anything I've forgotten. Is there anything you can think of now I've missed?" I was mentally organizing what we would need. Warm turtlenecks, long underwear, jeans and wool socks.

"I'm not going."

"What...?" I whirled around and stared at him. Please don't let this be happening, my mind screamed.

"I'm not going; I don't feel like it." He turned and walked out.

"Barton, why are you doing this? You know Charlie and Ally have already made the reservations. We both have the time off. We need this, please." I was whining like a pathetic child but I couldn't help myself.

"Please, Bart, you know how disappointed Matthew will be. Don't ruin this."

"He's my son, Jessica, and I said we aren't going. The only reason you want to go is because it sounds trendy to go skiing." His face was unreadable.

The tears were flowing and I never hated him like I did at that moment. He could always find a way to hurt and torment me. He seemed to wait for just the right moment. The right moment hurt the worst. Now I doubted he ever planned on going on this trip. That was just like him. *Any glimpse of happiness, the abuser will snatch it away.*

An hour before I was to report to roll call, I was placing cold compresses on my eyes to reduce the swelling I'd cried so much. Bart was blithely outside working on the car. I could hear him whistling. I was glad I didn't have to look at his ugly face.

I pulled on my Kevlar vest and the long sleeve uniform shirt. Long sleeves required a tie. I discovered why men hate ties. The ties were clip-on because the department didn't want someone choking us to death with one. As I laced up the last boot, I heard the door from the garage below slam. Bart made his way down the hallway to the bedroom door. He stood looking at me, not saying a word. As I pulled on my gun belt, he gave me a look of contempt, shook his head and walked away. I pointed my finger at him like a gun and emptied the chamber of my fictitious weapon.

The fury I felt was unbearable. Like an adolescent, I then gave him the double finger and made a face behind his back. God, was I pitiful or what? I left for work without either of us speaking a word. Work and Matthew were my solace and all I needed.

CHAPTER 69

1983

The sergeant walked to the podium and called the roll. I cringed at the short supply of officers. Some were on general leave and two had called in sick with the flu. Two others were away at required academy training. I was the only beat car for my sector and most of the others were running only one as well. It would be a hellacious night.

I usually phoned home a few times during my shift, but there was not one moment of time until I took a meal break. As I heard the phone ring, I began to think Bart wasn't at home. Finally, he picked up, knowing it was me.

"What?"

"Hi, sorry, I couldn't call before now." Our conversations often began with an apology from me for one thing or the other.

"If you didn't want to call, why are you calling now?"

"I did want to call, but we're short, and I haven't stopped since coming on duty."

"So, what you want?" He asked.

"Have you changed your mind about this week-end?" I held my breath, hoping his mood had improved.

"If all you called about was the trip, I'm busy." He hung up on me.

I stood in the dark listening to a dial tone. The continuous humiliation he dished out was beyond demoralizing. I wanted to cry again but I was standing in the middle of town in uniform. But I was tired of crying and disgusted and pissed off at myself. Somehow, the uniform gave me strength. What was I doing? What was I going to do? I handled problems and faced dangerous situations every day, yet my personal life was a disaster.

I was going crazy. I remembered the conversation between Ted and me during my review. Maybe I should talk to him. He would be working at the mall after the shift ended. He worked security off duty. Most cops worked outside jobs to survive. Bart and I got by with our two salaries without moonlighting, but money — at least my money — was always tight.

I tried my best to push the wretchedness out of my mind for the next few hours. I finally caught a break and stopped for coffee, before I was half-finished, dispatch hit the alert tone. I left what remained of my coffee and donut and ran toward the patrol car. People were staring, wondering what was happening. I figured the emergency was either an officer needing assistance or an armed robbery in progress. Those were the two most common protocols, which warranted the emergency alert tone to be activated.

"All units, 10-45, Armed Robbery just occurred, Two J's Package Store. Only description on suspect is white male, dark clothing, last seen running down McCoy Avenue, use caution, armed and dangerous."

I was five blocks away and tires screeched as I pulled into traffic headed toward the area. The beat car arrived at the scene and reported no injuries; he radioed the description of the suspect.

"White male suspect armed, small handgun, ran to rear of business, last seen wearing black tee shirt, blue jeans, clean shaven, wearing a knit cap."

The unit on scene continued to get information, process the scene and do the written report. The rest of us began setting up a loose perimeter around the area, hoping to box in the suspect. In reality, he most likely parked a getaway car on one of the back streets or disappeared into a house. The sun was setting and dusk fast approaching. Unless he was spotted, chances of capturing him were slight

I've always been intuitive, so much so, some of my partners thought my sixth sense was spooky at times. That my *sixth sense* might be good police work didn't cross their mind.

As I slowly patrolled two streets behind McCoy, I remained vigilant for anything suspicious. I stopped and questioned anyone I saw on the street. I noted the driver of every car, his race, and shirt color. Anyone who looked hinky. He had probably already tossed the knit cap.

The west end of the city was once upper middle class but declined during the last twenty years as the upper class moved east. Slumlords now rented the two-story houses as cheap apartments. Many smaller dwellings were in disrepair or boarded up and vacant. In the late sixties, a HUD apartment project was added to the mix and crime soared. The complex attracted even more drugs and criminals in a section of town already rampant with crime.

I slowly rolled down the street, and for some reason one old dilapidated house seemed to beckon me. I'd noticed it on numerous occasions and often saw young men lolling near the porch. I rolled to the curb half a block away.

"Fox One will be out of the vehicle at 19 Gray Street checking an empty house."

"Standby Fox 100, I'm one block away." Cal, who was working the adjoining beat rolled silently up behind my patrol car.

"Fox 200 out with Fox 100."

"Thanks, let's do this." We made our way through the thick shrubbery, stopping momentarily to observe the house. We could hear nothing and there was no movement in any of the windows. We stepped on the long porch and Cal reached for the door and saw the lock was broken. We drew our weapons. The door swung open revealing an empty room. As Cal stepped inside, I heard a thump from above.

I motioned for Cal to continue and I pointed up. He nodded having heard the same thing. I backed out to get a look at the upstairs window and covered second story veranda. Suddenly I saw movement in an upstairs window.

It all happened fast. The suspect jumped out of the window onto the veranda. I began yelling for him to halt. He didn't. He ran to the end of the veranda and jumped to the ground below. He never slowed. Still yelling for him to halt, I took off in pursuit. He turned once, a black object in his hand and pointed it back in my direction. I fired one shot as he turned, disappearing into the darkening woods behind the house. I radioed my position to other cars in the area and I could hear Cal calling my name, trying to close the gap between us.

Another police car blocked the subject's path as he barreled out of the kudzu on the next street. The next thing I heard was the officer yelling for an ambulance, saying the suspect was shot. I went cold with dread as I finally exited the woods and observed the suspect in custody, but bleeding profusely from the face.

As I tried to catch my breath and take in the

scene, the officer held up what first appeared to be the weapon. A closer look revealed it to be two small blocks of wood wrapped in black electrical tape. At a glance, as intended, it looked like a .25 automatic. Shit. I just shot an unarmed man? Fear gripped me. It took a moment for it to register; I realized I couldn't have shot him in the face. He had turned as I fired and his back was to me, diving into the woods.

I walked up and took a closer look, by this time needing my flashlight. I could see a gash in his forehead and blood was streaming from his nose. He wasn't shot. The sound of gun fire scared him so bad that he apparently tripped and fell flat on his face.

Relief flooded through my body. It would have been a justifiable shooting. The suspect's black-taped blocks of wood worked well enough to rob a liquor store, and it fooled me. But I was glad I hadn't shot a man. I was thankful he would get his punishment in a courtroom and not posthumously. This sad sack just needed a few stitches on his gashed head. I could hear the ambulance and threw my keys to Cal Larson.

"Can you shuffle my patrol car over to the E.R.? I'll keep this one company."

"Consider it done." He turned and disappeared into the woods cutting through to the street where we parked. I climbed into the ambulance with the suspect and paramedics. Once they cleaned his face and checked his vitals, they had no qualms about leaving him handcuffed. The ambulance ran silent to the hospital. I was met by the detectives and night commander.

Commander Harris was eager to speak to the news media and I could see his relief, just like me, when he learned the guy only busted his head and nose from a fall. The news media would have been all over the story "Female Cop Shoots Suspect." I was glad they didn't have much of a story.

By the time I completed the report, the detective assigned wanted the suspect transported to their office for interrogation. They wanted to question him about other unsolved armed robberies and were hoping to clear a few. I reached for my keys and remembered Cal was supposed to secure my vehicle.

"Has anyone seen Larson?" I asked the night commander.

"Forgot, Jordan. Here. He dropped them by a while ago."

"Thanks."

"Good job, by the way. I just talked to the Chief and you can bank on a commendation for this one," Captain Harris said. He was a 38-year veteran, and could have already retired. But it was easy duty since taking over as night commander. He continued to ride out his time.

As I took the keys, I felt disappointed that I'd missed seeing Cal. I wanted to discuss everything with him. My adrenaline was still high. At least, I told myself, that's all I wanted to do.

With my armed robber safely in custody and all the reports completed, I pulled into The Koffee Klatch for the best coffee in town and the proverbial donut. They served the coffee in heavy stoneware mugs, not Styrofoam cups. Her donuts weren't half-bad either.

I picked up the mike and told dispatch I would be 10-10 (out of the car but available for calls) at the corner of Main and Park Hill. Everyone knew that any officer out of the car at Main and Park Hill was at the Koffee Klatch.

Reedy View was still in the grips of old man winter. After the sun set, temps dropped to the lower 40s and with a strong breeze, it felt colder. The coffee was good and I accepted a refill, wondering if I would ever fall asleep with so much happening, and all the caffeine.

The bell above the door jingled and as I turned to look, Cal entered the shop. He smiled and I realized I had been waiting for him. We had replayed the chase and the arrest a dozen times.

"What made you decide to stop and check that one particular house?" he asked.

"It's hard to say. Just a feeling I guess."

"Gut instinct from a good cop," he said, reaching to shake my hand.

"Thanks, Cal. I think that's probably the nicest compliment I've ever gotten." I smiled and then suddenly we were both quiet. It was an awkward moment. Then the waitress broke the silence by refilling our cups.

"I'll be awake until sometime next week with all this caffeine tonight." I remarked.

"Doesn't seem to bother me, I just need the warmth. Coffee, I mean," he smiled. "Say, Jess. It's none of my business but is everything else okay with you?"

"Same ol', same ol', I suppose." I tried to sound upbeat but apparently failed.

"So is 'same-ol' the pits?" he asked, looking into my eyes.

"I don't know, Cal. To be perfectly honest, it's been a long time since my life was anything but the pits." I couldn't believe I was being so candid with him but I was past caring what others thought. My emotions were in a desperate state. I'd just been through what could have been a life-and-death situation and I didn't have any inclination whatsoever to share it with my husband. He wouldn't care anyway. But Cal did care.

"The truth is, Cal, nothing is right in my life except for Matthew. He's my heart and soul." Suddenly the emptiness overwhelmed me, for even imagining Matthew not being in my life brought on an excruciating despair. Yet, how could I continue living as I was? I wanted to spill out my guts to Cal but something held me back.

"You appear unhappy to me, Jess." Cal said quietly. I didn't respond and he didn't say anything for a long time. We just sat and sipped our coffee and listened to the chatter on the portable radios.

Then, seemingly making a decision, he turned and began to speak. His demeanor said this wasn't easy for him.

"I've been debating if I should tell you this. I consider you a friend. I think you consider me a friend. No, don't say anything." He held his hand up when I tried to respond. "I don't want to lose my courage. Aside from being a good cop, you're a good person. I think you're beautiful in uniform or civvies. I have no right to say this but I really care about you. I mean I care, Jess. You don't deserve the crap you put up with and everybody knows it. Everybody talks about how much you've changed since you and Quinlan got together. Changed for the worse. I don't know the guy, but I do know he doesn't deserve you."

He began to stammer, then, "I guess I have nothing else to say. Just remember, if you ever need anything, anything at all, you can count on me. And if you ever decide to leave your present situation, you won't have far to go."

I was speechless. I shook with the enormity of emotion that enveloped me. He had given voice to my own feelings. I was unable to speak for several minutes.

"Cal, you don't really know me. Please don't think... I could never leave my son. I willed myself not to show how deep my emotions were. Somehow I remained strong. I could not let Cal Larson know I felt the same way about him. My whole body was shaking. This must stop.

"Thanks for being my friend, Cal. But that's all we can be." I got up and put my money on the counter. "I better hit the streets, just a couple more hours and we will have it made." I started to leave but his voice stopped me.

"I'll wait, Jess." Then he turned and continued drinking his coffee. I couldn't move. I couldn't speak. Finally, I forced myself to put one foot in front of the other and made it to my patrol car. I kept hearing his voice over and over, *I'll wait. I'll wait, Jess. I'll wait.*

CHAPTER 70

1983

In the beginning, I couldn't see the ominous reality, I could only feel it. If I had foreseen the consequences of my choices, would I have done anything differently? We all make choices in life. The most we can hope for is to have as few regrets as possible. My life was slowly being eaten away by a terrible darkness and clarity came only when my own mortality was at stake.

After leaving Cal at the Koffee Klatch, I drove as fast as I dared back to headquarters. It had started raining steadily and was now raining harder. I quickly turned in my equipment. I didn't want to see Cal again and I was still in turmoil over the Gatlinburg trip Bart had nixed.

What's more, it had been an unsettling tour of duty with the shooting incident. But my high stress level was about much more than a cancelled trip and a shooting incident. Depression threatened to overtake me as I pulled away from the parking lot at police headquarters. I suddenly made a decision and turned toward the mall. I would talk with Ted. He and Bart were both sergeants and he was Bart's best friend. He had offered to lend an ear anytime I needed it.

Screw whether I got home on time. I drove directly to the mall, ignoring a fateful premonition of what I was about to set in motion. I no longer cared.

The mall had closed hours before and only a few abandoned cars remained in the vast lot. I went directly to the security office in the back where I knew I would probably find Ted.

His car was parked next to the building and I pulled in beside it. I walked up to a heavy metal door marked **"Security"** and rang the buzzer. Footsteps sounded and the door flew open.

"Jess? Is everything all right?" He seemed shocked to see me.

"Fine. No, actually, Ted, it's not fine. I need to bend your ear."

"Come on in out of the rain, I've got a fresh pot of coffee." I entered and took off my heavy uniform jacket. We responded often to the office when shoplifters were arrested at the mall. Security officers would bring them here and then we would transport them to jail. Ted handed me a mug of coffee. How many did this make for the night?

"Suddenly I feel rather foolish, Ted."

"What's Bart done now?"

"You know us too well. I wanted to think once we married, you know, a real home and all… he'd be more secure. I don't know what I thought."

"You mean you thought he wouldn't be as jealous? I know how he is, but it's not about you, Jess. I love the guy. He's one of my best friends, but, it's about control. He won't listen to me. Jess, I know you don't want to hear this, but Bart will never change. You've got to accept that reality and go from there."

The truth of what he said hit me so forcefully I thought I might actually fall to the floor. I had never felt so defeated, so helpless, so lost. *He will never change.* I knew it was true. We continued talking for almost an hour. I needed to get home. Bart would be asleep, but the day was catching up with me.

"Thanks for listening, Ted. You're a good friend."

"I'm sorry, Jess. I love both you guys. I wish it could be different. If he doesn't go skiing, then you and Matthew go without him. Let him stew in his own juices."

"I just might. Instead of feeling sorry for myself, I'll leave him to his misery. I just hope he lets Matthew go. I don't have a say in that."

We promised we would all get together soon, but I knew we wouldn't. Bart didn't want to socialize with anyone. I drove home slowly and, as I pulled into the garage, I could see most of the lights were on upstairs in The Quarters. Oh, shit, I thought. Bart was hardly ever up when I got home.

As soon as I walked into the kitchen from the garage, I knew something was wrong.

"Where have you been?" Bart hissed the words at me.

"I've been at work." I told him. "Why, what's wrong?"

"I called downtown and they said you left over an hour ago." His eyes were actually glittering with rage. My first instinct was to lie, but instead I just told him the truth.

"I stopped by the mall and talked with Ted."

"So now you're broadcasting our problems to everyone?"

"Ted is our friend, Bart. He isn't everyone."

I walked toward the bedroom, exhausted in spite of all the coffee I'd consumed. I wanted nothing more than to get out of my uniform and fall into bed. My legs felt numb, as if I were in a dream where I was in danger but couldn't move to escape. It was the strangest feeling.

I removed my uniform and pulled on sweats. I cleaned the grime off my face and felt a little better. I walked back to the family room and he was just sitting there staring at me, with a look of deep hatred on his face.

"Tell me what's going on, Jessica," he demanded.

"A terrible day at work, a bad day before I left

335

for work. You know what's wrong."

"Boo hoo, poor little Jessica, you have bad days all the time," he mocked me in a singsong voice. "You should never have gone crying to Ted."

"I didn't go crying to Ted, Bart. I badly needed to talk to someone. I'm sorry, all right? It won't happen again. I was just so disappointed about the trip and I know Matthew will be, also. Not to mention I had to fire my weapon at an armed robber..."

Although it was a big deal when cops drew their weapons and shot, he ignored what I'd said. He wasn't interested. "You're so damn right it won't happen again, Jessica." He continued to glare at me. I wanted him to leave. On other occasions when he was this angry, he usually left for two or three days. On those occasions, I begged him to stay. Now, I silently willed him to go.

"I'm going to bed," I told him and turned toward the bedroom. The drone of the television continued. He wasn't leaving. I laid awake a long time before I drifted into a troubled sleep. Fifteen minutes later, I suddenly awoke with a start, feeling something was terribly wrong. The first thing I saw was Bart standing over the bed, staring straight down at me, his eyes flashing fury.

For years I lived with his black moods, the days of him not speaking, and the many times he left and stayed gone. I don't know if he sensed that I was at the limit of my endurance, I'll never know. All I knew was that every instinct in my body was screaming; get out now.

I got out of bed and went to the kitchen. Like a menacing apparition, he silently followed. "You want some milk?" I asked, trying to sound normal.

"I want nothing from you," he snapped. He stopped and stared out the window at the steady rain.

"Fucking rain, I hate rain," he said, more to himself than me.

I poured a glass of milk and as I did, I took notice of where my carrycase with my off duty weapon and other paper work, and keys were. I had plopped them on the bar in the kitchen when I walked in the door. It was a bad habit that I was grateful for at the moment. I took my milk and sat on the barstool, meanwhile nonchalantly pushing my keys and case over to the end of the counter.

As I sat there, I surreptitiously made sure the double keyed deadbolt was not engaged. Good, it wasn't. I had gone to bed in my sweats and slipped my feet into tennis shoes when I got up.

I tried to act as nonplussed as my pounding heart would allow. Bart was watching my every move, a steely glare as his anger palpitated just below the surface. I sat motionless for what seemed like an eternity, sipping my milk. In reality it was only a few minutes. He picked up his empty water glass and walked across the kitchen to the sink. Counting the steps, one, two, I took my keys and firmly held the deadbolt key forward. I slipped off the stool—three, four. He turned the faucet on and began to fill his glass.

With his back to me I made my move. I grabbed my case and was out the door. I turned the key hearing the sweet sound of the deadbolt click into place. Bart never left his keys in the kitchen. The place for his keys was in the bedroom in his change tray. Everything had a place and everything in its place. For the first time, I was indebted to his obsessive-compulsiveness.

I raced down the steps and hit the switch to the electric garage opener we'd just installed—another reason to be thankful. I was backing my car out into the street when I saw Bart bolting down the steps. He was actually howling like a wild animal. I gunned the motor and peeled off into the night.

CHAPTER 71

1983

Casey's bungalow was near the North Carolina border. It was close to three in the morning when my lights illuminated her front porch. I parked beside her jeep and turned off the ignition. My hands were shaking so violently that I didn't trust myself to stand yet.

I kept a constant vigil in my rearview mirror, but never saw Bart behind me. I had no idea if he tried to follow me or anticipated where I would go. I stepped from my car and made my way to the front door. I knocked and waited. The porch light came on and Casey pulled the curtain back on the side light and flung the door open.

"Jessie, what has happened?"

"Nothing really, I mean I'm alright. I really don't know what happened." My emotions finally took over and I broke down.

"Did that bastard hurt you, Jess?"

"No, but it was different tonight. I was afraid of him." I related how he backed out of the ski trip at the last minute and how I stopped by the mall to talk with Ted. I told her my feelings at the seminar, it all came pouring out.

"Of all nights, he was waiting up for me. He never waits up, it's like he knew I was doing something I shouldn't. It was creepy. He was so mad and I figured he would leave. But when I finally fell asleep, I woke up with him just standing over me with eyes full of hate."

"We'll talk about what to do in the morning. You get some sleep. I keep the extra bedroom ready. Do you want something to eat? A drink?"

"No, yes, I think I do." I never drank with Bart, we never had even a bottle of wine in the fridge. He made me feel dirty if I ever had a glass of Sangria. "You got Vodka?" Casey grinned a toothy grin. "Bet your sweet ass I got vodka."

"I'm fine. I'm going to call Bart, just to let him know I'm all right. I don't want him calling my mom and waking her up in the middle of the night."

Casey looked at me like I was losing my mind. But she didn't comment. She began making us both my favorite drink, a Hairy Navel. A delightful concoction of orange juice, Peach Schnapps and vodka. I walked over to the phone and dialed my home number.

"What do you want?" Bart practically spit the words into the phone.

"I just wanted you to know I'm okay. I'm staying with Casey tonight." I grew silent.

"I don't give a damn where you stay." He slammed the phone down.

We had our drinks and I began to feel a pleasant buzz. Casey pulled an extra quilt from the linen closet and gave me flannel pajamas, a new toothbrush, towel and washcloth. I was exhausted, yet I felt safe until I saw Casey pulling her Smith and Wesson from her bedside table and lay it by the phone. It was then the trembling began again. I pulled out my own detective special and put it by my bed.

CHAPTER 72

1983

I finally slept, but it wasn't restful. The morning sun was pouring in the window when I awoke groggy and disoriented. Then the unpleasantness from the previous evening flooded my consciousness.

My legs were stiff and I moved as if I were made of wood. I could smell coffee and found Casey reading the paper.

"Aren't you supposed to be at work?" The kitchen clock displayed nine AM.

"Nope, I'm off for the rest of the week. I needed a vacation." She didn't look at me, just continued to sip her juice and mark the crossword puzzle. My eyes began to fill with tears as I took stock, yet again, of what a good friend Casey was to me.

"Thank you," I whispered, but didn't attempt to speak again.

"Coffee." She pointed to the Mr. Coffee on the counter without looking up. "And I've got brioche in the oven. Mom always makes me some for the freezer when she's up."

"Your mom's brioche? There is a God." I realized I was starving. I practically inhaled two of the luscious rolls. She served them with butter and marmalade.

"A good sign, you're hungry." Casey noted as she reached for a third brioche.

"How can you eat so much and not gain weight?" I shook my head. "No matter what the crisis in my life, I can still eat, but it shows. You never gain an ounce."

"One day it will catch up with me. It did on Mom. I'll wake up one morning and be Big Bird." We laughed. For the first time in years I didn't feel a heavy emotional burden under my careful façade. I almost felt free and it was a welcome change.

I had taken off work until the following Monday anticipating the trip, so I didn't have to worry about calling in sick. I did decide to call Charlie and fill him in on Bart refusing to make the trip. I stopped short of telling him the whole story and I didn't mention what transpired the night before. I got the feeling that Charlie understood more than he let on.

"Then you and Matthew come."

"I don't think Bart will let me take him."

"Then come alone or bring Casey," he added.

"You guys can shop or ski or just laze around. That's something you could probably use. How 'bout it?" I knew he was probably worried about me. Slowly but surely Bart had isolated me from family and especially my brother, who I missed terribly.

"Actually, that's a great idea. Casey is off; I'll see if she wants to come."

I promised to call Charlie back, then went looking for Casey. I found her in her bedroom, her suitcase already open. She was pulling out snow clothes from her closet. I was perplexed until I saw the big grin on her face. "I heard you talking," she said, "You don't even have to ask. It'll take me about a half hour to get ready!"

We drove first to Casey's office where she picked up a few files to review over the weekend. I was in a nervous quandary trying to decide how I might sneak home to retrieve my bag. Finally, shortly after noon, I dialed my home phone and held my breath. "Hello?" Matthew's voice answered.

"Matthew, sweetie, when did you get home?" I was surprised because Barton hardly ever picked up Matthew. That was always my responsibility.

"Daddy came to pick me up this morning. Where are you, Mommy? Are you coming home now?" My heart was gripped with both fear and longing for the child.

"Soon, Matt. May I speak to Daddy, please?"

"Here, Daddy." I could hear Matthew

344

handing the phone to Bart. My ears were ringing and I couldn't hear well. "Hello?"

"How are you?"

"Okay. Matthew called begging to come early. He won't shut up about the ski trip."

"Well, I'm going, Bart. I'm not going to disappoint Charlie after all the plans he made. Please let Matthew go, Bart."

"Okay." It was that simple. I knew he'd partially been swayed by Matt's anticipation about the trip, but I also knew that he didn't like to take care of a small child on his own. He didn't say whether he'd changed his mind about going with us, and I didn't ask him. I'd already decided he was no longer welcome. Anyway, I needed some time away to think about my life, all that was happening and what I was going to do about it. But, deep down I knew I had made a decision

Casey refused to let me go home alone. She put her pistol in her purse and promised to wait in the car while I dealt with things inside. When we got to The Quarters, Matthew ran out to meet me. Bart stood at the window and his dark penetrating stare spoke volumes as to how he felt upon seeing Casey in the car.

"What, you got your body guard with you, Jessica?" He smirked. "Or maybe she's a little bit more to you than just a friend. Big ol', tough girl like her..."

I ignored his smarmy insinuation. This time his words didn't hurt, it put a spotlight on his pathetic, prejudiced, bigoted chauvinistic attitudes about gays, blacks and women in Law Enforcement. And he didn't like Elvis. I really didn't like Bart.

I quickly finished packing for Matthew and grabbed a few toys to take along. My own suitcase was ready to go. All I needed to add were a few toiletries. Bart suddenly loomed in the bathroom doorway.

"You won't need this." He suddenly grabbed my left hand and wrenched my wedding band from my finger. Then he shoved me against the vanity and walked out. I was feeling too good to let his actions upset me and I didn't want Matthew to realize anything was wrong.

"Kiss Daddy goodbye and tell him we'll call as soon as we arrive at the lodge," I suggested. Matt ran into Bart's arms and hugged his neck. Bart didn't take his eyes off me, sneering. In response to his hostility, I forced a big smile and waved, "Bye now. Have a nice weekend." I then pulled both heavy suitcases out the door and down the steps.

Casey jumped out to help me load the car. Bart followed Matthew out, not saying a word and not offering to help. He fastened his hateful stare on Casey. Neither acknowledged the other. When Matthew jumped into Casey's arms and gave her a big kiss, I could see Bart's anger rising.

Casey and I gave each other knowing looks without commenting and listened to Matthew's excited chatter. We were really going! Charlie and Ally wouldn't arrive till the next day, but we were lucky the chalet was available a day early; we were ready to get out of town.

We'd been driving for about forty-five minutes when the first snowflakes began to appear. Great. Sudden snow storms in the Smoky Mountains could sometimes make traveling perilous. The steep mountain roads between Reedy View and Gatlinburg often closed for safety reasons when it snowed. The farther we drove, the heavier the snow. As we entered Asheville, I exited the interstate to get Matthew a snack, Casey and me coffee, and to get the latest weather forecast and road conditions.

A trucker, who'd just come over the mountains from Knoxville told us that west of Asheville the snow was much lighter. He assured us roads were dry not fifty miles ahead. After eating a late lunch, we all climbed back into the car and headed for Tennessee.

The remainder of the trip was uneventful. Matthew was sound asleep when we arrived at the lodge. I left him in the car with Casey and went in to register. The desk clerk gave me directions to the chalet and then handed me a note. "You received this call just an hour ago."

My heart dropped. As I took the slip of paper, I saw the name Barton Quinlan and our home number. "Thanks," I murmured. For a few short hours, I had wiped Barton from my mind. I dreaded calling him.

We located our assigned home for the next four nights and Matthew was jumping up and down by the time we got the last of the luggage inside. After getting everything put away, we braved the icy night and walked to the lodge restaurant and found a table by the stone fireplace. It had been almost five years since I had been to the lodge. Now I remembered how much I loved this place and missed it. Matthew was in awe over a huge bear rug in front of the roaring fire. Casey and I ordered a cocktail and the waitress brought Matthew chocolate milk. The food that followed was delicious.

It was a fun evening. But always in the back of my mind was the dread of returning Bart's call. When I told Casey about it, she said, "Fuck him. Ignore it. Tell him you never got the message." At first I followed her advice but I knew I needed to call in case it was something important. Still, I was proud of myself for waiting until after dinner.

The phone rang six or seven times before he finally answered.

"Hi, we're here. We just finished dinner."

"I heard about the snow in Asheville, I've been worried. Why didn't you call?" He sounded worried and relieved at the same time.

"The roads west of Asheville were fine. Then Matthew was hungry when we did arrive so we went straight to dinner." I started to apologize to him, but caught myself.

"Let me speak to Matthew," he said.

"Daddy, Daddy! There was a big bear where I ate my hamburger. He was in front of the fireplace." Matthew was shaking his head in answer to whatever Bart was telling him. "It was, it was a bear, wasn't it, Mommy?" He then looked at me for confirmation.

"Tell Daddy it was a real bear rug."

"See, I told you, it was a real bear rug." Matt continued to shake his head then handed me the phone.

"Sounds like he's having a great time. Take care of my boy, Jessica." But it seemed his anger had finally dissipated. "Listen, Jessica, I..." His voice broke and I froze listening to something I had never heard in all the years I had known Barton Quinlan. He was crying. "I'm sorry, Jessica. I'm really, really sorry."

CHAPTER 73

1983

The next morning, I was awakened from a deep sleep by banging on the front door. It took me a few groggy minutes to realize I was at the lodge. As I grabbed a robe, I saw it was already 9:30.

"Hey, Sis!" Charlie hugged me, grinning from ear to ear. Ally was there with their brood all yelling for Matthew. The kids ran to wake Matthew, everyone squealing with laughter.

"We threw the kids in the car before six this morning and they slept all the way here," Charlie said. "Now we're all ready for pancakes."

"Umm, pancakes, let's go. Give us 15 minutes..."

Charlie and his family headed for the restaurant while Casey and I hurriedly dressed. Matthew announced he could dress himself and was ready before we were.

"Just so you know, I may not put on makeup until I return to Reedy View," I announced as we joined everyone at a big table across from the fireplace.

"I know I won't," Casey added. She and Ally were already discussing a case involving a teacher friend of Ally's. The teacher's oldest son had been arrested for petty theft, more a teenage prank. Casey was explaining how the system worked and as we made our way back to our rooms, I thought about how relaxed and enjoyable the morning was and how everyone got along so well. What a difference it made when I didn't have to censor my every word and gesture.

I thought back to the last trip Bart, Matthew and I had taken. It had been with Ted and his family to Six Flags in Georgia. Matthew loved it and I was as excited as him. We were having lunch and my plate was piled with more fries than I could ever eat. Knowing Bart loved fries, I plopped some extra on his plate using my fork and knife as tongs. He became angry and told me not to ever do that again. I was stunned at his reaction and could tell Ted was trying to act as if he hadn't noticed the exchange. Needless to say it ruined the day and the trip. Bart had known it, too. He didn't speak directly to me for the rest of the day. He wouldn't ask me a direct question; he went through Matthew.

"Ask your momma if she's ready to go, Matthew." Or "Ask your momma if she will take you to the bathroom." The situations that would make him angry were always so outlandish I had long before stopped being shocked.

We spent the rest of the day in Gatlinburg skiing. Matthew was up after the third try and mastered the bunny slope by afternoon. Casey insisted on staying with Matthew while I tried the higher slopes. We were all exhausted, happy, and cold when we finally headed back to the lodge.

After steaks and wine for dinner, I was looking forward to getting a good night's sleep. As we walked into the room, the phone was ringing. My heart plummeted. Again, I had not thought about Bart for hours.

"Hello?"

"Are you having a good time?"

"Yes, actually a wonderful time. Matthew is an expert skier now."

"I'm glad, but I'm asking about you, Jess?"

"I said I was having a wonderful time. I am."

"If I thought I could find you, I would just drive up there." I didn't respond. I knew he was fishing for an invitation, but I didn't want him to ruin my vacation. Driving to Gatlinburg didn't take a rocket scientist. His reclusive tendencies now just made me angry.

"You don't want me to come, do you, Jess." He was crying again.

"I love you so much. I'm so sorry. I don't know why I act like I do. I'll get some counseling if you will just forgive me and tell me you are coming back home."

"Let's talk after this week, okay, Bart?" I'll be damned if I was going to give in to a few tears. I thought of the buckets of tears I cried over the years to no avail.

"I've just realized how much I love you. When are you coming home?"

"Sunday afternoon."

"Can we talk when you get back?" I must have hesitated too long.

"Please, Jessica, please sit down and talk to me."

"Yes, we need to talk."

"You're not going to leave me are you Jess?"

"I haven't said I'm leaving you, Bart. Let's talk when I get back." He continued to sob loudly for a few more minutes, then, he begged me to call him the next day. I agreed and finally disconnected, exhausted from the exchange.

"You will not talk to him alone, Jess." Casey looked at me pointedly.

"Case, I've never heard him like this before. Maybe he's seen the light."

"Oh, please, God, let him go, please, toward the light," she sarcastically intoned as she held her arms toward heaven. "Don't you see what's going on? For the first time in this relationship, you have shown a little backbone. He can't stand it. You've got him scared shitless. Well, I say let him wallow in it for a little while. And please, do not try to talk to him when you are alone. I have tried too many cases..."

I just looked at her, befuddled. I didn't know what I was going to do. I did realize that something in me had finally snapped and I was thinking seriously about divorcing Barton. But every time I looked at Matthew, my heart felt like it would break.

CHAPTER 74

1983

It's mystifying how people can't objectively look at their lives and see the reality while still in those lives. After five years of angst, like an escaped prisoner, I had tasted freedom and knew unequivocally freedom was my choice.

Sunday morning in Gatlinburg arrived much too soon. It had been a great few days and we all enjoyed every minute of the trip. There was no doubt in my mind that half my enjoyment was because Barton was not anywhere around. We packed our bags into the car and said our goodbyes to Charlie, Ally and the kids.

"Be careful, Jessie," Charlie said. He hadn't called me by my childhood nickname for a long time, and I felt comforted as he gave me a final hug. Ally made me promise to visit them in Charlotte. This time I knew that I would.

All too soon, we were headed through the

mountains back toward Reedy View. I felt in total limbo, my future uncertain. I didn't know how I would do it, but I knew what I would do. I was leaving Bart. I decided to stay with Casey for a week or so, and thus ease into telling Bart I wanted a divorce. Bart seemed remorseful and I hoped he was serious about counseling. But, it was too late for him and me. After all the times he left over the years, he should agree he owed me a few days. I was not going back to Barton.

CHAPTER 75

1983

Bart was still so emotional, it was unsettling. When I called to tell him that Casey and I would bring Matthew by, he begged for me to stay and talk, just the two of us.

"Please Jessica," he sobbed. "I just want to talk and make you understand how sorry I am. Please? Is that too much to ask?" His pleas slowly brought me around and I finally agreed to talk. After all, this was about the rest of our lives. I could never love Bart again, but any contact with Matthew hung in the balance.

Casey was furious when I told Bart we could talk. She just couldn't understand my willingness to go the extra mile. She begged me not to give in to Bart, or at least to allow her to accompany me when I went home. But I felt that I owed him privacy to express his feelings. I stood my ground and, for the first time in many years, felt that I was finally back in control of my life.

There were several reasons returning to the house was necessary I reasoned. It was my place, after all. I was paying the mortgage. Also, I needed my uniforms and service weapon and gun belt. It would be humiliating for Bart if Casey came along. His earlier insinuations about her ran through the back of my mind.

In the end, it was just Matthew and me who drove into downtown Reedy View toward home. Matthew was ecstatic, wanting to show his father the souvenirs we'd purchased and his picture taken on the bunny slope. He bounded in the front door and Bart was standing there waiting.

"I'm so glad you're home," he said. "I've missed you so much. I don't know what I would ever do without you."

"Bart, we need to let things settle down. I just need to think. Things can't continue like they have. Maybe we could both go for counseling."

"I'll do anything, but please just stay. What will Matthew think if you leave? He'll think you're leaving him." He always used Matthew to arouse my emotions.

"Matthew is going back to his mom's house. I have to work tomorrow. Let's just take a break, all right? How many times have you left, Bart? At least I'm being honest with you."

I began to gather what I needed in the bedroom as Bart followed me like a puppy, taking every step I took. With everything I needed for work in my arms I started out of the bedroom.

"Let's make love, Jessica, please, let's just do it right now." He was sobbing again and his bizarre behavior was getting worse. I was becoming uneasy. The idea of him touching me made me nauseous.

"Bart, please. Matthew is in the den."

He continued to cry, trailing behind me, pleading for a second chance. The crying was the first red flag I overlooked; he had never cried before this past weekend.

"I'll change, I'll change," he continued to sob. "You'll see. At least give me a chance!"

I tried to explain yet again that I needed a little space, and time to think. "We can talk more in depth when Matthew isn't around," I patiently said. "I promise you that we will get everything settled. It's just that right now is not the best time."

I moved down the hallway from the bedroom, struggling with the weight of my gun belt hung over my shoulder and five uniforms on hangars

Without warning I was slammed to the floor with such force that I bit my tongue and tasted the metallic tang of blood as my mouth filled. He jerked me onto my back and his hands pressed against my throat. He was on top of me and it felt like he would push me through the floor. I could barely breathe. For a split second I wondered if this was it...was I about to die? Then I was sucking in air. He released my throat. Just as suddenly I felt the cold stainless steel of my .357 service revolver pressed against my head. How he managed to get his hands so quickly on my weapon I don't know. I heard the hammer as he slowly pulled it back. *Single action* the words come unbidden to mind. I closed my eyes and wondered if I would hear the gunfire or would my brain explode first? No sound, just a silent eruption into eternal darkness....

Instead, I looked up into Bart's rage-filled eyes, the eyes of a madman spiraling out of control.

"Please." I whispered...then I remembered Matthew. Oh God! Where was he? How I managed to turn my head to look across the room, I'll never know. Matthew stood frozen in fear by the front door. His eyes were wide with horror, an innocent fawn caught in careening headlights. The look of terror on his precious face would be seared into my mind and heart forever.

My voice was weak and raspy as I pleaded with Matthew.

"Go next door to Anne, now!"

"Don't go out that door, son!" Barton's deep voice boomed over mine. Matthew looked at his father, then at me. He was terrified and bewildered. He was panicky trying to decide who to obey.

"Run, baby! Run to Anne!" And suddenly he did, he was out the door running, as fast as his 6-year-old legs would carry him.

360

Barton continued to hold me down but he took the gun and put it to his own head and began praying. "Forgive me, God..." He was whimpering.

"Bart, please don't do this, please, I love you."

"You're lying," he said scathingly. "Our Father, who art in heaven..." His eyes were insane, the gun still pushed against the temple of his head.

Suddenly there was banging at the front door and the doorbell rang. I heard my neighbor, Anne O'Reilly, yelling my name.

"I've got to go see about Matthew," I whispered. "I have to make sure he's all right."

And abruptly, Bart rolled off me. I ran to the door but he held it so I couldn't open it. "Please, please, Bart," I cried. "I love you. I have to take care of Matthew!" And then the door opened and I could see Anne's panicked face. Matthew was standing behind her, peeking from behind her legs, his little eyes displaying total shock. I squeezed through the partially opened door, but Bart had to have let me go through the door. I didn't have the strength to force it on my own. Once I was outside, I grabbed Matthew's hand and told Anne to run.

We reached her house next door and scrambled inside. She quickly locked the deadbolt.

"My God, what happened? Are you all right, Jessica?" She looked closely at my neck.

"I think I am." I was shaking all over.

I then looked at myself in the foyer mirror. My neck was red and badly bruised. My lip and tongue were cut from hitting the floor. He hadn't struck me, so no other marks were visible. but my back hurt and my head throbbed.

"Call the police, Jess," Anne pleaded.

I looked out the foyer window, but could see no one outside Anne's front door. My mind was racing, trying to decide what to do. I picked up the phone and dialed the sergeant's office at Headquarters.

"Sgt. Evans," Ted answered. I was relieved when I heard his voice.

"Ted, I need you to come to our place now. Bart and I have...he threatened me with a gun, Ted."

"Are you all right?" he asked quickly.

"Yes, but he's gone crazy. Matthew and I are next door. Please hurry. I don't know what he might do. At one point he put the gun to his own head, but I haven't heard a shot." It felt surreal having this discussion about my life.

"Should I come alone?" he asked. Then I realized he was asking if he needed a backup. I was torn as to what to do. Part of me still wanted to protect Bart. If he were arrested, it would mean the end of his career and what would happen to Matthew?

"I don't want anything to threaten his job, just do what you think is best."

"I'm on the way."

I watched from the window until Ted's patrol car pulled to the curb. Anne's teenage daughter took Matthew into their family room to watch television. I looked in before going to the door.

I ran out and met Ted as he walked up my short driveway from the street. I reached in my car and pulled my off duty weapon out and put it in my pocket. I prayed I wouldn't need it.

I was terrified of what we would see when we entered the house. I remembered that long ago Christmas Day and the call to the Chief Deputy's house. I touched the butt of my gun in my pocket.

Ted and I quietly opened the door and saw Bart sitting on the barstool. He stood and walked over to Ted. He wouldn't even look at me.

"Sorry you got dragged into this, Ted. It's really between Jess and me."

"Maybe so, Bart, but I can't leave until I'm sure you're both safe. You are both my friends, but I'm also trying to settle this just between the three of us. Jess wants it this way, Bart, your career could be on the line."

Bart then looked at me with dead cold eyes and said nothing. He turned to sit back down and I saw my service revolver stuck in his pants in the small of his back.

Ted looked at me and asked what I wanted to happen right now. He said he'd stay while I got whatever clothes I needed. He could see the uniforms in disarray on the floor.

"I just want to get my uniforms and I want my

service revolver that Bart has in his pants."

Ted reached and Bart pulled it out at the same time. Without further incident he handed the gun to Ted and Ted gave it to me.

I didn't say another word but immediately began getting my things together. I picked up my gun belt and replaced my .357 in the holster. My hands were trembling badly and my neck ached.

I piled as much as I could into my car, then backed out of the drive and pulled into Anne's driveway. As I got out of my car, I saw that Ted was leaving. He and Bart exchanged a few more words and Bart shut the door. Ted walked calmly across the small lawn toward me.

"I think he'll be okay, Jess. God, what did he do, choke you?" He suddenly noticed the ugly blue whelps on my neck.

"Yes, but the worst was that he put my own service revolver to my head and threatened to kill me." The tears finally flowed, I couldn't stop them.

"Dear God, Jess, I'm so sorry. Do you want me to take you down to file a complaint, what are you going to do?"

"I can't jeopardize his job, Ted. Could we just keep all of this between us? I'm leaving him, I won't be back. He made sure of that today. All I asked was for a few days to think things through. He was furious when I came home last Tuesday evening late, after you and I talked. It's a long story. Today he was crying and promising to change and then he all of a sudden went crazy. If there was any chance we could ever work it out, there's none now."

I was so drained physically and emotionally that I could hardly speak. It was difficult to remain standing. I went back inside and told Matthew I was taking him to his grandparents' house.

"What's wrong with Daddy, Mommy?"

"Daddy will be fine. He was upset, but he will be fine, Matthew." He was standing beside me in the front seat as I backed out of the drive. He then looked to me with his big brown eyes, his look too worried for such a small child.

"I should have stayed with my daddy." he sighed. He sounded more like an adult than a little boy who was not yet seven.

Matthew, I knew, was lost to me in that instant.

CHAPTER 76

1983

Divorce is an ugly, all-consuming hell. For months I walked around like a zombie. Bart allowed me to see Matthew only a few more times. Those few days that Matthew and I spent together, I tried to fill with happy memories. I could only pray that he wouldn't hate me for leaving him. I tried to explain but how could he possibly understand? I memorized his every look, every laugh, the dimple in his cheek when he smiled, the twinkle in his eyes. I tried to store enough memories to last a lifetime. I didn't know when or if I'd ever see him again.

Bart pressured me in every way he knew to change my mind about the divorce. I gave in and played along with his insidious games at first because I knew it was the only way he would allow me to see Matt. One night when Matthew was staying over with me, he suddenly looked up as I tucked him into bed. "Mommy, do we have to say the prayer tonight?"

"Lay me down to sleep?'" I asked.

"No, Mommy. The one where we ask God to bring you home to me and Daddy."

Matthew and I repeated the prayer that Momma Alex had taught Charlie and me "now I lay me down to sleep..." every night. Neither Bart nor I attended church, Bart refused. I wanted Matthew to have an understanding of spirituality. Although my experience with the Baptist church was troubled; the church did instill in me a belief in God and strange as it seemed, I maintained a strong faith. I wanted Matthew to have the opportunity to make his own decisions and be exposed to the church and God. I worried about what he would believe when he was older.

I was livid that apparently Bart was putting the responsibility upon Matthew to pray for me to return. I agonized that Matthew would blame himself when his prayers went unanswered.

"Daddy said we have to pray every night for you to come home."

I swallowed the lump in my throat and kissed his cheek before I replied. "No Matthew, you don't have to say that prayer tonight. Remember when I explained how you grew in my heart, not my tummy?" He vigorously nodded his head. "I'll always be there in your heart. I'll always be with you, Matthew — here." I took my hand and placed it over his heart. "I hope you remember this as you

367

get older. I will always love you and you can always call me if your other Mommy or your Daddy will let you."

"I love you, Mommy, you'll always be here." He clutched his chest with both hands. I sat on the side of his bed, my eyes brimming. I sat that way until he fell soundly asleep. "My beautiful boy," I whispered over and over. "My beautiful child."

CHAPTER 77

1983

I had toyed with the idea of taking Matthew and running. But where would we go? How would I provide for us? Common sense told me it was a stupid idea, worse than stupid even, and could only end in tragedy. I'd be a fugitive from the law charged with kidnapping. And there was no doubt in my mind that Bart would kill me if he found me before the authorities did. In the end, Matthew would grow to resent and maybe hate me for taking him away from his father.

It infuriated me that Bart used Matthew to try to control me. It was always about power and control with him. When he finally accepted the fact it was over, the only way left for him to hurt was to take Matthew away from me forever.

When Bart finally did that, I grieved as if Matthew had died. I obsessed over what his daily life was like and what it would become. I found myself wanting to drive by his mother's house or school just to catch a glimpse of him. That first Christmas without Matt was sheer torture. The loss and emptiness was almost unbearable.

But for all the sorrow I felt in losing Matthew, I also felt relief and joy at being free of Bart. It was as if I'd been sick for a long, long time and was finally recovering. I smiled more and began to reestablish connections with old friends.

Work was my salvation. Casey's domestic violence program became a regular community event; it was offered bi-monthly at different venues. I hadn't been strong enough to participate in it, however, since I'd separated from Bart. Casey understood and didn't push. Cal Larson stepped up to the plate and was one of the most popular speakers. I found myself watching for Cal at roll call and always felt disappointed on the days he was off duty. I even forced myself to attend one of the programs where he spoke. I arrived late and left early, hoping I wasn't noticed.

Bart finally agreed to a divorce on physical cruelty, which allowed the divorce to go through in three months' time. He agreed only after my attorney threatened assault and battery charges at the least, attempted murder at the most. Now we waited for a court date before a judge.

Bart continued to live in my home—the one I was paying the mortgage on—proving he would not go without a fight. But the court decreed he would move from the marital home by the end of

July. Meanwhile, I stayed with Casey. She was afraid to let me out of her sight. She was incensed that Bart remained in my home. After the prior owners had subdivided the estate into half acre lots and two, half-million dollar homes had gone up adjacent to the small place that was my home. Thankfully one of those homes had been Anne O'Reilly's, and Matthew had known her and went to her that dreadful Sunday.

Casey had a security system installed in her house and we both slept every night with our guns nearby. "Surely he wouldn't try anything again." I sighed.

"Just listen to you," she retorted, exasperated. "I wanted to go with you before that last event but, oh, no, you were so sure everything would be fine. I will not even start quoting statistics, you of all people should be aware. I don't want you going anywhere near that man until we are both satisfied he won't go crazy again."

"I have no intention of going near him."

"Good." I felt safe with Casey and was grateful for her friendship.

"By the way, I meant to tell you, your Cal spoke last Tuesday at the Morningside Community Center. He did a great job."

"I'm glad you weren't left scrambling for a speaker. And what do you mean by *my* Cal?"

"He's a great guy and not at all bad looking. For some reason he seems to think you hung the moon. And seems like you're always mentioning his name, too…" She smiled conspiratorially.

"Sure, he's nice. So what?"

"I mean, come on, girl. He's got the hots for you bad."

"Casey!"

"Jess!"

"I'm not even divorced yet. I don't want to date anyone; so don't you start."

"Well, you're not dead, that's all I'm saying. If you don't start living again, you might forget how. And if you don't like him, maybe I'll go after his cute little buns."

"You keep your damn hands off of Cal, Acacia Demarches."'

"Atta girl!" She patted me on the back and winked.

CHAPTER 78

1983

Working weekend midnights was usually so busy that time flew. On other nights, the hours sometimes slowed to a crawl. It was a Sunday and I was experiencing one of those crawling nights. I yearned for a little excitement, anything. I knew it was not exactly right to wish for bad things to happen, but I figured they were going to happen anyway and so might as well happen on my watch and beat. I long ago moved up from rookie to veteran, but I would always be that *hotdog rookie*.

I backed into a parking space on Main Street and completed a theft report. There was peacefulness about the city in those wee hours of the morning. Streets empty, stores closed, silence. At times, a cop could feel like the last person on earth. I found tranquility in those moments of solitude. It was during such times I thought about just how much I loved my job. I could faintly hear far off traffic from the interstate occasionally or the infrequent time-check crackle from the police radio. I so loved this city.

As I tucked the finished report inside the metal clipboard, I saw headlights top the hill and a vehicle slowly made its way down Main Street. Anything moving was suspicious, but by the time it was within a block, my patrol car was clearly visible to the driver. If it turned off I would make a traffic stop for no other reason than it was moving at three a.m.

But it didn't turn, it continued toward me. It slowed as it neared my vehicle and then the headlights went off. I recognized Cal Larson's vintage pickup as he pulled in, his driver side to mine. His windows were down, as were mine.

"Can I buy a lady a drink?"

"Not unless you want me dancing naked on the patrol car. I don't handle liquor well."

"Now there's a pleasant thought."

"I assure you, it's not."

"Oh, try one anyway." He handed me a large coffee from the Koffee Klatch, the Styrofoam cup sitting inside a ceramic mug. He had remembered how I disliked coffee out of anything other than a real cup. In all the years I'd been with Bart, he'd never once remembered, or more likely, never cared. I was touched.

Out of the blue, my heart began pounding. I was happy he had ventured out on his night off. I pushed a pang of guilt over those feelings aside. If

I admitted it, I had been having those feelings for a while. As I took the cup, I saw it was hand-stenciled with "The First Day of The Rest of Your Life." There was a big grin on his face.

"Thanks, but you're really corny, Larson. Anybody ever tell you that?" Yet, I couldn't stop smiling over the sentimentality of the gesture. We were both grinning like a couple of pre-teens.

"See, I knew you'd like it." There was a yearning building inside me as I took in the sight of this handsome man and basked in the realization he came out to see me. Not meeting up with another officer, but me, little Jessica Grace Jordan. I waited all my life for the storybook romance, the big screen happy ending. I almost decided it didn't exist. But now Caleb Larson made me believe it did exist, just maybe. We seemed to share an ethereal bond. We communicated without words. He had never so much as held my hand. But in my most secret dreams, I longed not only to hold his hand but to feel his touch on my body. I yearned to feel his lips on mine.

He had not spoken to me on a personal level since the night he pledged to be waiting if my situation ever changed. His eyes sometimes sought me out at roll call, then he would quickly smile and look away. We both began to seek the other out at the beginning of every shift, just for a brief glimpse. I was always checking to see if he was looking at me. Frequently, he was. At the end of shift, I began to hang back, taking my time going to my POV. Cal seemed to always be headed in the same direction at the same time and we would make small talk. But something much heavier hung in the air between us. He always seemed to find a parking space next to my mine, as well.

Coincidence?

Cops don't believe in coincidences.

The final divorce decree would be signed soon, but I still wasn't sure I wanted the complications of a relationship. Somehow Cal sensed this. I was never unfaithful to Bart, no matter his accusations. Casey convinced me that Bart's suspicions alone constituted an insult. The exhilarating sense of freedom I felt after leaving Bart, often made me wish I had been unfaithful. Maybe I would have left sooner. But, just the thought would throw me into a fit of guilt. I also knew, If I had, I may not have survived.

Since I left Bart I was learning to view our relationship in a healthier light. I now realized that we had been unconnected from the beginning. We were much better friends than we ever were lovers. Once we became more than friends, that was the beginning of the end.

Before we became involved, Bart often talked about the love of his life, his high school sweetheart. According to him, they were the proverbial star football player and cheerleader couple.

He assumed they would marry. The last time he'd seen her was from his hospital bed in Texas after he had been wounded in Vietnam. He claimed she walked away before the doctors knew whether his paralysis was permanent. He told me she'd jumped into bed with someone else while he was off fighting for his country. Whatever the truth was, she'd left him angry and bitter. But I knew enough about Bart now to realize that not everything he saw as true was true.

As I tried to psychoanalyze Bart's bizarre personality, I concluded it was a mixture of his experiences and something deeper, maybe biological, that put him on a collision course with me.

As I sipped my coffee with Cal I shared something with him that I'd grown to loathe with Bart—silence. With Cal, silence was tranquil and natural. Odd, how silence can be twofold. I never felt more alone in my life than when I was with Bart, especially during his long periods of brooding silence. Now, the stillness Cal and I shared was almost intimate. I didn't want it to end.

"Better head home," he finally said. "How about a date later tonight, say 2300 hours?"

"I'll be there."

"Good. See you at roll call." He backed out and drove off into the night. The warm feeling was something I'd never felt before. I was 32 years old, and as smitten as a school girl. As I held my new cup, alone in my patrol car, I realized I was grinning like an idiot. I could hardly wait for my tour to end.

CHAPTER 79

1983

August turned into September and the weather was hot and muggy. Not a day went by without rain. In one month I worked more traffic accidents than I had the previous six months together.

Cal asked me out to dinner a few times, but I was still afraid of Bart and afraid to pull someone else into such a sticky situation. So the relationship between Cal and me remained at work. But, we talked on the phone every day about everything imaginable, everything except our future.

One night, we were working adjoining beats when we were dispatched to a possible burglary in progress at a government housing complex. The month before, four units were damaged by fire in the apartment complex. Doors and windows were boarded on the upper and lower floors of the townhouses until roof repairs were completed. A neighbor saw someone going in one of the apartments through an upstairs balcony door. The furnishings were still inside, but it was doubtful anything was salvageable. The water damage would be severe. When we arrived, we saw that the bottom floor remained secure; the only way in was through the balcony.

I pulled my patrol car directly underneath. With a boost from Cal, I was able to pull myself up. Being taller, he grabbed the edge and in short time we both entered the darkened apartment. It smelled heavily of smoke and I couldn't see why anyone would want to scavenge through such ruins. The perps must have come to the same conclusion. The apartment was empty. We made our way back to the balcony. Cal went over and lowered himself onto the hood of the patrol car. He looked up and said, "Jump, I'll catch you."

"I don't think so." As I stared down it seemed like forever between the balcony and the hood of my patrol car.

"I can't come down. I can climb up, but coming down...I can't." I was embarrassed, but it did look impossible.

"Yes you can."

"No, really, I can't. The last time we checked a roof, the fire department came out with a ladder truck. Call the fire department."

"I am not calling the fire department," he insisted. "You can do it."

Oh, shit, I thought. What was wrong with

me? I had always been a little afraid of heights. I could handle armed suspects and violent drunks, but here I was cringing at a 6-foot drop from a balcony onto the top of a car.

"I'm not coming down so you might as well go ahead and call the fire department."

Cal looked at me with those beautiful eyes but his meaning was twofold when he said, "You've got to trust me sometime, Jess." He held out both his arms. "Please trust me." And I did. I jumped. For the first time I felt his arms as they held me momentarily when he caught me. The feeling his arms gave me sent electricity through my entire body. We looked at each other, then quickly resumed our professional cop's demeanor.

"Well," I said. "That wasn't so difficult."

"No, it sure was not," he grinned.

I finally agreed to go out to dinner with Cal. On the day of our date, I spent all afternoon tinkering with my hair, makeup and clothes, trying to decide exactly what looked best. He showed up at Casey's driving his roommate's Corvette.

"I couldn't take a lady to dinner in a pickup truck," he explained. I thought it was sweet, but what he didn't know was I would have gladly ridden a jackass to dinner with him.

Our relationship continued on a slow and careful progression. We continued to talk daily before and after work. We often took our meal breaks together when the call load allowed. It was only a matter of time before Bart learned I was seeing Cal. He confronted me in the parking one afternoon as I arrived for work and he was going off duty. I wasn't afraid, just angry he would not leave me alone.

"So Larson is the reason you left, huh, Jessica?" he smirked.

Suddenly, I was consumed by an almost uncontrollable fury; incensed as the full realization that his sick obsessive, negative, insufferable thought process would never end.

"Go straight to hell Bart."

"The truth hurt, Jessica?" He kept pushing. A few of the officers from shift change stopped to watch the exchange. I was embarrassed, yet my anger was reaching a boiling point.

"The only reason I left you, Barton, was you! You will never admit it, maybe you can't even see it, but it's true. You and your sick, cruel, pathetic attitude."

He was showing off for the cops who were watching us. "You know what, Jessica. You're a slut."

"Fuck you!" I screamed. "Fuck you and the horse you rode in on!" He always said 'ladies didn't talk like that.' Well, by God, I did and it felt good! Several of the nearby eavesdroppers snickered. That seemed to enrage him. He stalked off in a huff.

The release I felt was like a lightning bolt. I was finally completely free of Barton Quinlan.

While I would always miss Matthew, I knew if I had not left, without a doubt, I would have been murdered. Murdered by someone who claimed he loved me. My first call of the day would drive the point home.

CHAPTER 80

1983

"Trust me. You will see this over and over on domestic calls Jordan. It's the victim who will post bond to get them out of jail. So I say, they make their bed, let them lie in it."

How well I remembered Ted's words the first time we'd responded to this address. Then, I was a fresh-out-of-the academy rookie and took offense at his cynicism; then, I was still the idealistic cop, out to save the world. After seven years on the job, my approach was more practical.

I was working solo when I got the call to East Pennsylvania Avenue. Before I even pulled to the curb and saw the crowd milling about the front door, I knew this probably wasn't the routine domestic call dispatch implied.

"Fox 100."

"Fox 100, go ahead," I responded

"Possible domestic. Victim down 532-B East

Pennsylvania Avenue; situation unknown."

"Fox 100 en route 532-B East Pennsylvania." I made a U-turn and headed east. I was only a few blocks away. As I exited my patrol car, several people in the crowd pointed inside the door to the front of the familiar old Victorian. I had a sinking feeling as I climbed the steps. The front door was ajar.

"He hauled ass outta here, Miz Officer," an old black man spoke from the doorway of an adjacent apartment. "He's drunk as a skunk and I heard'em yelling' and takin' on. Then he got to shouting, 'get up, get up'. When I looked out, I saw him moving down the sidewalk at a pretty fair clip. I looks inside and that's when I sees her on the floor. She ain't answered when I axed was she okay."

I entered, careful not to disturb the scene. I reached down to feel for a pulse on her neck. There wasn't one and from her pallor and stillness I knew there wouldn't be. When I pulled my hand away, it was sticky with blood. It was before the time AIDS changed the world; we didn't yet worry about contact with blood. No one carried disposable gloves. The EMTs arrived and deduced the same thing. She was dead.

I felt despair and anger building as I looked down at the woman's frail and broken body. She was wearing her usual cotton housecoat, now soaked in blood from the open wound on the side of her head. As I looked around the room, now a crime scene, I saw much the same wretchedness as I'd seen seven years earlier when I first entered this apartment. Near the sink lay a metal walking cane obviously smeared with blood. Dark red splatters were splashed across the filthy floor. I didn't touch anything. The Crime Scene Unit would process and collect evidence in due time.

"Why, Loretta? Why in God's name did you come back to this hellhole? You were safe, a thousand miles away." I shook my head, not realizing I had whispered the words aloud.

"You losing it, Jordan?" One of the forensics officers was squatting beside the body. I hadn't noticed him.

"No, it's just...I've been here before. I thought the lady had finally left this place. Instead...looks like she's...well this time she left for good." The CSU guy looked at me quizzically and began processing and photographing the scene. The ambulance was parked in front, waiting for the county coroner. Once he declared Loretta dead, then she was officially dead and could be transported to the morgue for autopsy.

I radioed a suspect description of Dewey to be relayed to all units. A warrant would be forthcoming. After talking further with the neighbors, there was no doubt he was the doer.

I spent just over an hour on the scene. The body was transported to the morgue, and the next-door neighbor was driven to headquarters to give a statement to detectives assigned to the case.

There wasn't much else left for me to do but the paperwork and sign the warrant. As I returned to my patrol car, all I could think was; *there, but for the grace of God, go I.* I shuddered. It so easily could have been me. I said a little prayer of thankfulness. Feeling morose, I pulled my patrol car away from the curb and headed downtown.

There was a bridge spanning the river before reaching the business district. It was as if the river separated the squalid part of town from the arts center, museum, and library. As I approached the bridge, my intuition kicked in. I suddenly knew. I pulled the patrol car to the curb just before the bridge. A well-worn path, littered with trash, led down and under the bridge.

This was home or a hangout to many of Reedy View's derelicts. On any given day you could see blankets neatly folded with brown-sacked empty pints of liquor on top. As I made my way down the path I saw feet sticking out from behind a rusted oil drum used by the homeless to burn scraps of wood to keep warm. I crept closer to see if the supine figure was asleep, drunk or dead. Cautiously I circled around the drum and there was Dewey, stretched out and sound asleep. his upper body covered with a flattened cardboard box.

I drew my gun and nudged him with one foot. "Get up and keep your hands where I can see them, you son of a bitch." I drew out the last part, remembering how he hated a woman calling him

387

that. It gave me little satisfaction this time. He jumped up and grabbed a brick as he fought to stand, still drunk and unsteady.

"Dewey, drop the damn brick, you really want to give me an excuse to shoot your sorry ass?"

He dropped the brick, looking dazed. "That old bitch hit me first," he whined. I felt my hand tighten on the 9mm Sig the department now carried. *It would be so easy....*

"She did, she hit me first, don't care what she says. She can be a mean woman." *He doesn't even realize he's killed her.*

I ordered him to drop to his knees and I holstered my weapon and cuffed him.

"Dewey Crawford, you have the right to remain silent, anything you say can and will be used against you in a court of law. You have the right to an attorney, if you can't afford an attorney, one will be appointed for you. Do you understand these rights?"

"What are you talking about...?" He was genuinely confused. He was often arrested for drunk but was never read his rights.

He stumbled several times before we finally reached my patrol car. As I opened the door I grabbed his handcuffed hands pulling them straight up behind him and he yelped in pain. I held him here momentarily with his arms contorted as I fought to control my anger. Finally, I spoke. "You are under arrest, Dewy Crawford, for the murder of Loretta Wilkins."

"What in hell are you talking about?" he whimpered. "I didn't hurt her..." I shoved him in the car. He was silent and seemed to be in shock as I slammed the door. As I got behind the wheel, I could hear a wailing sound that seemed to be growing louder. I looked in my rearview mirror to see Dewey's face contorted and sobbing.

"Fox 100 to headquarters." Dewey's loud sobs could be heard over the radio, I was sure.

"Fox 100, go ahead." The dispatcher was anxious hearing the background noise.

"Fox 100 has prisoner in custody for the 10-89 (Homicide) from East Pennsylvania."

"Fox 100 prisoner in custody, 10-4?"

"10-4 Headquarters, en route to detention."

"Fox 100 go to channel four." I switched to the talk-around. Barbara, the dispatcher, groaned. "Jessica, I hate it when you do that!"

"10-9?" the code for repeat, message not understood.

"You know exactly what I'm talking about. 10-4?"

"10-4 Thanks Barbara."

"Unit C-1 to Fox 100" Oops, now the lieutenant was calling. I picked up the mike knowing I was in trouble.

"Go ahead C-1."

"Come to the office when you clear detention."

"10-4."

I would have rather taken the ass-chewing

from Barbara. I drove slowly to the detention center with Dewey wailing all the way. I wasn't really worried about the LT. I knew he would just remind me to always call for back-up, cover General Orders and then tell me good job.

I should have been pleased with my single-handed arrest—but my mood was somber. My mind suddenly jumped to another time, 1974, when Daddy became Momma's first fatal victim.

CHAPTER 81

1974

"Daddy's gone."

I couldn't quite grasp Charlie's words. Gone? Gone where?

The clock read four in the morning when the doorbell rang, almost immediately followed by pounding at the front door. Startled out of sleep, I ran and peered through the peephole and saw my brother and great uncle standing in the dark, blowing on their hands. It was a frigid January night, 1974. Vietnam was still raging and my brother was a senior in college. I was newly divorced and enrolled for my second semester at Reedy View Tech.

As I saw Charlie's grief ravaged face through the door, my immediate thought was my grandmother, Momma Alex. My heart caught as I swung open the door. Oh, dear God...

"Daddy's gone. Daddy's dead, Jess." Charlie blurted as he stepped in the door. His face etched in pain. I'd never seen him like that. All I could do was scream.

"I'm sorry sugar..." Uncle Bert said kindly. "I think a massive heart attack. We didn't want to call and tell you on the phone." My grandmother's older brother grabbed me as I felt my knees buckle. Charlie couldn't speak; tears rolled silently down his cheeks. I flung myself into Charlie's arms and we held each other and sobbed. I felt trapped inside a nightmare and could hardly grasp hold of reality. Everything was happening in slow motion. Charlie called our mother and she drove over as Uncle Bert made a pot of coffee. Through the pain I could not help thinking, Momma shouldn't be here right now. She doesn't deserve to be here with us.

The last time that I'd talked to Daddy was New Year's Eve, a week earlier. I'd fallen asleep reading a text book "Criminal Evidence", when the phone rang just past midnight.

"Happy New Year!" I could still hear his voice. He was the only person to call wishing me a happy new year. It had been so good to hear his voice and we chatted for a few minutes about school, work and how I was doing since the divorce (my first divorce). He was a taciturn man who didn't particularly like chatting on the telephone. He ended the call by saying, "I love you, Jessica. You're a strong girl and everything will work out fine for you."

"I love you, too, Daddy," I responded.

Luther Alexander Jordan, who everyone called Lex, and I called Daddy. My world never felt as empty knowing he was not in it.

That telephone call from Daddy had been comforting and later profound, because when I had moved into that small apartment after I separated, it was the first time in my life I had ever lived alone.

Growing up, my nights were often filled with nightmares. I can't remember ever falling asleep without first straining to hear the unknown entity that was waiting in the dark. I continued to be afraid of the dark until well into adulthood. When I finally slept, the dreams would come. Sometimes they would be Indians attacking our home, shooting arrows into my bedroom window, circling our white clapboard mill house like a wagon train in the movies. At other times, I was falling off a cliff. I couldn't hold on to anything, just falling and falling and crying for help. But this wasn't a dream and I wouldn't wake up.

I watched Momma as she cried with my brother and uncle. I could still remember vividly that sickening sight of Momma seven years before when I was still in high school. She'd awakened me in the middle of the night, panicked, telling me get up and take her to the emergency room. There was a cut over her eye, a gaping gash, and it obviously needed stitches.

"Look what your Daddy did! Get up!" I don't know why I was so shocked. Hadn't I grown up with the yelling and cursing? Yet, I never saw or heard a physical altercation in all those years. My father was usually a quiet, gentle man. However, they could, and did, hurt each other with words. I could recall only a few times in my life when they were not angry at each other. I came to doubt that they had ever been happy together. But they must have been at some point. They'd married as teenagers. It was five years before I was born.

There were dim memories of Sunday drives into the mountains; Momma and Daddy in the front seat, Momma Alex sitting with Charlie and me in the back. "How 'bout you kids singing for me." Momma Alex would say. Then my parents would begin singing gospel music in perfect two-part harmony. The hymn I remember best; I can only recall a few lines:

"Up Calvary's mountain one dreadful morn. Walked Christ my Savior weary and worn..." Momma was an alto, Daddy a tenor. I remembered their beautiful voices.

Now I shuttered as I remembered their voices. Mostly, what I remembered was Momma's voice grating in anger and irritation. She didn't miss many chances to say something demeaning.

"Hurry up and finish," I would hear Momma say in disgust. The bed springs in their room would be squeaking and I wasn't sure what was happening. I just knew it was something secretive

and adult and whatever it was, Momma hated it.
The only time Momma's voice calmed down and
sounded happy was when Harvey came over.

On those nights when Daddy didn't work at
the mill, Momma always went to bed with face
cream smeared on her face and her hair rolled up
in pin curls. Later, when the styles changed, she'd
wrap old panties around her high-teased hair, to
protect her "hair-do" until the next beauty parlor
appointment. But there was usually at least one
night a week, when Daddy was working
graveyard, that she'd put on her best nightgown
and lipstick and wouldn't pin curl her hair or
wrap the panties around it. She even blew in my
face one night and asked me if her breath smelled
fresh. I wanted to slap her.

Looking back on those events through adult
eyes, I saw how humiliating Momma's blatant
behavior around Harvey must have been for
Daddy. Yet, I never saw Daddy hit Momma. I
never heard so much as a push or a slap during
those many nights when I listened to angry voices,
grunting and displeasure. I never saw an injury
until the night she startled me out of sleep,
wanting me to take her to the hospital.

As the days passed after Daddy died, I knew
Momma killed him as surely as if she put a knife
in his heart. The doctors said it was a cardiac
infarction, but I knew-Daddy died of a broken
heart.

The bruises inflicted upon Daddy weren't

physical. Charlie and I suffered through whippings, maybe some we deserved. Charlie always seemed to get the worst of it. Charlie was always the spitting image of our Daddy and grandfather. I think Momma looked at Charlie and saw Daddy. There's no other way to explain her dislike for him.

Momma smugly divorced Daddy after the trip to the emergency room claiming physical abuse. It was the start of my Senior year of high school. Momma Alex and Daddy packed his belongings and somberly carried them to their cars. I could only stand and watch, my emotions tumultuous. I didn't know what to do or say. I wanted to chase after him and tell him how much I loved him, but those words were foreign in our family. My Daddy was 39-years old the day I watched him and my grandmother drive away. Seven years later he was dead. I lost my Daddy twice.

CHAPTER 82

1974

One month after Momma divorced Daddy, she married Harvey. Surprise, surprise. It was strange having Harvey in our house instead of Daddy, but he'd already been around so long, it was an easy adjustment.

The nice thing about Harvey was he was even-tempered and happy; you couldn't help but love him. He was always there to offer advice if we asked, but he also knew when to keep his mouth shut. He treated my brother and me as individuals with brains and not just an inconvenience or stepchildren. He treated us like his children, the only children he would ever have. I somehow understood that, after a while, Daddy probably forgave Harvey from heaven, because Harvey became Momma's next victim. I think Momma was happy for only a few years. By the time she became disenchanted with Harvey, I was a cop and there was little time for visiting with the shift rotation I worked. She thought the grass would be greener on the other side but it soon became obvious her pastures were never green. Nothing ever seemed to please her except Matthew.

Both Momma and Harvey became enamored with Matthew and he became the only grandchild Momma ever acknowledged. She never liked Ally and all but refused to acknowledge Charlie and Ally's two girls.

When the pressure became almost unbearable between Barton and me, I tried confiding in Momma one time. It was right after the first choking incident and I badly needed to talk.

"Well, I guess we won't ever get to see Matthew again," she responded. Like clockwork, the guilt washed over me and I immediately went into fixer mode. I didn't leave Bart then, of course, I was in too much in anguish over Matthew myself. But she couldn't seem to see any unhappiness beyond her own.

When I finally left Bart, I avoided telling her. But, eventually it had to be explained why I was staying with Casey. She immediately broke into tears. "How can you put me through this?" she cried. "It's going to take me a long time to get over it."

It's going to take me a long time to get over it. That was a phrase Momma repeated so often, it became the family joke. If I drank the last coke, or ate the last piece of chicken, Charlie would say,

"It's going to take me a long time to get over it." If, when we were adults, Charlie changed jobs or drank more than two beers, I'd scold him, "It's going to take me a long time to get over it!" Then we'd both howl with laughter.

Faye's Fury slowly, but surely began to take its toll on Harvey. She would degrade him no matter who was within earshot. She treated him just as she had Daddy, Charlie and me.

She told people he was stupid and could never do anything right. Yet, Harvey never raised his voice to her. He covered his discomfort with his sense of humor. When he could no longer perform in bed, Momma decided to discuss her problem with anyone who would listen, including me. She was embittered about the lack of sex and called him a "eunuch."

"Well, I'm a damned handsome eunuch," he would retort. She never once indicated concern for his physical health or emotional wellbeing. I often wondered if Harvey's "inability" might actually be his *choice*. How could a man make love to Faye's Fury?

When Momma wasn't within earshot, we all joked about Faye's Fury. Harvey said he never seen a woman who could get so mad, so quick, over so little.

After bouts with health issues over the years, Harvey's health began to fail in a major way during the early '90's. He suffered a heart attack and three years later was diagnosed with lung cancer. After surgery and chemo, he was in remission for three years. By the time the tumor returned it was too late. We brought him home from the hospital to live out his last few months. I was working days at the time, and told Momma I would stop by after work every day. A hospital bed was brought in for Harvey and within a few weeks he could no longer walk.

One afternoon after work, I came into their house and found Momma struggling with a bedpan. There was a wild, angry look on her face. "I'm up to my elbows in shit!" she spewed out with venom. I looked at Harvey, helpless, a man who was now my father, and all he did was sadly shake his head. His face held only sad humiliation.

For the first time in my life, the anger I felt at Momma exploded. "Get out of my way and do it now!" I ordered as I made my way to Harvey's bedside. I took the bedpan and finished the ministrations he needed.

There were tears in his eyes. Momma hung back and whined, "Well, you don't have to be so hateful about it!"

I turned and stared hard at her. "Shut your damned mouth now!" Whimpering, she ran into the kitchen. I looked back at Harvey and saw a weak smile cross his face. "Let her go stew in her own sour juices," I whispered.

Over the years I often wondered why Harvey stayed with Momma. I tried not to think about how he wronged Daddy. Somehow, Harvey transformed into the honorable man I'd grown to love as a father. By his actions toward Charlie and me, I'd forgiven all past resentment. He probably stayed because he felt it was the right thing to do. We became his family, and we needed him. Maybe if he'd known we wouldn't have blamed him if he left Faye, he might have lived longer. If the nagging and yelling didn't actually kill him, I firmly believe it hastened his death.

CHAPTER 83

1998

Long before he was dying, Momma had alienated Harvey's family. He was one of seven siblings and Momma, over the years, claimed every one of his brothers and sisters insulted her. So they weren't allowed in *her* house. While she did give in and let them briefly visit during Harvey's last months, she made it as uncomfortable as she could. She would leave the room, or sit glaring, her arms folded.

I moved back into Momma and Harvey's house to help with the nursing after the bed pan episode. I hired help during the days and after work, did the nursing myself. I will always be thankful for those weeks I spent with Harvey. We said our goodbyes and would talk way into the night about his childhood and experiences during the Korean War. He loved peach ice cream and I made sure he had his favorite from Pap's. His appetite dwindled but Pap's homemade peach ice cream was the one thing he could always tolerate.

"You know you've have been my only parent for a long time now." I told him quietly one evening. Mother long since gone to bed, passed out in a drug induced coma.

"I know, sweetheart," he whispered. "It's been wonderful for me to be your father." In that moment I felt elated in the love he felt for Charlie and me. And I completely understood it, for it was exactly the same love I still felt for Matthew.

Matthew. So many years since we last saw him. Harvey loved and doted on Matthew and now would never see him again.

For the first time, I thought of contacting him, but then thought better of it. What would I say? The man you once loved and called grandfather is dying. It would be unfair to contact Matthew at a time like that. One could only guess at what Barton told him about me over the years. Maybe I was only a shadowy memory...or not remembered at all. Maybe he hated me.

My husband would often be at my side and Harvey loved him like a son as well. They would talk about the Army, about fishing, about planting their gardens. Those were serene moments for me that I would always cherish. Harvey was dying. I did everything possible to make his last days on earth peaceful.

On Easter morning that year, I decided to attend church services and would return afterwards to prepare lunch for Momma and Harvey.

I was a police officer with years of experience with drug addicts, but somehow, when it's in your own family, you fail to see the signs. I couldn't get past the anger I felt at Momma long enough to realize that her erratic actions went beyond being just plain mean. Charlie had always said she was just mean as hell.

I soon learned she doctor shopped and with two or three different doctors providing prescriptions for pain killers and tranquilizers that she had filled at different drug stores.

It surprised me that one of Momma's daily medications was a narcotic, hydrocodone. She explained that she took it for her headaches and arthritic pain. In addition, she took tranquilizers many times a day. Mother insisted upon taking care of Harvey's medications, which I soon learned were the same brand of hydrocodone and the same tranquilizer.

One morning he was in a great deal of pain. He always waited as long as he could to ask for a pain pill. Momma crushed them for him like she did her own pills. She could have been a pharmacist, naming every kind of pain pill and sedative and what milligram dose was needed for relief.

Momma was busy crushing the pill as I walked into the kitchen. "Oh no, I've crushed an Equanil and he wanted a Lortab. What will I do with this?" The question was apparently rhetorical because before I could comment, I watched in amazement as she turned the foil up and downed it herself, then reached for the pain meds and began to crush the correct one.

"Momma! What are you doing?"

"I needed something anyway for my nerves."

"You just took something at breakfast, Momma."

"I know what I need. I need something to get me through the day. I just can't believe this is happening to me. What am I going to do? Harvey does everything for me. Why am I having to go through this?"

"Momma, Harvey is going through this." I replied through clenched teeth, "He's the one in pain. He's the one dying." I tried to keep my anger under control. "We're all going through this together, that's why I'm here." I softened my voice, trying to comfort her when she started weeping.

"I'm afraid you all will just forget about me; I don't know what I'm going to do." She began to wail.

"You need to stop taking so much medicine for one thing," I said. "Why don't you try Tylenol or aspirin first for your headaches, before using a narcotic?"

Her tears immediately dried and she fixed me with an angry glare. "Tylenol is no more than taking a drink of water for all the good they do," she spat. "I know what I need and the doctor prescribed them for me."

"Does he know you take them like candy?" I shot back, as I started out the door.

"You sure are acting like a bitch this morning." She chased after me.

I slowly turned and glared at my mother enraged, but, in a measured tone said, "I was taught by the best." I then turned my back on her and walked away before she could respond.

CHAPTER 84

1998

"Momma, come on, let's get out of here! She's goanna bust hell wide open when she gets there." My step-cousin almost ran over me barreling out the door one afternoon. Her mother, Margaret, was Harvey's youngest sister. I never knew why she always received more of Momma's wrath than the others.

"Dear God in Heaven, what has she done now?" I asked as Margaret stormed out right behind her daughter.

"Your Momma has to be the biggest bitch on earth," she wailed. "She just cussed me out because I haven't stayed overnight to help with Harvey. She told me she has to clean his shit and vomit while I run around and go shopping and have fun. If you needed me, Jessica, I hope you know I would have stayed. I wanted to stay but I thought she didn't want me around." She dissolved into tears.

Only Momma could wreak such havoc. I soothed Margaret and tried to comfort her as best I could. She consistently offered many times to take her turn staying with Harvey. I knew it was better for me to stay every night, in an effort to prevent exactly what happened. Margaret never came back because Momma told her to stay away, and Harvey died two weeks later.

Every night I would tuck Harvey in as I would a child. I bought a bell he could ring if he needed me during the night. I would kiss his forehead and whisper, "Goodnight, sleep well."

When morning came, I held my breath until I checked on him, always afraid of what I'd find. It was a relief when I stuck my head in and he would wave.

"Good morning. What do you want for breakfast this morning?"

"Honey, I would love an egg and a pancake." Sometimes it was an egg and toast, but his requests seldom varied. It was difficult for him to eat. Making his breakfast and then eating with him became a meaningful time for both of us. Momma was always still sleeping off her drugs. So Harvey and I sipped our coffee and I would tell him about work, this case or that. I'd bring in the paper and we'd silently read, just being together in comfortable silence.

Pauline, the day nurse, arrived by eight and I would kiss him goodbye, praying he would be there when I returned that evening. Every day I prayed for one more day.

One morning, I got up as usual. The night before had been rough, with several bell summons. He was having difficulty catching his breath. I tried to suction his throat as the hospice nurse taught me but finally he asked me to quit, he couldn't stand it any longer. I admitted to him I couldn't stand to make him suffer any longer myself. But it gave him enough relief to allow him to finally fall asleep. I sat by his bed for about 15 minutes, watching his shallow breathing.

The next morning when I stuck my head in, he was still asleep. I could see the gentle, steady lifting of his chest as he took even breaths. As usual, I was relieved. If anything, his breathing was not as labored as the previous night, and I hoped he was catching up on the rest he'd lost.

When Pauline arrived, he still hadn't wakened. I told her about the rough night and that I hoped he would rest for a while. At noon, the hospice nurse phoned me to say that he still had not roused and had drifted into a coma. By three that afternoon, Harvey's battle was over. Thankfully, his last hours had been peaceful. He simply fell asleep.

I felt my chest knot with the knowledge that he was gone. Even though we knew it was inevitable, his death was still devastating. Part of me wanted to scream with despair—why does such a good life have to end like this? And another part of me thanked God he was finally out of his misery.

True to form, Momma made the funeral arrangements as painful and chaotic as possible. She insisted upon having her hair done before the first viewing of the body by the family, then, kept everyone waiting for almost an hour. The funeral director explained that he had been given explicit instructions that no one was to view Harvey until she arrived.

With that emotional hurdle over, she decided to keep the casket and viewing room closed until the family received friends later that evening. This was against all custom in our small community.

Harvey had many friends from church, work and childhood who wanted to pay their respects at times other than the formal reception, but Momma decided otherwise. I figured the main reason Momma was doing this was that she feared Harvey's old flame, whom he hadn't seen in 30-something years, might show up when she wasn't there. Just as Harvey took Momma from Daddy, she took him from a woman who he'd promised to marry. Momma had never once met Delores but she was bound and determined to have the upper hand when she did. Whether Delores even knew that Harvey had passed on was anybody's guess.

I dressed for the funeral in a daze, but Momma prepared as if for a trip down the red carpet. Months before, she'd purchased an expensive Liz Claiborne black dress. As I walked

CHOICES

by her bedroom before the service, I heard her on the telephone and stopped to listen.

"This is Mrs. Harvey Farrow. I don't want any other family members seated in the church until I arrive."

Would she ever stop! I wanted to scream. Sure enough, when we finally arrived at The First Baptist Church of Reedy View, the vestibule was uncomfortably packed with Farrow kin, everyone waiting for Faye's arrival. She entered through the front doors and suddenly all talking stopped. Long live the Queen, I thought. Then regal and dramatic, she removed a lace hanky from her black bag, dabbed at her carefully made-up eyes and entered the church sanctuary. With the organ playing "I Come To The Garden Alone", she marched solemnly to the front pew followed by 30 or 40 others.

CHAPTER 85

1983

"Want more spaghetti?" Casey glanced over her shoulder as she heaped a second helping of pasta onto her own plate.

"No thanks. But I see the baby is still hungry," I teased.

"She is always hungry. Her father's Italian genes, combined with my Greek genes, has given this child an insatiable appetite!"

Casey's baby was due in September and she'd just learned it was a girl. She had been two months pregnant when we were on the Gatlinburg trip in February. I had not even suspected when she feigned a pulled muscle and insisted upon staying with Matthew on the bunny slope. Instead, I had been grateful she was watching Matt and I could try the steeper runs.

By the end of April, her condition was obvious. I was both thrilled and concerned for her.

I was thrilled because I adored babies, but even more concerned because she wasn't married and didn't want to be. But Casey finally convinced me she never did anything without careful planning. She chose to become pregnant and wanted this baby.

"I'd rather have a baby than a husband any day," she matter-of-factly stated.

Casey was essentially a free spirit. And, no doubt, she would be a wonderful mother. She refused to say much about the father other than that he was, of course, married. The baby's father was relieved when she told him she wanted nothing from him, but that an abortion was out of the question; she was keeping the baby. "I doubt I'll ever see him again," she told me. "I don't want to ever see him again."

It was near the end of August and the baby was due in a few weeks. Casey finally took leave from work to prepare for the birth.

I was working third shift again when dispatch asked for me to give them a 10-21 (phone call). Expecting to hear dispatch's voice, I was surprised to hear Casey instead. "What are you doing up at this time of night and why are you at headquarters?" I asked.

"Livvy was bored and wanted to ride around with her auntie."

"Dear Lord in Heaven, are you crazy, Casey?" I asked, shocked that she would consider putting herself in the unnecessary danger of riding around in a police car. She would name the baby Olivia Casey Demarches and was already calling her Little Livvy. I loved the name.

"Quit being such a worry-wart, will you. I'm not used to having so much free time. Pick me up out front. I brought my gun."

I could only smile. "Okay, I'm on the way," I said.

Casey, an assistant solicitor, was cleared to ride on patrol and she knew I enjoyed having company. In addition, she was still a cop at heart. Once a cop, always a cop. It was a Tuesday night, not usually a busy time, which she also knew. I picked her up at headquarters, glad to have someone with whom to talk. We drove the empty streets and talked about the baby. Then suddenly the topic turned to Cal and me.

"You know he's in love with you, Jess. I mean in love, the wants to marry you kind." she told me.

"Casey, I'm not ready," I sighed. But even as I said it, my heart skipped a beat. "As a matter of fact, he wants me to come by his apartment when I get off work this morning. He wants to cook breakfast for me."

"He can cook, too? I may drop your body in an alleyway and take him for myself," she teased.

"Keep your hands off, he's mine." She winked.

"Well, how good is he...?"

"Casey, you are absolutely incorrigible."

"Please do not tell me you two haven't done the Big It yet?"

"As if it were any of your business. But, no, we haven't. Of course not."

"Why not?"

"Is it so hard to fathom that I might go out with someone and not hop into bed with him?"

"Possibly, but I don't know why anyone wouldn't want to." We both laughed.

"There are only so many pleasures in life and luuuvvve is by far the greatest." As she gave me a wicked smirk.

"Well, ol' buddy, ol' pal, since you brought it up," I smiled knowingly.

"Yeah...?"

"I'm thinking this morning just might be the time. But I didn't know ahead of time and I'm afraid..."

"What?" she prompted.

"Well, I need you to do me a favor. There's an all-night pharmacy over on South Street..."

"Pharmacy?" She looked perplexed.

"I'm not on birth control and..."

"Oh, no, Sister," she cut me off. "I'm all for a good romp in the hay and I can't believe you haven't done it yet, but I am not—let me repeat that—NOT—going to buy you rubbers from an all-night pharmacy."

Suddenly we both giggled. "I don't want those; I want the foam stuff. But I'm in uniform, and you know I can't go in there and buy spermicidal foam while I'm on duty. I have ethics. I don't buy liquor, condoms or spermicidal foam on duty."

"No. Period. No, no, NO! I will not walk into an all-night pharmacy and be the only customer in the store and buy contraception foam and me eight months frigging pregnant! I love you, but no. Forget it."

"Here's the money, I'll wait outside." I pulled into Walgreen's parking lot.

"No!"

"Yes, you will."

I wish I could have seen the pharmacist's expression when Casey waddled in to make the purchase. As Casey got back into the car, she was shaking with laughter.

"Go Go Go! I can't believe what I just did for you," she crackled. "You cannot ever say I'm not a friend. You should have seen that old geezer's face when I took it to the register. He looked at me like I'd lost my mind. You owe me big time, girl!" We both laughed until tears rolled down our cheeks.

For the rest of that night, we'd look at each other, snicker, and then crack up again. We couldn't stop laughing and it made the time fly.

CHAPTER 86

1983

Cal shared a two-bedroom apartment with a young intern who was working a residency in psychiatry at Reedy View Memorial. Steve Steiner was a divorced, native New Yorker. I liked Steve immensely because he was unpretentious, smart, funny, and a great friend to Cal. He was self-effacing, which made him even more endearing. To be from such different backgrounds, he and Cal became fast friends, referring to themselves as "the cop and the doc." They golfed together, hit the sports bars together and liked to hike in the mountains. I felt sure they had discussed my situation, at great length. Nevertheless, being a gentleman, Steve never said a word.

I always kept a set of gym clothes in the trunk of my car. When I got to Cal's apartment, I quickly changed out of my uniform showered and pulled on my shorts and tee shirt. The aroma of frying bacon wafted through the air and made my mouth water. Cal was in the kitchen busily flipping bacon in an iron skillet. Homemade biscuits were browning in the oven and a bowl of eggs were waiting to be scrambled.

"Umm, smells good. What's this, hash browns?" I lifted the foil from a plate on a warming tray. "I'm impressed. You are going to be so disappointed when I cook for you."

"Who said I was interested in your cooking?" He gave me a suggestive grin. The table was set with checkered placemats and white china. I was amazed he was such a wonderful cook. Neither of my former husbands ever cooked me a meal—I felt like a queen. We lingered over breakfast, talking easily. He talked about growing up on a farm and what a great cook his mother was.

"So she passed on her culinary skills to you?"

"Actually, no, Uncle Sam did. When I grew tired of Army food and fast food junk, I bought a cookbook, a grill and found the best meat market near every Army post. I taught myself."

I loaded the dishwasher and cleaned the kitchen while Cal went to shower. I was excited but also nervous because I knew our relationship was about to change.

Cal stepped out of the bathroom wearing a dark brown terrycloth robe. His hair was still wet, and fell over one eye. I thought he was the sexiest, most handsome man I had ever seen. Including Rock Hudson. My apprehension disappeared as he pulled me to him and put his lips to mine. I fantasized about those lips for a long time... now I couldn't get enough. I could feel my wetness as we sunk to the floor right there in the den of his tiny apartment. We were like two frenzied animals. We shed our clothes in a rush and he spread his robe underneath us. When I at last felt him inside me, the ecstasy of the moment took my breath away. I had never made love with such passion.

We made our way to the bedroom and made love a second time. This time, we took it long and slow. He was a sensuous, skillful, gentle and considerate lover. After I came the second time, I realized how starved I was to be touched and loved. I wanted to completely envelope him, to pull him inside me and drown in his body. I wanted to be greedy and he let me.

Then I let him and we were in perfect sync. Afterwards, we lay together on the rumpled bed for a long time, bathed in pleasure. I could feel his heart beating against my own.

We showered together and made love for a third time. This time we climaxed together as the warm spray beat down upon our soapy bodies. I was like a sex-starved teenager and so was Cal. We collapsed onto the bed still damp from the shower, with no thought of clothing. Our nakedness was liberating. We fell asleep almost immediately, wrapped in each other's arms. Six hours later I awoke to his hands softly caressing my breast. I turned toward him and took his hardness in my hand. "Oh yes, please..." And for the fourth time he gently entered me and we made sweet, amazing love.

Later as he held me, he whispered softly, "You know I love you. I have for a long time."

I turned and kissed him softly, then deeply, afraid to speak. "Is it too soon to say those words? Is it too soon for me to be in love you?" he asked.

"No," I whispered. "No. Please say those words."

"You do know getting rid of me will prove complicated since I plan to marry to you." It wasn't a question.

I stared deeply into his kind, green eyes. "I love you. I whispered.

"I love you, more."

CHAPTER 87

1983-1984

Bart made sure the final divorce decree was postponed and dragged out to be as long and painful as possible. But he couldn't drag it out forever, and it was final the week before Olivia Demarches was born. Bart finally moved from my house and I could move home at any time. But, with Casey so close to her due date and so far from the hospital, I decided to stay a few more weeks with her. Anne, my neighbor, assured me she would keep an eye on things, so I didn't worry.

Since that harrowing Sunday afternoon Bart went crazy, Anne and I spent many hours over coffee, talking. In the years since I'd lived there, we'd always been friendly acquaintances, but it took the crisis to step our relationship up a level. I visited her sometimes when I knew Bart was working. She became such a close confidant and friend, that I don't know what I would have done without her.

Casey's labor began on a Sunday morning and Livvy made her grand entrance into the world late that afternoon. She weighed seven and a half pounds with a head full of dark curls, just like Casey. I was so proud of the thoughtfulness Cal showed when he arrived at the hospital with a dozen red roses for Casey.

I drove Casey home the next day and stayed at her house to help for another week until her Mom arrived from Tarpon Springs. I picked Mrs. Demarches up at the airport and when she arrived at the house, there was an emotional moment between her and her daughter. Then Mrs. Demarches was introduced to Livvy. She took the baby in her arms and was lost in the love and wonder of her first grandchild.

"I hope you enjoyed your daughter while you could because I think you've just lost her," I whispered to Casey as she watched her mother cuddling the baby.

"You know, Jess, I was always such a pain in the ass to my folks. Then to have Livy, without being married—they're orthodox and I wasn't sure how they'd feel."

"I think you can quit worrying. Livvy will be as spoiled as you were. Maybe more."

"I know."

"I'm off little Momma. Please let me know if you need me at any time, day or night." I said. I knew she was now in good hands. I was ready to get back to my life.

"I promise, don't worry about me. Mother loves taking care of babies, and once she's gone, I have a wonderful lady who will be living with us when I go back to work." We said our goodbyes; I packed the last of my belongings and headed south to the city.

* * * * *

By Thanksgiving, Cal and I were spending almost all our time together. He seldom slept at his own apartment. When Steve announced he would be taking a position at a hospital in Orlando, it seemed the right time for us to live together.

The Quarters was great—I loved it. But since Bart, and especially that horrible afternoon, it held too many disturbing memories for me. Cal never said a word but I sensed he wanted a home that was ours, I know I did. After Christmas, The Quarters was placed on the market, and it sold within a week. Cal and I quickly began looking for a house of our own.

We found a wonderful old farmhouse on ten acres in the foothills north of town, just a few miles from Casey. There were overgrown meadows, pinewoods and a pond in back. The house was handcrafted of native stone and I fell in love with it the first time I glimpsed it from the road. It was almost 60 years old and needed some "fixing up" but we immediately made an offer.

We came up with the down payment by pooling our savings. The next few months were spent painting, refinishing hardwood floors and updating the kitchen and bathroom. We moved in permanently in March and planned our wedding for April. Happy endings did come to pass off the big screen, and I almost missed it.

CHAPTER 88

PRESENT

I left my husband sipping wine on the patio, and left the house in plenty of time to meet a young man I had not seen in many years, and feared that I would never see again.

For over twenty years, I had been married to Cal Larson and loved him more with every passing day. He had proven his love for me in every way possible through the years, no more so than today when I was going to meet again, Matthew Quinlan.

Matthew and I had spoken several times during the previous weeks and e-mailed constantly. Making contact with him after twenty years was something of an accident. Casey insisted it was fate. As I lost loved ones through the years, I began to see and understand life as a fine tapestry woven with the threads made up of family and friends. Sometimes threads frayed or unraveled but they still lent color and substance to the whole. Births, deaths, childhood, puberty, marriages, jobs, laughter, illness, tears, sadness, anger and all the many, many joys that life brings—they were all part of my life's tapestry. It seemed as if the most heartrending events somehow pulled the threads tighter together, making the happiness and laughter and love more precious.

I chose the Koffee Klatch as the place to meet Matthew for the first time after all these years because it somehow seemed appropriate. The little coffee shop still stood unchanged in the shadow of the Police Department where my beloved career unfolded and where Matthew first burst into my life with such joy. I had nice memories of sitting at The Koffee Klatch counter with Matthew, myself enjoying a cup of Peggy's good coffee, Matt, sipping milk through a straw, both of us sharing nibbles of a donut.

A silver BMW pulled into a parking space at the curb. I held my breath as a young man emerged—no, unfolded—from the driver's side. There were only a few customers at four in the afternoon. I clutched a silver-framed 5 x 7 photograph tightly in my hand and peered closely at it once again. It was the picture Casey had given to me a few days before. A picture of a beautiful, blond little boy with his Auntie Casey and me on the bunny slope in Gatlinburg, Tennessee. Matthew had his small arms linked through ours, all of us light-hearted and beaming.

I planned to remain seated until he entered the coffee shop, but sheer emotion made me suddenly leap from my seat. Would he recognize me? I'd changed outfits several times, unable to decide what to wear. It isn't everyday you're reunited with your long lost child. I'd finally settled on simple black slacks with a silk shirt and wool blazer. It was unusually cool for October, the sky so clear and blue it looked endless. The crisp day felt cleansing and redemptive.

Without further thought, I rushed out the door to meet the tall, muscular young man. My eyes took in every inch of him, the fair brush cut, the chocolate brown eyes, the neat jeans and sweater. As soon as he saw me, his face broke into an all-consuming smile. It was then I saw that little dimple on his cheek. I was so overwhelmed that I suddenly I stopped, but then he ran toward me. My smile never faltered as tears flowed silently down my cheeks.

Without saying a word, we embraced. His strong arms lifted me off the pavement, grasping me in a tight bear hug. I caught a glimpse of Peggy's few customers staring at us through the plate glass windows. Then with the same warm smile Matthew whispered two simple words that made my life complete.

"Hello, Mom."

EPILOGUE

It's autumn again. I feel only peace as I sit on my porch, once again enjoying the magnificent seasonal color as the forest behind our house displays dazzling shades of yellow, brown, red and orange. I never tire of autumn.

My life has been a good ride; despite the bumpy roads I've traveled. They made me who I am. They gave me the wisdom I've been told I possess. I'm not so sure.

Matthew is on the periphery of my life. It made me sad that I had been right, his father had damaged him greatly. Matthew had wounds not seen and he battles the damage even as an adult. While, he did not have the depth of demons his father possessed, he had his own, which, like his father, he could not see.

Because his father could not show love, I think Matthew tries to ensure love in his life by monopolizing all who enter. Demanding recognition and accolades and jealous of anyone or anything that he perceives will rob him of his due. Narcissistic in some ways, but something prevents or limits his happiness. Because he has a need to hold on so tight, he becomes a self-fulfilling prophecy and loses those most important to him. His father never learned that a person couldn't own another, cannot control and monopolize another person, how they think, who they loved. I prayed he would one day defeat his demons. Would one day be the man I always dreamed he would be.

When he married, his father, if nothing else, was consistent, said he would not attend if I did. So, I did not. I took it in stride, but was more disappointed that Matthew would not stand up to his father. Would not be his own person.

Barton had died two years before, and while I would always love Matthew and that precious child he had been with all my heart, I realized once again, he was not my child. Even in death, his father controls him. Someone who could not, would not, show love. *You are mine. You will love me. Momma. Barton.* Two hateful bullies. And two of the people I loved the most, Charlie and Matthew, I could not protect from their tormenters.

I've found a certain peace with the anguish and guilt I've carried because I chose to leave Matthew all those years ago. I'm free, because when the decision was sink or swim, and I chose

429

to swim.

I couldn't save Loretta, or protect Charlie or Matthew. I couldn't change who Matthew had as a father.

My reverie is interrupted by the pattering of little feet running across the foyer. I stand to meet my grandchild as he runs onto the porch and jumps into my arms. I clutch him to me and we dance around as I sing an off-key rendition of Que Sera Sera. This is the way we always greet each other.

Caleb Christopher, on this day is now four years old and our daughter and husband finally received a duty station back in the states. Caleb was born in Germany, and awaiting our first meeting was excruciating.

Alexandra is a Captain in the Air Force and a pediatric R.N. Her hair is a beautiful strawberry blond and Caleb is the spitting image, with a head full of her curly red hair. Momma Alex would be happy and love her namesake. Alex's husband, Liam Connelly, completes our Irish family. Which, is something of a joke. I have always been obsessed with Native American history, especially the Cherokee. Such a proud people, who suffered the greatest injustice by the United States government. I had been told that my family had some Cherokee blood, so I sent off a DNA test, anticipating a link with these great people. It came back Irish. I quipped that my Native American ancestors must be from a former life.

"The Birthday Boy!" I laugh as I swing Caleb around.

"Yeaaahhhh! Do we have cake?"

"Of course we have cake. A great big, chocolate birthday cake. Momma Jessie will show you in a minute. Where's Mommy and Daddy?"

"They're outside with Papa," he whispers conspiratorially. "They have to help Papa wrap my present I think."

I have brought Momma from the nursing home to join us for the festivities. She keeps asking who that little boy is, but Caleb seems to understand and treats her with gentleness. I watch as she hugs Caleb with real joy in her eyes. She smiles at something he tells her, oblivious to everything in the room but him. Dementia has made her as much of a child as he is.

"Now what are we doing today?" Momma asks again, bewildered as usual.

"It's Caleb's fourth birthday, Momma. We are having a party."

"I'm a big boy today!" Caleb chirps, taking her arm and pulling her toward the door. We all three stroll outside arm in arm. "You can help me open my presents," Caleb gravely informs her.

"Oh, I love to open presents," she answers.

Alex, Liam and Cal, are looking at the new pony Cal brought home just this afternoon. We three walk out toward the pasture. Suddenly Caleb notices the pony and stops dead in his tracks. "A horse!" he whispers in awe.

"Yes, and if you want to, Papa is going to let you sit on his back and…," I start to say but Caleb doesn't hear me, he's off running toward the brown pony.

"Can I ride him? Can I ride?" Caleb is jumping up and down. Momma smiles, as excited as Caleb is.

I have no doubt that my Momma Alex's spirit is always with me. I know this with every butterfly and each red bird I see.

"Blow the red bird a kiss and make a wish." I can still hear Momma Alex tell me. And, I do, every time. As my eyes take in my wonderful family, husband, daughter, son-in-law, mother and grandson, I know without a doubt she was right. My wish did come true.

"Oh, my, it's a horse," Momma mumbles, astonished.

I gently grasp her frail arm and lead her toward the pasture, discovering the world again, through the eyes of a child.

ABOUT THE AUTHOR

B.J. King is a retired police sergeant having served twenty-six years with the Greenville Police Department in Greenville South Carolina. She was the first female uniform patrol officer for the City Police Department and the first woman promoted to the rank of Sergeant. She worked sixteen years patrolling the streets. The last ten years she was commander of the Communication Center, overseeing the implementation of a computer aided dispatch system and the Enhanced 911 system.

Since her retirement, Bj has her own Private Investigation business. She works domestic cases where abuse is often present; helping the victims start new lives has become her passion.

She is currently writing a second novel, TRAVESTIES.

ACKNOWLEDGEMENTS

It would be impossible to thank all who have inspired this book. The writing has been a journey that at times I thought I would never see to fruition. To the countless, I thank you all.

To my brother, Ronnie Carroll Bates, for his love; he made that first journey with me through our childhood. To the memory of our beloved grandmother, Jessie Duncan Bates Cooley, who always made that journey worthwhile and showed us what love looked like.

In memory of my father, Herbert Luther Bates, whom I lost much too soon, just as I was finding him again. In memory of our mother, Hazel Styles Bates Forrester; she unwittingly taught us perseverance and fortitude. In memory of my kind, loving stepfather, Samuel Forrester, who was my only parent for a long time and taught me loyalty in the midst of turmoil. My love and gratitude to Timothy, who is a special hero and a distinguished Sheriff's Deputy in South Carolina.

To Jean Montgomery Stewart and Debbie Brown Barefoot, whom I love dearly. Daughters of sisters, who were our mothers. My sisters sent to me as cousins. They are survivors in their own right, and understand the meaning of this journey.

My love and gratitude to my best buds and writing pals, The Novel Four, Charlcie Hopkins, Jim Christopher, and Rebecca George. All amazing published authors and friends beyond measure. You encouraged me, even when I gave up. To Carol Christopher, whose life's work was with non-profits and Safe Harbor, and who understood the message I needed to convey on domestic violence and encouraged me to finish and publish this story. Thank you.

To my childhood pal Sarah Hammett Johnson, my cheerleader, who struggled through the first draft of my manuscript and pretended it read like Conroy. To Julie Felton, graphic artist extraordinaire. Without the expertise and editing help from Rita Seaborn and Cheryl Duttweiler and the formatting help from Ellis Vidler, a published author, this may not have been a reality.

My love to my grandchildren, who are such a big part of my heart. Christopher Lucas Yearwood, David Jacob Yearwood, Caleb Griffin Yearwood, Allison Jane Yearwood. Our daughter Stephanie King Yearwood and our son-in-law David Eugene Yearwood. I love you all to the moon and back!